C000023485

TRAIN, TRAIN

TRAIN, TRAIN

A Novel

GRAHAM COSTER

BLOOMSBURY

All rights reserved: no part of this publication
may be reproduced, stored in a retrieval system, or transmitted
in any form or by any means, electronic, mechanical, photocopying
or otherwise, without the prior written permission of the Publisher.

First published in Great Britain 1989
Copyright © 1989 by Graham Coster

9 8 7 6 5 4 3 2 1

Lyrics from 'Peace Train' by Cat Stevens
© 1971 Cat Music Ltd, administered
Worldwide by Westbury Music Consultants Ltd.

Bloomsbury Publishing Ltd, 2 Soho Square, London W1V 5DE

British Library Cataloguing in Publication Data
Coster, Graham, *1960*–
Train, train
I. Title
823′.914[F]

ISBN 0 7475 0394 X

Photoset by Rowland Phototypesetting Ltd,
Bury St Edmunds, Suffolk
Printed in Great Britain by
Butler and Tanner Ltd, Frome, Somerset

A green road, level and empty, winding its way across the Lake District landscape, is the central motif of this brilliant first novel. Once, this green road was a railway, built to serve the mines, boasting vast feats of civil engineering in its viaduct and mile-long tunnel, linking the town of Carrock with the main line and ultimately with London. By the mid-1980s it has long been closed, and its track reverted to grass.

But when Greg, a refugee from the Big Bang dealing-rooms, comes to the Lakes to work in Carrock's youth hostel, amid the thunder of juggernauts through the town and the summer invasion of car-borne holidaymakers, he discovers a campaign to reopen the line. Why reopen the railway? To the movement's leader – another London émigré – it will be the catalyst of Carrock's industrial rebirth and a blow for democracy. For the uninterested townspeople, such as the hostel warden (a man so retiring Greg can never quite ascertain his name), it might be a useful tourist attraction. And to the elusive Ruth, repeatedly seeking Greg out while staying just out of reach, it is simply grown men playing at steam trains. Over the course of the following year – a post-election year of controversial government measures and radical political division – the project inches from plans and dreams towards a kind of reality.

On one level this is a novel about the land, set in a region long commemorated for its sublime wilderness, less often for its mining and railway history, but always shaping profoundly the lives that can be lived there. On another it is a quirky and funny look at England in the 80s: a nation preoccupied as much with shopping as with work, and discovering its industrial heritage just at the point when most of its industry has disappeared; a nation of consumers rather than community. At the heart of the novel, above all, is Englishness itself: that strange, complacent, often fantastic way in which England makes use of its history to create its present. Rarely has there been a critique of Thatcher's Britain as subtle, as thoughtful, and as satisfying as *Train, Train*.

FOR TODD McEWEN AND FOR
MONICA McSTAY

Railways were often believed . . . to be symbols of 'democracy', in Doctor Arnold's words 'destroying feudality for ever'.

Asa Briggs, *Victorian Cities*

Self-drivers may curse their luck,
Stuck on new-fangled trails,
But the good old train will jog
To the dogma of its rails,

And steam so straight ahead
That I cannot be led astray
By tempting scenes which occur
Along any permanent way.

W. H. Auden, 'A Permanent Way'

Train took my baby
Away from me . . .

The Count Bishops, 'Train, Train'

FIRST SUMMER

Chapter One

There was a green road, winding across the landscape. A perfectly empty road: not a lead-grey road for glinting cars, but a green road, a grass road, a natural road — running level and still like a river. It started, as far away as Greg could see, in the pale plain that blurred into the horizon over to his left. As it came nearer it was a green string across green fields, and then it disappeared behind a hill. Greg scanned to the right, and picked it up again, a stretch as straight as a Roman road, passing first some kind of disused quarry works, then a tiny house, intersecting with a grey minor road, before vanishing once more among the belt of trees fringing the outskirts of the town. He traced the green line back again, now to try and join it up to where he had lost it. The causeway by the toy house merged into a gently, then steeply shelving hillside, and the line laid itself along a ledge around it as the ground dropped away beneath. Then, as a great river gorge cut down deep into the hillside and the olive-green water curled through, Greg saw the line stop, turn dull brown and cross the river in, he counted, twenty slender, arched steps, and realised that the green line was an old railway line, the massive viaduct still keeping its course uselessly complete.

And the air hummed, a deep humming that swooped into buzzes and growls, beneath Greg as he looked out over the landscape from the top of the fell, and around him. Far below, tiny cars, lorries and coaches raced to and from the town on the wide white dual-carriageway. The noise was incessant: three thousand feet up, it was all he could hear. The road seemed to part the land, to push the hills aside in order to make its way, and its groaning hum seemed like the energy constantly needed to keep it so. A metal, pylon-sound: you climbed this high, so you could see all the land, and hear its silence; instead the air whined like a fridge.

With the evening coming on, the sunlight had become richer and weaker at once: now the light seemed to come from the ground rather than the sky. Greg stood up to begin his descent. He had scrambled up the fell along one of its steep rocky promontories, which had gradually narrowed into a ledge as thin as him so that he'd had to crawl along splayed on all fours, breathless with tension, to reach the summit; now he was heading for the grassy fellside that ran down to the town. He lingered to run his eyes once more back along the old green line he had discovered – even now Greg knew it was a railway line he still found himself studying it with the landscape – watching how it rounded the side of the valley, traced the trees, tiptoed across the river. The line did not split the hills and the fields, like the road, but sewed them together. It seemed to introduce the landscape to itself: it seemed a green road made by the hills to take you through them. As his gaze came to rest on the town below, with the low sun splintering up from the lake beyond, Greg shaded his eyes, and then set off over the wide, evenly-sloping down.

Not that the advertisement had said anything about railways. Greg had been leafing through the youth hostelling magazine at the dentist's. They had wanted Assistant Wardens for the summer; he had been wanting out of London and the City, out of green screens and dollar rates and sandwiches at your desk so you could shout into the phone over lunch. Four years out of college, and the interview in the hotel suite during his final term had led to here: paid to have the jitters; paid to be steeled with euphoria; paid to make money for someone, or something. It was the responsibility, you assured anyone who asked, mostly yourself, alarming responsibility. This was why it was an important job. This was why salaries were . . . *comparatively* high. But Greg had come to feel no responsibility at all for fluctuating decimal points on wall screens: which ought to have been alarming, for him and his employers, but was only boring. He was haunted, rather, by a recent newspaper report of a long-distance coach driver convicted of reckless driving after

4

his coach had ploughed into a queue of stationary vehicles at a contraflow. A second's inattention, after thirty years' service, and six people dead: a second was all you needed, if you were only a bus driver.

No experience was necessary to be an Assistant Warden, and certainly none that Greg had had. It was easy; he prepared by finding out as little as possible. He had been assigned to Carrock Hostel, the double-breasted suit and the red tie could stay hanging in the wardrobe: and Carrock was in the Lake District. Wordsworth country: Melvyn Bragg country: televised sheep-dog trials from green dales on the television: a Bluebird power-boat backward-somersaulting off the water and fragmenting: something to do with Beatrix Potter books. Lakeland – up north, near Scotland. Greg had never been there.

On his last day in the dealing room his colleagues had taken him out to a wine bar and got a lot drunker than he. Back in the office his boss had consoled him that he wasn't mercurial enough for this line of work, perhaps, and Greg wondered if the man really meant stolid, or ponderous, which were the words that sometimes occurred to him about himself. This time, however, it felt like a compliment, since usually such thoughts came to Greg when he was standing at a crowded bar waiting endlessly and unsuccessfully to be served. His flat in Lewisham had been let for the summer, and the June day he left London was the morning after election night. On the television Trafalgar Square in the early hours had danced with blue rosettes; as results were declared town hall after town hall had swelled with a belligerent roar. On the steps at the victorious party headquarters tender words were spoken about the inner cities: 'So much to do . . .' Greg sprawled on the floor in the dark cradling a bottle of Scotch, flicking frenzied then listless V-signs at the grey screen.

That next morning London felt like him: hungover and shabby. There was bright, hot sunshine. It seemed a day of somnolence, quiescence: a day to take the deckchair out into the garden: a day for the head to loll sideways and the newspaper to fall into the lap: a day for heavy, clogged drowsing. Who were all those exultant people? Who *were* they? Here, anyway, they were, not far away, the crowds and the headquarters and the Prime Ministerial constituency – in this city, and nearby. How could this day feel like a Sunday morning? Greg cancelled the papers at the corner shop, and had a late breakfast on a plastic tray at McDonald's.

By early evening he was hurtling his Mini in towards Carrock along the wide white road, windows down and hair astream: *such* a good road for getting some speed up! Green steeps of fell were either side of him, and the sky seemed huge. Entering the outskirts of Carrock he found a small town by the shore of a lake so long the other end was out of sight, the fawn-coloured stone buildings straggling up the hillside around a sharply-climbing cobbled high street. There were wide tree-lined avenues of tall Victorian guest houses, half a dozen large hotels, several new closes of redbrick bungalows, and a boarded-up cinema. Cars towing caravans trundled round the one-way system. A cluster of youths drank cans of lager in the empty marketplace.

The Youth Hostel was an isolated grey house on three storeys at the top of the town, its back garden ending in a fence beyond which the open fell rose away. Greg picked past rucksacks and cycle panniers in the hall and found the Warden in the kitchen. The Warden wore a green plastic badge that read YOUR WARDEN IS – and the space for the name was blank. A man pushing sixty, perhaps: grey hair Brylcreemed smoothly back, grey moustache thick and nicotine-stained. A white shirt and a bottle-green tie, and a stiff striped butcher's apron reaching nearly all the way down to polished brown brogues. All prior communication had come to Greg direct from YHA head-quarters – Greg couldn't remember if any of the letters had mentioned the Warden's name, and anyway he had left them back in London. Now the Warden was offering his hand with a grim nod, but only countered Greg's self-introduction mystify-ingly with, 'Head Office led you the usual dance, then?' before about-heeling to attend to some new arrivals who were ringing the reception bell. Greg wandered around the hostel under the high, ornately-plastered ceilings, his shoes clicking on the black and white tile floors, wide wooden banisters creaking under his hand. Posters of Lakeland views curled off walls, stiffened with age, all fluffy clouds and azure skies and brown at the edges. People lugged heavy bags past him, burst out of steaming shower rooms on a dripping tippytoed run for a dormitory. Skylights laid slabs of corn-coloured evening sunlight across landings.

The Warden was toiling up the staircase, cigarette in hand. 'You're there,' he said, halting halfway up and pointing across to a short dark corridor, down which Greg saw a door with 'Assistant Warden' on it, and then was on his way down again, remarking as if bearing a doubtful brief from a superior, his words bitten out around the cigarette, 'The . . . understanding was . . . for you officially to begin tomorrow morning . . . if you can therefore occupy yourself until that time . . . ?'

So then Greg had meandered out into the garden. The other side of a gate in the bottom fence a path twisted up the tussocky slope, and when Greg followed it he found it ascending across the slopes of the fell to the rocky crag, and above the town.

Slumped back in bed that night, Greg picked up the new paperback of Wordsworth's *Selected Poems* he had bought in Waterstone's in Charing Cross Road, and flexed it experimentally for a while. He was going, now he was here, to read Wordsworth: he should read Wordsworth. Squinting hard, he counted the number of lines in the bar code. He tilted the book this way and that to see how the glossy cover reflected the light from his bedside Anglepoise. Eventually he riffled through the pages looking for the shortest poems, until he found a section where there were several different ones on each page. A series of sonnets: poems only a couple of inches long. Greg's eyes skated over the pages and eventually, to his surprise, he read:

XLV
On the Projected Kendal and Windermere Railway

Is then no nook of English ground secure
From rash assault? Schemes of retirement sown
In youth, and 'mid the busy world kept pure
As when their earliest flowers of hope were blown
Must perish . . .

But already Greg's mind was wandering. Throat-clearing, he thought, Get on with it . . . He skipped to the next one:

XLVI

Proud were ye, Mountains, when, in times of old,
Your patriot sons, to stem invasive war,
Intrenched your brows; ye gloried in each scar.

(What pompous bullshit, thought Greg, yawning. Falklands
rhetoric.)

Now, for your shame, a Power, the Thirst of Gold,
That rules o'er Britain like a baneful star,
Wills that your peace, your beauty, shall be sold,
And clear way made for her triumphal car
Through the beloved retreats your arms enfold!
Hear ye —

There was a knock at the door. He was left with a mental
picture of Wordsworth standing by a McAlpine's Portakabin,
stern sideburns and wooden staff, beholding earthmovers and
concrete mixers flattening the wide white dual carriageway
across the valley. 'Mm-hh?'

Beyond the furthest pale reaches of the Anglepoise a tall girl
in a short nightshirt was letting herself in, parting her dark,
waist-length hair away from her face.

Greg put down his book. The girl — she looked in her mid-
twenties — drifted about his room, peeping round the curtain
out at the dark, studying herself briefly in the mirror, drawing
a finger down the label of his Scotch bottle on the mantelpiece.
'Can I lie on your bed?' she said, curling up on the foot of his
bed and closing her eyes.

Greg nodded an open-mouthed yes, but the girl was
smoothing her nightshirt over her thighs and sighing luxur-
iantly. He watched her lying there, now still, her head on her
hands, her mouth in a solemn smile. Eventually he picked up
his Wordsworth again.

– Hear ye that whistle? As her long-linked Train
Swept onwards, did the vision cross your view?
Yes, we were startled; – and, in balance true,
Weighing the mischief with the promised gain,
Mountains, and Vales, and Floods, I call on you

(*There was a tall girl with long hair lying on his bed.*)

To share the passion of a just disdain . . .

– and a railway line was just a green road with tracks on.

The girl sat up suddenly and scoured her eyes with her fists, and beamed brilliantly at Greg. 'I'm doing a survey,' she said, and sighed. 'Bunk beds are so narrow! It's like . . . sleeping to attention!'

Really, Greg thought. He wanted to guffaw out loud. A po-faced poet ranting about railways, and the most forward girl in the world . . .

The girl burrowed her chin into the counterpane again. 'I'm Ruth.'

'When did you test the bunk beds?'

Ruth looked hard at him. 'I'm sleeping in the dormitory,' she said. 'Here all summer, for some reason that escapes me. It's for my thesis: on the geology of the Lakeland mining regions. I muck in with all the cooking and shit and get free board and lodging. I had the dormitory to myself a couple of weeks ago, but now the place is full of people every night – all *staying* here.'

Greg said he was Greg, and all that, and asked if it was a good hostel.

'I can't seem to exchange one sensible sentence with the Warden,' Ruth said. 'Food's crap. But he sells Mars Bars at reception'. She inclined her head in vague enquiry. 'Who won the election?'

'Where've you been?'

'I heard it was on . . . Out on the fell all day. I'm in the middle of mapping the tungsten deposits on Scale Fell – the old mine was on the far side. It's about three miles away.' She shook her head. 'But I don't talk to anyone here.' Ruth bounced off the bed and raised her bare foot to her knee in a *pas de deux* and said, 'Well, it's very nice to meet you, Greg,' with demure formality.

'Can I, maybe, come out to see this fell one day?' said Greg. 'I've never been to the Lakes before. I climbed up one today – this mountain behind the hostel.'

'Mm, the Lakes are OK,' said Ruth abstractedly. 'Thunacar.

The Warden disappears up that a lot. Yes – you got a car? I walk there along the old railway line.'

'I'd like to do that.'

'Can I take the car, then?' Ruth poured herself a swig of whisky from Greg's Scotch bottle into his toothmug and stared at him over the rim as she tossed it back. 'I'm sorry that woman won again,' she added afterwards, and pulled the bedroom door open again slowly. 'Her *hair* . . .'

Chapter Two

During Greg's first week the Warden, always on his way somewhere, immediately preoccupied, patting all his pockets for matches or cigarettes suddenly mislaid, successfully limited their exchanges to edgy pleasantries, conversations-to-avoid-conversations about the weather and the advantages of microwaves for cooking quick meals. But talking to him for a few moments about the view from the top of Thunacar, Greg did manage to elicit that the Warden had been up there once at midnight, and you could hear the lorries grinding by even then; and that the old railway you could see went from Carrock down to the main line at Wetherbeck fifteen miles away: it had closed in the early seventies. That new road did for it, said the Warden, but no one ever used it anyway, and all the hostellers came by car these days. At one time there had been talk of the council turning it into a nature trail, but that had been a while back.

The Warden talked to Ruth even less. She stared out of the window a lot while they were cooking, cheek pressed to the glass, or read the sheets of old newspaper the Warden had torn up to wrap the peelings in. Whenever she was cooking something the Warden hovered nearby and darted in every so often to turn down the gas; everything burnt to a frazzle, he muttered, no wonder she never ate a thing.

Towards the end of that first week, in the quiet middle of the day between all the hostellers departing and the next lot arriving, Greg walked down the hill to take a look around the town. After following the road signposted 'Town Centre' at a crossroads, however, he soon found himself passing a park he hadn't remembered driving past; then the road began to climb, and there was a no-through-road sign. The High Street was down below: some kids must have turned the notice round. But it was a wide and pleasant tree-lined avenue, curving steadily uphill ahead of him, so Greg strolled on to see what was at the top, and on the crest of the hill the road opened out into a wide forecourt.

In front of him was an enormous, solid building, with three tall gables, built in large blocks of grey stone. Ivy trailed across the stonework, the windows were boarded up, the chimney stack had sagged askew. But the padlocked front door was a freshly-painted plum-red. Greg peeped through the letterbox – the dim light he could see by was filtering in under lopsided doors at the opposite end – into a high, murky hall, the marble floor scattered with old newspapers and broken wine bottles. He took a few paces back. Over the entrance portal in the centre was the stone inscription: 1877 CARROCK STATION.

To the right of the building stood a large hotel, the Carrock Grange, built in the same grey stone and obviously at the same time. Through one of its picture windows an elderly lady sat sipping at a cup of tea. To the left was some kind of council depot – blue dustcarts, vans and flatbed trucks parked behind the gates, and a muffled drilling coming from what looked like the old goods shed, its doors now blue like the lorries. The gates were ajar, and Greg meandered into the yard – no one else seemed to be around. Pushing between two bushes in the dense wall of hydrangea at the side, and scrambling up the earthy bank behind, he came out on to the platform.

It was hugely long. It stretched away to his left until it was terminated by a high wall, back to his right to the station building, and from there on quite as far again. It must have been a hundred and fifty yards. Greg tried to imagine how many carriages could fit alongside: a hugely long train. In front of the platform was a broad expanse of hummocky grass, perhaps fifty yards to the tall hedge screening a row of houses. You could fit a football pitch here where the tracks would once have been.

From the station building a great glass canopy hung out over the platform – more like a conservatory suspended in mid-air. All of its panes were smashed, and the platform was covered in glass fragments. Against one of its supporting pillars a notice was propped up: BEWARE UNSAFE. Greg crunched across under the skeletal roof to stand in front of the booking hall doors. They had also had the plum-red repaint.

He counted one hundred-and-sixty-three paces from the council depot end of the platform to the hotel end, where the platform sloped down to the ground and the old line went on, a thin footpath disappearing into straggling hawthorn bushes. Greg looked back towards the station. This was a big place! Room for perhaps four tracks side-by-side on the football-pitch area; one long train departing from this platform, another maybe arriving at another in the middle, and still space for all the wagons and engines and shunters and spare carriages you also saw at stations, rows of them; and all the yard where the council lorries were now . . . Here was the end of the old railway Greg had seen from the top of Thunacar. And yet, somewhere on from here, outside Carrock, that smooth green line – the idea of the one did not continue from the idea of the other. Visible from the top of the fell, out beyond the big road, had been a country railway – a part of the countryside: a quiet, slow, mostly empty line, it would have been, the little train an occasional interruption to the deserted calm just to mark the periods of the day. So Greg conjured it to himself. But this station's vast residual emptiness bespoke a former hectic crowding: a terminus for long, snaking express trains – trains that hammered along behind large locomotives, and disgorged hundreds of passengers onto the platform in the simultaneous swinging-open of every carriage door: a station too for freight trains longer still – wagons heaped with coal, cylindrical tanker-wagons, trucks loaded with cable drums, racks of girders: a loud, ringing station, sending passengers and goods across the country!

How had it all survived so long – if the line had closed back in the seventies – and what was to happen to it? The green line curling through the fells: lush and even, naturally undisturbed: somewhere people didn't need to be any longer – it was as if, out there, it had grown its own path. Whereas this tousled piece of waste ground and its boarded-up station-emporium, abandoned among the avenues of houses and the trees, had no use, but needed one.

A railway in the Lakes: the kind of thing Wordsworth wrote

13

sonnets about. Something would happen to this, the derelict scene said to Greg, as it had itself once happened to other things. Who had just painted the doors like that?

Inside The Bookshop, Prop. A. Edwards, halfway up the High Street – this time Greg had taken the right turning – a man with an unkempt ginger beard and rimless glasses sat at the counter reading a fat paperback of *Aneurin Bevan* by Michael Foot. Greg rotated the postcard spinner and found a card to send to his parents, and the bookseller held out his hand for the coins without looking up. Behind the counter a sign pointed up a narrow spiral staircase to 'Politics, Women's, Nuclear, Green Issues, History, Literature'. Greg squeezed past and clambered up to find a large L-shaped room under the eaves. There was a whole bookcase of poetry, an area of green Virago spines, a display of a new book he had seen back in London about the modern cult of the Royal Family, and a corner devoted to Transport, which appeared to be entirely books on trains. I wonder, thought Greg, if there is anything on the old line here, about when it was open? The quiet space in the town; the quiet gap through the country – finding something that was not, but had been. Their emptiness was staying with Greg, simply saying, people were there once. But these railway books all had titles like *Great Western Motive Power of the Fifties*, and were only full of photographs of steam engines.

Greg went back downstairs to browse among the books on local history. And besides, this was the Lake District, not the Train District.

'Can you find what you want?' The man with the ginger beard flattened his paperback open and laid it face down.

'No, no thanks,' Greg said. 'I was just wondering if there was a book about the old railway line here.'

The man shook his head as though the two of them had already been discussing the subject for a while. 'These things just get forgotten. Under people's very eyes – but they're too busy looking at something else.' He looked up to Greg for confirmation. 'Very easy to get depressed about it,' he said, smiling a sanguine smile, 'especially when, inevitably and unbelievably, this cynical, brutish government's just been voted in for another four years . . . But people'll come to remember some day.' The man pushed his glasses up his nose, clasped his hands together on the counter before him, and leant forward. 'They'll look at the history again, they'll see how the National Health Service was founded, and why. They'll realise that there has indeed been such a thing as a Poll Tax before, but not since virtually feudal times. They'll find out that under this government the number of people living below the poverty line has for the first time in decades actually *increased*, and conclude that maybe, in such circumstances, company directors receiving golden handshakes of half a million a time isn't *strictly* necessary . . .'

What is this? Greg was thinking. Did this man bend everyone's ear with a speech like this as soon as they came through the door? All he'd said was 'railway'. 'I . . . saw someone had painted the doors of the old station red . . .'

'It's a step,' said the man. 'You have to do something. It's coming together.' He was licking his finger and peeling a yellow leaflet off a pile on the counter. 'Awareness in the town is just beginning to grow, and soon –' (passing the leaflet across to Greg) '– the time'll be right to have the launch meeting.' He offered his hand. 'Ashley Edwards. I'm the Chairman of the Preservation Group.'

Soon he was telling Greg how he'd come to Carrock a year ago to run the bookshop, after teaching English for ten years in Muswell Hill. Shortly before he'd arrived, the foundry in the town had closed, and a couple of months later – 'just like that' – the ballbearings factory had shut too.

'Town's two major employers both' – Edwards snapped his fingers – 'gone. I decided then that the railway had to reopen; all these people here suddenly cut off like that, cut adrift. If the town was going to hold together, have any future other than coffee shops . . . The line's still there: everyone can see what it's meant for.'

Now Greg had a chance to introduce himself. 'I was reading these two poems Wordsworth wrote about railways in the Lake District. About the Windermere railway.'

'The only one still open,' said Edwards. 'A little single-track trundle nowadays.' He got up and went over to the Lake District section and pulled out a volume of Wordsworth. 'All the others are lost.' He turned the pages. 'Scandalous waste, on every count – economic, social, ecological . . . Typical of the way things are nowadays. So typical I can't believe it . . . You mean these two?' pointing to the pair of sonnets Greg had read. 'Hadn't much notion of democracy, had he, in spite of all the French Revolution stuff. Didn't want the Windermere line because it would bring day trippers to Grasmere . . .' But Edwards's voice had tailed off. As he read on he began to pace up and down the shop. A smile slowly spread over his face; once he let out a quiet chuckle. He paused in thought. Then he shook his head. 'I do him an injustice,' he said. 'Quite remarkable. I'm quite wrong. I hadn't come across this one – number forty-eight. This one's about the building of the Bela railway viaduct – you know, over on the Furness estuary, by the abbey:

'Well have yon Railway Labourers to this ground
Withdrawn for noontide rest . . . blm blm . . .

'Here –

'Others look up, and with fixed eyes admire
That wide-spanned arch, wondering how it was raised,
To keep, so high in air, its strength and grace . . .'

Edwards raised a finger to signal the climax:

'Profane Despoilers, stand ye not reproved,
While thus these simple-hearted men are moved?

'There! It is the Carrock line's greatest marvel too, its viaduct. A phenomenal achievement. Go and have a look – you'll see what I mean. Never been surpassed: sums up everything that's best in human labour. There's the best reason for reopening a railway. Wondrous things – how can they ever be obsolete, left to rot? You'll see. And he's seen that. Wordsworth has *seen* that!' Edwards was staring into air.

'So how are you going to reopen the railway here?' asked Greg, but then a woman came in the door and stood waiting expectantly behind him.

'Read the leaflet and let's meet for a drink,' said Edwards.

*

That night in bed – waiting for Ruth to knock again, but she hadn't since that first night – Greg read Edwards's leaflet.

RAILS RETURN TO CARROCK

Fifteen years after closure by British Rail, the Carrock and Wetherbeck Railway is poised for a new life. This beautiful scenic line can reopen if *you* help. After so many years of neglect the work ahead is immense, but the prospect stirring. Aiming to provide a year-round diesel service for local people, and summer steam trips with preserved stock for tourists, the new company is starting by raising the funds to lease Carrock Station, and the trackbed as far as Force Road (one mile). Then line clearing can commence and the first sleepers be relaid.

Ultimately the company's plans are ambitious and exciting. Reinstating freight facilities along the full length of the line, connecting with British Rail's system at Wetherbeck, will mean the removal of heavy lorries from Carrock's roads, and with them the attendant danger to pedestrians and old buildings – but above all the overdue rejuvenation of Carrock's industrial base, which has in recent years suffered such catastrophic and unnecessary 'rationalisation' and decline.

Holidaymakers might once more travel together in their hundreds to Carrock by train, and the heavy burden of thousands of cars pouring individually through serene Forcedale can be diminished at last. Far from speeding unseeing to their destinations along the concrete waste of the A-road, people will once again be able to appreciate the full splendour of this part of Lakeland from the leisurely passage of the train.

Instrumental in Carrock's past, and crucial to its future, the Carrock Railway has been closed for too long. A railway is for everyone! Before the car kills the Lake District, and nature finally kills the Carrock Railway, join the growing movement to make its rebirth a reality!

The gawky fluctuation between hesitancy and effusiveness surprised Greg again – it was as if Edwards was trying not to sound like Edwards. Again, here was no puffing smoke, no Golden

Age of steam, no bucolic idylls or *Railway Children* echoes: rather, it seemed, hinted at beneath the stern reticence, here was a vision of the future for a present that had gone wrong, of a huge communal act of reclamation and tending. But how? How was all this going to happen? Hadn't the Warden said there were fifteen *miles* of the railway? A yellow duplicated handout, telling you at the end to contact A. Edwards at his shop, whose parish magazine prose made reopening a railway as simple as a garden fête; telling you, in fragmentary dreams of democracy and humility, not how, but that it had to.

Then Greg turned to Wordsworth's Sonnet 48 about the railway viaduct, and read that. Except it turned out actually to be entitled 'At Furness Abbey', and not to be about a railway viaduct at all.

> Well have yon Railway Labourers to this ground
> Withdrawn for noontide rest. They sit, they walk
> Among the Ruins, but no idle talk
> Is heard; to grave demeanour all are bound;
> And from one voice a Hymn with tuneful sound
> Hallows once more the long-deserted Quire
> And thrills the old sepulchral earth, around.
> Others look up, and with fixed eyes admire
> That wide-spanned arch, wondering how it was raised,
> To keep, so high in air, its strength and grace:
> All seem to feel the spirit of the place,
> And by the general reverence God is praised:
> Profane Despoilers, stand ye not reproved,
> While thus these simple-hearted men are moved?

It was the *abbey*, the derelict abbey that had the 'wide-spanned arch' – an ancient ruined church to whose peaceful haven the railway workers had adjourned. Who did Edwards think the 'Profane Despoilers' were? What was Edwards talking about?

Chapter Three

'I think probably my best bet is the Diplomatic Service,' Ruth was saying ahead of him, as they pushed on through the tall bushes overhanging the narrow trackbed path out of Carrock. 'Meet people all the time ... travel ... help to sort things out ... I suppose once I'm shot of this thesis I ought to take some exams or something.'

Greg, brushing aside the branches that waved back into him in Ruth's wake, and finding that his mind would only project her in defiant, self-absorbed solitudes – Ruth striding out in measured paces over her fell, Ruth curled up into herself like a cat – couldn't think of a reply. Eventually, recalling the Mars Bars, he said, 'And the food? The enormous banquets you'd have to eat all the time?'

'And the chance to learn languages,' said Ruth, as if food were one more language she would automatically be taught and grow gifted in once she arrived at her consulate-university. 'You'd learn so *much*, just from travelling all over the world.'

This Diplomatic Service, it became clear to Greg, was British Airways' long-haul division.

'Do you have an idea what the ... average day in an embassy would consist of?'

'Oh, administration. Conferences. Receptions. Releasing hostages.'

Was the airy tone indication that she'd lost interest in the subject, or reproving him for his laborious curiosity about details she knew far too well to need to relate?

The trackbed emerged from the overgrown corridor of trees to run along a grassy levee. Their boots skidded on hidden lumps of ballast.

'There's Scale Fell.' Ruth pointed at a tapering, almost conical mountain in the distance, its summit capped with a grey puff of cloud. 'We're about halfway there. I really like this part of the walk.' The embankment stretched ahead far into the morning haze, curving evenly left. To their right, a wide, grassy plain dotted with sheep; to their left, ancient, twisted rowan trees climbing up a hillside. Here was Greg knowing less about Ruth now than when they had first met, and he could think of nothing to ask or say to her. Although they were kicking along side by side now, it was as if she was still out in front, and he left only with her hair swaying down her back. The sun was easing through a milky sky, but he thought he could feel rain in the sliding, tingling air. As the sun burned through and then drew back the cloud shadows deepened and stretched across the fields. For the next half hour they walked in silence, stride for stride.

After a while Greg thought suddenly, this embankment is entirely man-made. It isn't a hill; it hasn't always lifted the land up like this. People built it. Once upon a time we would have been walking across the fields. He said to Ruth, 'Do you know when this railway was built?'

'It was opened when the lead mine at Force started working its main seam. That was in 1870. We passed the old workings back there – the siding's all overgrown with bushes now.'

'Force . . .' mused Greg out loud.

'It's Norse for waterfall. There must be one somewhere nearby.'

'And how would men have dug things in those days?'

'Picks and shovels and barrows,' answered Ruth.

All by hand, then.

So this huge causeway, thought Greg, is spadefuls and bar-rowfuls of earth; twenty feet high all along its length: earth dragged here in carts behind horses, it would have to be, then heaped up on the ground with shovels. These two miles of earth to make the railway's level course through the hills were dug like you pile up soil for a rockery.

Again Greg had the feeling he had had on top of the fell, but down here it was a sensation, not a deduction. It's man-made, but it makes itself part of the land. Obviously, everyone was used by now to seeing railways as natural landmarks, but a motorway, say, as a raw scar. Railways had always been there, it seemed, throughout the lifetime of anyone alive now; motorways were new. The grass had had far longer to grow on railway embankments than motorway cuttings. But that main road —

He stopped. As Ruth's boots crunched to a halt he caught the wavering, ebbing buzz. He answered her glance with a shake of the head and they walked on.

— That road: they hadn't even tried to merge it with anything. Perhaps it was simply too large to bother: two wide lanes each way, a central reservation in between, lay-bys either side — if it was going to be there, it would look like that. But perhaps it had been too easy. With those enormous hinged earthmovers and JCBS you could make it as wide as you wished, put it anywhere, move anything for it.

Greg found all perspectives in the landscape around him realigning. Now he saw the embankment not as massive against men, but narrow and low against the mountains. A train, even a train the whole length of the platform in Carrock, would be a short, thin centipede on just one point along it — this level green curve that held the line of the hillside, brought the plain up to it, and sat at its foot. When you were building by hand the easiest way was to accommodate the land, to go round, and join in. Then it came to him with simple, surprising clarity: the realisation that hundreds of people could be taken across this landscape all at once in that single train: that they would be tiny and insignificant to the mountains, and the mountains Yes! would be stupendous and towering to them: a realisation that subsumed and sang out the strange magnanimous euphoria that had been gathering behind his reverie! . . . and returned him suddenly self-mocked to Ruth and her steady scrunching steps by his side. Greg halted for a moment and looked around him. This is my first time in the Lake District, he told himself, and still all I've thought about is trains.

When they reached the site of Ruth's current survey on the side of Scale Fell, Greg stood and watched as she slid her finger across the large map unrolled on her knee, took compass bearings, and then wandered around on the grassy slope. Occasionally she would break into a marching stride. On each return she would dab the map with a pencilled cross.

Several times Greg strolled over afterwards to inspect these pencil-cross sites. Once he found a chunk of glittery rock protruding from the turf. Another place was a patch of dusty heather. At a third there was an ancient pitted sheep's skull and some rabbit droppings.

'I'll have to talk to you later,' Ruth said with faint irritation at his beaming, baffled look. 'I have to remember how many steps and which one I'm counting to.'

Eventually, as a distant Ruth was disappearing around the side of the fell, Greg called across, 'I'll find you here in an hour', and set off – just catching her belated, disembodied, 'And a half' – down towards the stocky church tower he could see among the trees at the bottom.

When the path Greg was on reached the tree-line, however, it must have followed the spur of the hill rather than the decline into the valley, for he came out of the plantation on to the top of a cutting, and found himself looking down on the old railway again.

The sides of the cutting were sheer, chiselled faces of rock. Peering over the edge carefully, Greg at last found a way down across to his right, where the striations of the rock descended to the trackbed in a thin, precarious stair. He dropped the last step onto level ground with a gulp, twenty yards from where the line was suddenly truncated in a tunnel mouth, the fell framing it massively. The tunnel – therefore this was the main rise of Scale Fell above it – was walled up with grey stones, but in the middle a rusty iron door, its corners rounded as on a ship, hung ajar.

Inside, the doorway immediately receded as an outline of pale, peachy, one-dimensional light. All around Greg, as he stopped still, was a quiet, pouring roar, as if the blackness itself was falling in a torrential curtain. Inside him, at the same time, he could hear his own breathing. He walked further in until he was not sure when he looked back whether he could see the light at the doorway or not. The floor felt slushy and uneven under his feet; his boots kicked invisible sharp stones, splashed into puddles. In the darkness it seemed to Greg, standing with hands clasping his knapsack straps, that the roof must be hanging swimmingly high above him like cathedral vaulting;

the walls, placed only by the sound of the water he could imagine quivering down in innumerable rivulets, felt vastly distant.

Finally he clicked on the torch Ruth had insisted he bring for fog on the fells, and arced the beam over his head to discover the crusty, streaked dullness of brick only feet from him. Now he was in just a long, narrow tube bored through the bottom of this hill to get out the other side. Greg shone the torch back until he picked out the entrance only twenty yards off, and then forward, where the ray of light seemed to fall away to the floor after an uncertain distance. He retraced his steps to the door, and then turned to try and pace out the tunnel's full length.

He walked on into the tapering white beam for four hundred, four hundred and one, four hundred and two steps, until the silent counting of his voice in his head seemed as continuous and unvarying as the thin rushing of the water. He stopped and said out loud, 'Four hundred and three': the sound that sprang away could have been a murmur or a shout. When he played the torch up above there was the same jaggedly level arch over him joining the two darknesses together. He thought, A quarter of a mile already, and knew a cool, incontrovertible shifting in his mind that said, 'And with one more step all this will be exactly the same.' He turned round, looked down hard, examining the minute, coarse cording on his parka sleeve, searching the burnished water on the tunnel floor for the filmy shapes that he could know were unique to that one pool, and sighting the last number at the distant dip of his torchbeam, started counting from one again.

Once Greg climbed out to stand in the cutting again his mind became furiously, discursively rational. A quarter of a mile, and no end in sight – but the other end could have been completely blocked up: in any case the doorway at this end had soon disappeared from view: so the other end might have been two steps away from where he had finally halted: or the tunnel could have been as long again – or twice as long: the only way to know was to look at the map, which Ruth had: therefore return to Ruth. When he looked at his watch, however, he saw he had only left her twenty-five minutes ago.

As he walked back along the line towards Scale village, the exhilaration he had felt bestriding the embankment now seemed ridiculous and mawkish. *This* was the railway: not some lucid, pastoral paradigm of social engineering, but that endlessly black, cold, stone hole. Greg tried to imagine seeing the tunnel from the window of a lighted train swaying and grating through it – the sudden lurches and bangs that clutch the carriage – but all he could remember was the unceasing brittle pouring-like silence. The sun came out, warm on his cheekbones, and made his limbs feel loose and flaccid. He thought angrily, Why do they want to reopen this? Has that Edwards man been in there? Why don't they just lock the door and leave it alone?

The cutting walls sloped down and the line ran through the trees. Soon a narrow road crossed the trackbed, and ahead Greg could see the land gradually falling away and the embankment lifting up. He turned off on to the road up the hill. At its summit there was a row of four dark terraced cottages, and a hedged grassy trackway next to them signposted 'St Martin's-in-Forcedale'. Greg walked for a quarter of an hour up the steeply, evenly climbing track before he came upon the lych-gate in a dry stone wall.

It was a tiny church, in a small clearing among the trees, with the heathery fell swelling behind. Its deep slate roof seemed to reach nearly to the ground; its low stone walls showed their patching and filling over the years. Banks of bright yellow forsythia at the edge of the clearing were palpitating gently in the breeze. The churchyard was crowded with grey headstones that came close to the church walls.

Greg turned the iron ring on the door and went in. It was bare and cool inside – the sun had been striking the door – and the latticed windows at the sides were dull and watery. He counted ten rows of pews, seats for perhaps fifty people. A small iron cross at the altar, a faded brocade altar-cloth, and three uncovered bulbs hanging down from the roof-beams over the aisle. Looking around him, Greg felt chilled and content. You could not imagine Harvest Festival here, or even Christmas: in this church you would have to make your festival with the people who came; it gave you nothing itself. It was not a church for visitors, or rather a visitor was turned back on his own simple being. Nothing to beguile: a welcome if you wanted to be there.

Greg dropped some money in the box at the back, took one of the thin, heavily-letterpressed guide-books, and went to read the slate plaques on the walls. He found one dated 1722, read on others of Churchwardens of This Parish, Devoted Christian Families, and then at the far end, tucked between two windows, on a small brass plate, saw:

IN MEMORY OF THOSE DILIGENT AND SELFLESS
MEN WHO LOST THEIR LIVES DURING THE
CONSTRUCTION OF SCALE RAILWAY TUNNEL.
THE REWARD OF THEIR EFFORT IS WITH US ALWAYS.
    Geo. Manning (Sec^y.) C.W.R.C. 1871

How many, thought Greg, his hand at his lip, and how?
  He sat down in the front pew to look in the guidebook.

In the eastern corner of the CHURCHYARD are the graves of the ten navvies who died during the building of the infamous Scale railway tunnel nearby. Some were killed in explosives accidents while the mile-long tunnel was being blasted through Scale Fell. Others died in a cholera epidemic at the sadly insanitary tunnel mess (situated at the Scale end of the cutting, but now disappeared). Only three of the men's names are known, and all the graves are unmarked. A small plaque . . .

Outside Greg found the ten grassy hummocks, and, standing in the sun and light wind, could think only, A patch of ground; a small patch of ground.

By the time Greg got back to Ruth again – a quarter of an hour late, after toiling right up to the top of the fell so as to look down and find her – the sky was grey marble and the air had the stirred-up rain-feeling again.

'We'd better get down off here quick,' said Ruth, already packed up and starting off.

'It didn't come to anything this morning.'

'It will now,' Ruth said ahead of her.

She led the way straight down the hillside, the route Greg

had descended earlier, and the rain hit them just as they entered the trees, a thin, seeping fall that seemed to thicken as soon as it started. While Ruth stopped to rummage in her knapsack Greg thought, licking the water off his top lip, how much daylight he could see between these trees, how much rain they let through. Ruth yanked on a long orange cagoule and overtrousers, and pulled the cord in her hood tight. The small circle of face left showing seemed to accentuate her frown. 'Haven't you got any waterproofs?' The rain was running down her nose.

'Only this,' Greg apologised, shrugging his now-heavy parka reasonably.

Ruth set off at a run, billowing and orange, shouting back, 'You'll get *drenched*,' and Greg lumbered after her blindly as the rain turned solid, streams of it crowding in to pelt him.

They hurtled out of the plantation at the end of the cutting, and ahead Ruth was yelling, 'We can shelter in the tunnel.' He jolted out, 'Yes-I-know', as she sprinted for the iron door. Then she was holding it open for him to stumble inside, clanging it shut behind her, and there was only their gasping for breath in the blackness.

Greg switched on his torch, and Ruth took off her waterproofs to spread them wet-side-down on the floor. She sat cross-legged and erect, and Greg knelt down next to her. They listened to the rain flinging itself on the door.

'I'll go to the camping shop as soon as we get back,' said Greg.

Ruth said, 'You can put the torch out now.' She was scraping the wet strands of hair from her forehead.

Greg turned the torch off experimentally. 'Then we just have to listen to water pouring down in here as well.'

'I really love it in here,' came Ruth's voice after a few moments, calm and pensive. 'I've been coming in here lots. You stand in the middle of this . . . and it's so cold . . . and this constant rushing noise . . . and it's as if you're speeding through outer space . . .'

Greg wondered if Ruth was hurling her arms out as she spoke. He could feel her still looking straight ahead, and then her voice turned towards him. 'Where did you go this morning?'

'I came in here,' he said slowly. 'I didn't like it much. I tried to walk to the end, but . . . It's all right with you now, but I think it's awful to be here on one's own.'

'So why did you stay so long?'

'I didn't. Then I went to Scale church.' As he was about to tell her about the navvies' graves, he had the sense that Ruth's mind was tuned to a quite different frequency. He just said, 'This tunnel is a *mile* long?'

'Mm. There's some very hard rock in this mountain, too. Shales and stuff.'

'You know there's this movement in the town to reopen the railway?' Greg tried the monologue anyway, even if it was only leaving Ruth to her own thoughts and falling into the darkness. 'I've only been here a few days, but already I seem to have met the bloke who's trying to organise it, read his handout. And seen the old station, and walked along the line all the way to here, and now this massive, appalling tunnel. It has to be the most *ludicrous* joke. One little sheet of paper, talking about challenges, and tourism, and seeing the hills by train . . . When you've got this – this *huge*, horrid thing. I could see why they want to do it, as we were walking along that embankment this morning – but they're talking about taking responsibility for *this*. And that enormous viaduct you can see from the top of Thunacar . . . I suppose I'm fascinated by the theory and all the optimism of it, but sitting in here you realise it's just crazy, frivolous speculating.'

'A lot of people died,' said Ruth, to his surprise. 'If you compare it to what the miners on this fell were doing it's amazing. You almost wonder why they bothered, just to put a railway track underneath. I like to think of them seeing if they could actually get all the way through, digging deeper and deeper into all this darkness.' Ruth stood up steadily, and Greg heard her gritty footsteps receding from him – further into the tunnel or towards the door? He had no bearings; couldn't tell.

While Ruth was gone into outer space Greg thought about the navvies and their tunnel mess in the middle of nowhere: actually living out here – saw them under rain like today's, stamping mud into their shacks, dipping mugs into pails of stale water, lugging a coffin right to the top of that steep trackway.

TRAIN, TRAIN

That, all in order then to work in here, hacking this out. Where the men and their shanty-town had been: now just the hillside again. This tunnel they had blasted and shaped through the fell – for trains, for a dare, or merely for money, it didn't matter: a pointless sealed-up hole more useful if never dug at all. Greg understood then the simple rhetorical question behind those red-painted doors at the station: *What do you do with all this?*

Suddenly Ruth said, 'It's only raining inside now – hear?' and where her voice came from the door was opening for the sun to glow in. Greg hauled himself off his stiff knees in the gloom, gathered up Ruth's waterproofs and splashed after her.

During the walk back to Carrock Ruth broke the silence once to say, 'I really like the way you're always trying to work everything out – except you leave me to be completely Ruth-ish.'

Greg, who could not think of anything to say, or be sure whether Ruth were being indulgent or reproachful, or whether he were supplying both intonations, said nothing, and had no idea what this meant, except that in their strange symbiotic dislocation it probably didn't matter.

Chapter Four

The avalanche of summer holidaymakers had swept down on to Carrock. Since the day Greg had arrived all the hostel's forty beds had been taken nearly every night, and in the early mornings the corridors and staircases clattered with fixed-eyed cyclists in dazzling liveries and advertising decals, walkers with heavy clanking packs dangling mugs and map-cases, sunken-chested old men in shorts, and phalanxes of cackling scouts. Greg seemed to be busy all the time: he rose at dawn to stir porridge and fry bacon for breakfasts, and he was still booking in new arrivals and selling Milky Ways from the reception shop at ten at night. At meal times a bird-like old lady called Edie came in to help; she looked in all the simmering cauldrons saying, 'Lovely,' and with a rigid finger assigned sheepish hostellers to washing up. But otherwise the Warden and Greg, with Ruth's dogged but fluttering assistance, ran the whole place themselves. During the middle of the day, when the hostel was closed, there were still stairs to mop clean of wet footprints, doorknobs that had come away in people's hands, and paddy-fields to be reclaimed for washrooms again in time for the evening influx.

The Warden – still Greg had not found out his name, and Ruth had no idea either, and after this long how could you now ask him? – endured it all with harassed patience in the presence of the hostellers, and sighed in irritation once they were gone. He was formal and gruff with them, murmuring, 'And do you require –?' and, 'As regards –?', but when he stooped to pick up clods of mud in the hall or found cooking-pans still streaked with food after washing-up he would say quietly to Greg, his colour rising, 'We run a nursery, not a hostel.' Greg had to admit to himself, however, that though it was hard work looking after them, he couldn't say the hostellers were excessively slack or demanding: there were an awful lot of people passing through every day. Sometimes the Warden waved dismissively for Greg to go and sort out something that would probably only make him angry, and at reception Greg would find two girls from a guide company swathed in towels to say their shower was broken – who led him into the washroom as half a dozen others, with voluptuous shrieks, clutched up skirts and nighties just too late over young, pointed breasts. Or ten empty places at the breakfast table where an entire boys' school party was missing – and in the dormitory a master with the smudged face of having got out of bed instantly before, declaiming fiercely, '. . . And if you're *not* all down in *five* minutes not *only* will you miss breakfast but you will also *still* do all the washing up . . .'

The Warden, Greg realised quite soon, was simply tired all the time. He had been running this hostel, it emerged during one of their brief, grunted conversations, for twenty-one years. He mentioned 'my wife' once, but gave no clue as to when, or why, he had had to start doing it alone. He smoked heavily and intensely. Keeping the hostel open every week of the summer was exhausting him.

But also, Greg knew, the Warden made himself exhausted, with the demoralised anger he forced himself to feel whenever the hostellers were careless or destructive. The Warden worked too hard at keeping the place going, and not hard enough at letting it look after itself. On another occasion he had referred to his time in the army, and from the casual intimacy with which he used the word Greg was sure he didn't just mean national service. Greg decided that he must have been an officer – a leader, once – but by now the ambivalent army training of leadership and service had declined into merely service. The Warden served the hostellers, as he felt he ought, but had become unable to see how the situation – rather than the people, whom he couldn't corral like soldiers – could be led into improvement. He kept the hostel freshly decorated, but painted it in navy-blues and duck-egg greens so that it felt like a school. He tidied and cleaned it relentlessly, but his edgy, grim tolerance made it a dour, cowed place. And by remaining aloof, official, The Warden, he made himself a headmaster, and the hostellers

surly and conspiratorial. Greg came upon him one morning
standing quietly alone in reception after the last of the hostellers
had departed, and realised that he truly hadn't met a single one
of them.

When Greg had been there a fortnight or so he came downstairs one night after checking all the lights were out in the
washrooms and corridors, and heard the Warden call out softly,
'Telly's on,' as if there were a programme on that Greg had
asked to watch. Greg went into the Warden's darkened sitting-
room for the first time and found him stretched back in an
armchair, feet crossed, watching the snooker in black and white.
They sat in silence with the regular clicking and the breathy
commentary, and the Warden smoked coolly and reflectively like
the players. Greg could feel the Warden's relaxed contentment in
the presence of these smart, deferential individuals soberly and
smoothly tidying the table of balls.

Afterwards, as the Warden was turning off the set and collecting up his cigarettes and matches, he said to Greg, 'You happy
with this?'

Greg wondered if the Warden might mean the snooker, but
said, 'Yes,' in a considered tone, 'enjoying it very much.'

'Bit of a come-down after what you came from?'

Greg shook his head. 'I was selling money to other people
selling money, who sold it to other people selling money who
then sometimes sold it back to me. You spent your whole
day quoting figures and decimal points down the telephone. It
shouldn't be that easy to make money – in fact it's only so easy
because it isn't real.'

'Whereas here you just feed and water people, give them a
bed, and send them on their way.' There was quiet self-derision
in the Warden's voice.

'That's what I like.' Greg had in fact been assessing earlier
that day what he appreciated about his new occupation: how
prototypically practical it was; how anti-materialist the idea of
the hostel – offering accommodation as a necessity, not as a
luxury as well: how democratic, even – every kind of person
stayed there and all sat at the same table. And how already it
had chastened him: the number of UB40 cards presented for
reduced prices. 50p off: where Greg had come from such a

quibble would have been a laughable meanness, as you rounded up restaurant bills and taxi fares to the nearest pound. Here it was a factor in whether someone could have a holiday. So anyone could stay here . . . But what was expected of him, Greg sensed, was a response of reassuring, collusive dignity. He couldn't think how to say any of this to the Warden.

'And our young Ruth?'

Ruth would have stared away resignedly and said he was working everything out.

Greg didn't know how to reply about Ruth either. That morning she and the Warden had had an argument about frying eggs – Ruth for quickly and brown, the Warden urging slowly and smooth and white – which had ended with one saying, 'Do you want me to do this or not?' at the same moment as the other said, 'Do you want to do this or not?' And apart from running her out to Scale Fell each day since the storm – journeys soon established to elapse in easy silence – Greg had hardly been aware of her. At mealtimes there was too much cooking to allow talk, and in the evenings while he manned reception she borrowed his room to write up her notes and (he saw from the bottle) drank his whisky.

At last, 'Ruth is a person . . .' he began shrewdly, clueless as to how the pronouncement would end.

The Warden switched out the light as answer, and nodded goodnight.

One bright morning soon afterwards, when Greg returned from dropping off Ruth, the Warden was packing up a small rucksack and putting on boots and a floppy green hat. Greg half wanted to be asked to join him, half wanted to offer his company, but then decided to take the hint from the Warden's innocuously swift preparations to leave. The Warden went out through the back gate.

Greg now had the day to himself, and could think of nothing to do. He watched the Warden's hunched, leaning figure slowly diminishing as it inched up the fell, and saw himself made lonely by the departure – he was starting to notice how much his time had become dependent on the Warden, who in turn inhabited his own space. Ruth was away all day. As soon as the hostellers arrived Greg had work to do, and the work continued all the while they were there. In the morning, as the day became free, they left. Whenever the day was free, the Warden left.

Hanging around the hostel, Greg came upon a small poster on the notice-board, announcing a Second Public Meeting to be held that night, in the Methodist Church Hall, of the Carrock Railway Preservation Group.

Edwards, studying the hundred or so people in front of him, was looking soberly obligated – as if he had been invited to address this meeting rather than the one to call it. He was flanked, on the stage, by two men in suits on one side, three on the other in blazers or polo-necks. Greg sat near the back, next to a large elderly man with whistling breath who rested one hand on his walking-stick. Just as Edwards was getting up to speak the man turned slowly to Greg with a stern stare that seemed to read, 'Are you behind all this business too?'

If Edwards's leaflet had read like a halting address to a public meeting, his speaking wasn't. 'Things are moving,' he began simply, in the manner of resuming from last week's lesson, and went straight into a progress report that implicitly included them all as contributors. He spoke of consultations with the council, the National Park Board, the British Railways Board, of the interest of the local paper. Now, most importantly, the county council, which still owned the station site and buildings in Carrock, and the trackbed of the whole line, had, subject to certain conditions, given the go-ahead for essential renovation to start. 'The weeds and bushes can go,' said Edwards, 'straight away, and we can open up the station again.' He grinned with combative pleasure. The county surveyor would produce an estimate in a week of the major rebuilding work the station would need.

'The next step,' Edwards continued, regarding the audience with relaxed frankness, hands in pockets, 'is money.' How they were going to pay for reopening the line as far as Force Road. Not an appeal, but an affirmation: Edwards merely articulating the audience's own collective conclusions. There would be two stages. First, to pay for the things like paint and weed-killer needed in the short term, there would be all the usual

33

fund-raising activities – a jumble sale to start it off, and ideas and help welcome thereafter.

Then, the formation of a limited company to run the railway – to lease the land and buildings from the council, acquire rolling-stock, and put down track: to be capitalised by a share issue. 'It's something I hope the whole town will want to be part of. Can't promise any dividends; can't promise any profits.' Edwards's tone had become carefree, dismissive – such things were not to be apologised for, but rather a reassurance that Carrock's money would not be used in the wrong ways. 'I can only promise you that we'll get trains running for Carrock again.'

The applause was respectful and reserved as Edwards sat down, the light now catching his glasses and making his face appear inscrutably closed. It had been a curiously low-key performance; perhaps the panegyrics on viaducts and tunnels, the denunciations of Thatcherism, had come in the first Public Meeting, thought Greg. In any case, if the leaflet had been an uncertain combination of two different voices, and Greg had heard the first in Edwards's shop, then here was the second. Edwards knew, at this moment, what his audience did not want to hear. Meanwhile Greg's neighbour was shifting heavily in his seat again, and Greg followed his amazed eyes back to his walking stick, as though this blunt pole he thudded softly, testingly, on the floor were Edwards's speech.

The man on Edwards's immediate left glanced across – but Edwards was gazing ahead, calm and assured – then rose ('Geoff Parris, Environment Planning Officer, Cumbria County Council') and spoke guardedly of the council's interest in the preservation project, its regret back in 1972 when British Rail had confirmed that they were terminating services, and its awareness of the huge civil engineering task that would lie ahead if the railway really were to be reopened back to Wetherbeck. His brisk, cataloguing style made clear to all the council's attitude at this stage: tolerant, rather than encouraging. 'I can therefore confirm that the council is not opposed to any basic renovation work on the Carrock station building, or simple clearance of overgrown trackbed vegetation.' At the same time – Mr Parris sifted individual sheets of paper lightly like scenarios

– the council's ultimate intention remained, for the time being, to convert the longer sections of the line into a nature trail. Its intuition was that the combination of, say, a two- or three-mile steam railway running out of Carrock, to connect with a public path along the remainder of the trackbed, would be the most desirable, and the most feasible, co-operation of interests. He dangled his spectacles delicately, defensively.

The other man in a suit was writing down a few notes. Greg wondered who the other people on the platform were – Edwards hadn't introduced anyone. Presumably the other founders of the preservation group. Greg was also half-surprised by Edwards's easy and convivial manner as he had addressed the meeting. Obviously ten years' teaching had developed the public speaking facility, but how did this apparently gregarious, spontaneous organiser now endure sitting in his bookshop on his own all day? Then Greg thought, he plans all this.

The man in the suit from the Lake District National Park Tourism Committee was wistful and lugubrious, and soon his words drifted past Greg in snatches. 'Anything which cuts down the number of cars coming into the Lakes . . . grateful to Mr Edwards for taking this initiative . . . restore something of this example of Lakeland heritage, think by now we can call it that . . . pity we're now fifteen years on from when the railway originally closed . . . huge lapse of time . . . consequent decay and deterioration . . . prospect so much more daunting . . . indeed as I'm speaking to you now about the railway I've just had to spend the whole day discussing car parks and road improvements to keep this summer here from grinding to a halt completely . . .' He promised all possible help with developing a steam railway at Carrock Station as a new and valuable tourist attraction for the town, and sat down in righteous, self-effacing dejection.

The argument of the meeting – or at least of the authorities who counted – seemed to be crystallising as: 'Reopening the whole line is an exorbitant dream; do a small tourist attraction if you want.' But in the speakers' defensiveness, and in their disproportionate pessimism, there seemed certain personal homages and emotions – the acknowledgement, behind their official positions, of some larger, apparently familiar question. They weren't talking about reopening the railway as they would, perhaps, a swimming-pool; they tacitly recognised that more was expected of them. For each of them, and each differently, it seemed, the railway stood for other, large tasks which they knew hadn't been done, and which implicated them with every-one else.

It was time for questions from the floor.

A grey-haired man stood up and adjusted the silk handker-chief in his breast pocket, and said he was Norman Grice, the manager of the Carrock Grange Hotel. 'Well, I had wondered if something was up when I saw the station door had been painted bright red. I have to say that, as the neighbouring property, we would be very much opposed to the reopening of the railway as suggested. Steam engines, I know from my own distant experience, are horribly noisy and sooty things, and with this and the considerable influx of tourists into the station all the time there would, we feel, be an extreme inconvenience to our residents. It would be very detrimental to our trade without bringing any other benefits.'

Edwards looked angry, then secretly prepared, and said that of course the hotel had actually been built by the Carrock and Wetherbeck Railway Company in the first place, and originally depended on railway passengers for its custom to the extent that it used to have its own exclusive entrance direct from the platform. It was a little disappointing now that the hotel should be against the new venture, but he could assure Mr Grice that disturbance would be kept to a minimum, and that steam trains were simply the first phase, and a subsidiary aim. 'The over-riding reason for doing this is to get more people coming to Carrock again, and the Carrock Grange – more business for everyone – but coming by train.'

'We're full already,' said Mr Grice, 'and we want to stay that way.'

'Further to that,' called another voice, 'could I suggest an alternative, and cheaper, way of restoring the train service, which might also be of interest to our friend here?' A man in a white shirt with the top button fastened and no tie, stood up. 'It's how British Rail run their country lines these days. They now have these buses converted into little trains – like a bus on train wheels. You'd only need one to go up and down the Carrock line. You have a conductor inside to sell the tickets, and you don't need any station-masters. You have traffic lights for all the signals and level crossings. Then you just need one track for the train, and one platform at each station. The passengers wait in a kind of bus shelter. To pay for setting this up, you sell off all the spare land along the line, and you redevelop all of Carrock Station except for one platform – and that site alone should go for a really big amount of money. And by knocking all the station buildings down you also wouldn't have any to maintain. And these train-buses are very quiet. Just purr along . . .'

There was a horrified, glum settling around the hall in response to this sanguine reasoning. Whether those present were enthusiastically for or sceptically against a new railway for Carrock, such threatening sense was unwelcome. No one, evidently, wanted a railway like this. This would not be a railway.

One of Edwards's anonymous colleagues in blazers broke in: Yes, it would in theory provide the cheapest, most efficient railway, but it wouldn't work. A restored Carrock railway couldn't afford a fulltime paid labour force to do all the necessary work of track maintenance, train repairs, signalling and everything. It would depend for its operation on the help of volunteers, who wouldn't want to work on that kind of railway. Moreover, you couldn't realistically expect the year-round passenger service to make a profit – it hadn't under British Rail – but by running steam train rides for tourists you could generate extra revenue as cross-subsidy. For this, though, you'd need to preserve the stations and restore them with a proper 'period' feel.

Greg's neighbour eased himself up on his stick, muttering as he rose in an irritated phlegmy rumble, 'Why d'you think anyone's going to use the trains now when they didn't then? It's why they stopped them – wasn't a soul on them. The road's faster. Even the coach is quicker because it doesn't go all round the hills.' He sank down again immediately and glared at Greg for an answer.

More questions followed fast.

Wasn't reopening the railway as a tourist attraction going to

bring more cars into Carrock, not fewer, as everybody drove in
to park there for their ride on the train?

How many years was it going to take to get trains running
through to Wetherbeck again? Quite a few, presumably?

Wouldn't it be better, now that the railway had been closed
for so long, and the main road was here to stay, to leave things
be, let the line return to nature, and keep at least that part of
the landscape undisturbed, as it had now become?

Edwards heard them all out with disappointed, but not de-
feated, patience. I would have expected you to be with me, his
keen face seemed to be saying, but if you're not yet, you'll come
round; I just have some more work to do. They were all in this
together. His replies became fulsome, fraternal; he gestured
briskly, inclined his head deferentially. And yet all the time,
whether Edwards was arguing that indeed passengers had
dropped off before the closure, but only because British Rail
had run down the service, or that the number of accidents on
the main road through drivers going too fast was unacceptable
and increasing, some part of him seemed unengaged by all this,
or more deeply engaged elsewhere. It was like Edwards telling
his English pupils, You may not like this Shakespeare now, but
you'll be glad you did it later. *It will be good for you.* Edwards
seemed to know – seemed to perceive in the faces before him –
that it was *necessary* for Carrock to reopen its railway, and for
a reason too banally serendipitous to relate.

Another of the men in blazers talked about rolling-stock, and
a four-six-two that once worked on the branch, and Mark One
carriages, and an appeal to get the tank back from Barry.
Edwards followed him to close the meeting. He was apparently
on the brink of a final homily, but then simply stood regarding
the audience intently for several moments.

'Membership forms for the Preservation Group at the back,'
he burst out with a hearty clap of his hands. 'First working
party at the station, Sunday at ten.'

Chapter Five

For the rest of the week the weather was drear, and the Warden lost and mellow in front of the snooker, which was now on all the time. Greg went into town every day. On the Wednesday (the morning after the Public Meeting) he dropped in on Edwards at his bookshop. Already, as he walked up the High Street, Greg could see how many more people there were around, compared with when he had arrived a fortnight ago. They stepped off the narrow pavements into the road and then skipped back on as lines of cars nosed through. They peered out through smoke-glazed windows on tall, slabby coaches. They queued out of the door of the baker's for sandwiches and sausage rolls. By lunchtime they had bought all Edwards's stock of Lake District Ordnance Survey maps.

'Bittrix Pudderrr,' said Edwards as Greg set his pint down in front of him and joined him in the window seat in the Duke of Cumberland. 'That's all the coachloads of Amurrcans want. Don't want to know which are the best ones – just take a boxed set of the lot and flash a plastic card.' He rang up an invisible cash register with gleeful resignation. 'Hardly even about the Lakes – but she lived down at Near Sawrey and they've gyudda *hairv* it!' He hurriedly raised his beer glass to his face, and Greg turned round enough to catch an angry stare through a pair of thick chrome spectacles.

'Are they going to ride on your railway?' said Greg.

'You make it sound like my personal crusade,' said Edwards. 'Or toy.' He considered. 'Not the scheduled service, granted. Steam trains, Reverend Awdry books –' The windows of the pub began to buzz. Something giant throbbed along the street outside. As the roaring engine and buzzing glass drowned his words Edwards was shaking his head.

'This town,' he resumed when the din had subsided, 'is literally cracking up. Road up all the time because the lorries are fracturing the water mains. Needs more car parking space, we're told – but there isn't any more space. Main road's already as· busy as the M6 – should be widened, but even the council hasn't dared to suggest that yet. One of the most heavily used trunk roads in the country. The windows here rattle all day. Buildings are going black. Air is thick . . .' Edwards spread his hands.

'Why not just build a bypass?' said Greg. Shall I? he wondered, then went ahead. 'I thought people who preserved railways – like that Bluebell line, is it called?' (Edwards's expression was of someone listening very hard) ' – I thought they were for people who counted train wheels or something, wrote down numbers. Collected tickets, liked wearing peaked caps. And something to take the kids on . . .'

'It's people's lives we're talking about.' The look in Edwards's eyes said, *Got you.* 'The whole problem nowadays is that certain things – local government, education authorities, railways – are regarded as some kind of quaint joke. Sort of twenties period pieces, like Gilbert Scott phone boxes. The railway here would make people's lives better in so many ways. Townsfolk *and* tourists.

'This town is letting itself be run in radically the wrong way. It's putting itself entirely at the behest of individual wills, individual gratifications. It's stultifying its own collective needs, and by trying to pander to all the contradictory individual whims it's not even satisfying them.

'The town says, if you want to park your car here – fine; or there – fine; or over there, yeah, fine. Come on in. So everyone drives in to visit the town, and actually visits a vast car park instead. It's utterly emblematic. The town is paving itself over, abasing itself. The town says, we must cater for holidaymakers – they bring us money. And it's so busy opening tea-rooms and sweet-shops which the women of the town think they're lucky to have got afternoon jobs in, that it doesn't notice that all the industry in Carrock has gradually closed and there's no work for any of the men. *No work.* No foundry. No factory. When the nuclear plant over on the coast closes too the people who've started going all the way over there to work will be finished as well.'

'Why is that going to shut?' said Greg. 'I hadn't heard.'

'The disgusting pollution. Scandalous health hazard. It will. It has to.'

'So what do the men do?'

'Whatever little they can find. Bit of farm work. Painting and decorating. There's nothing else. This town says, come on in, take whatever you need – we've forgotten what we need.'

'How does this town compare with living in London?'

'Much friendlier. Much more conservative, small "c". Down in London you could get things *done* – through the council, the constituency party, even through the school. We had the parents' association, the community service programme, the evening classes. People knew what they wanted – or they went and found out – and then they did it.'

'Maybe there was less that needed doing.'

'Here they pretend nothing needs doing. As if the foundry or the factory are just on holiday. They don't realise how serious this is. There won't *be* any work.' Edwards's face was stiff with indignation.

'So the railway . . .'

'The railway will give this town a sense of itself again,' said Edwards. 'This place needs control over its own destiny again. It's been cut off. It needs a way out. It needs a future. A railway is something that belongs to a whole community. The railway network as a whole – you have to look at it in terms of the whole country; it doesn't work otherwise. It presumes consensus, common interest. And then when you get a government celebrating *individual* initiative, *private* enterprise, *self-*improvement, drive your own juggernaut anywhere . . .'

'Wouldn't the railway still be open if people here really cared about it? Or if there was still any use for it? They let it close. They didn't try and preserve it back then when everything was still intact.'

'It was decided in London. The British Railways Board. All the Beeching closures: the good doctor who lives down in Sussex closing railway lines in Cumbria. Same as the nuclear plant: run from London. The locals here don't have any choice – if it's

41

open, they can work there, and never mind the leukaemia. If the railway's not, it's because they weren't asked, and never mind the traffic. Have you seen the viaduct yet?'

'I went in the tunnel the other day,' said Greg.

'The *tunnel*,' said Edwards.

'How ever are you going to look after that? A *mile* long?' The words came out more fiercely than Greg had intended.

'Amazing, isn't it? That is one of the miracles of nineteenth-century railway engineering. Should last for ever.' Edwards looked at his watch, and drained his glass. 'You going to join in, then? Didn't you think that meeting went well? It'll be fun! Fun for the *town*,' he added, in serious plea, as if it shouldn't need saying.

The following morning Greg was wandering down through the town in search of a coffee-shop, and found Dorothy's, the other side of the market square. Heavy high-backed wooden chairs, bare knotty tables and earthenware crockery; the whole place had evidently only been open about six months. Inside it was busy, and soon Greg was joined at his table by three other people, all thirties-ish.

'You don't look like a hiker,' one of them said, a man in a thick, sloppy jumper. He set down his mug of coffee. 'Your shoulders haven't got the backpack-bow.'

Greg introduced himself and said he was working up at the hostel till the autumn, and all three seemed pleased at his arrival.

'Peter Fellows. Run a phototypesetting business here.'

(Would any of them know the Warden's name, wondered Greg fleetingly.)

'And this is Jane Bradford, Carrock Cheeses,' (a woman with a spiky page-boy haircut and salmon-pink dungareees). 'And Bernard Day, theatre director. Cottage retreat out near Force.'

'Carrock's Belsize Park community,' said Day through a thin cigar.

'I was just talking yesterday to the man who runs the book-shop,' said Greg to the woman. 'He told me there wasn't any work in Carrock.'

'There isn't, except for people like him and us.' All three of them, she explained, were dependent on London for their business. Bernard directed there, and came to Carrock for long weekends; Peter worked for London publishers and posted down his disks and proofs; she sold most of her hand-made cheeses to Harrod's and Fortnum's. 'We don't need to be down there – we just need the communications. Even with the tourist trade and all the holiday cottages property's still miles cheaper up here. I don't have to tell you it's nicer.' They had moved up from London during the last three years. 'Della here,' – Jane gestured at the woman behind the counter – 'is the newest émigré.'

'Ashley's been bending your ear about trains, I suppose?' said Fellows.

'Has he yours?' said Greg.

'Tried.' Fellows looked at Jane – seemed to be wondering whether he now wanted to pursue the subject. 'It took him nine months to get his bookshop going, and then he had to cast around for something else to do.'

'It sounded like a good move,' Greg said. 'I mean, English teacher in North London to bookshop in the Lakes.'

'We don't talk about that,' said Jane. 'His wife and kids are still down there, aren't they, Peter?'

'Something to do with one of the girls in his Upper Sixth.'

'Ah,' said Greg. 'Well. The railway – do you think it's a crazy idea of his?'

'No, no. I'm sure he'll pull it off in some way. Don't know how much, or what it'll all signify. What did you get from him?' Fellows added politely, obviously already knowing very well.

'It's a huge project,' replied Greg. 'I've seen quite a bit of the old line, in fact. Keep coming across it. But he's not one of these people who drools over the thought of steam, is he? He seems to see the railway as a means to an end – to revitalise the town.'

'Revolutionise,' said Jane. 'He gave you all the hopelessness and haplessness stuff – the locals need something done for them, don't realise the horror of their plight?'

'Ye-es. What do you think of that?'

'Don't like being preached at. Any more than the people who've always lived here do.'

'But if there *isn't* any work . . .' said Greg.

'They know that!' exclaimed Jane. 'Ashley says they don't, because they're apathetic. They're apathetic because they don't all go into his bookshop and buy his Pluto paperbacks that say how unemployment means hideous entropy. They know there's no work – but they have to carry on. Ashley simply patronises them for not being despairing enough. They also know that running steam trains for tourists won't bring any jobs, and resent this ridiculous fantasising of his that somehow it will. There won't be a *single* job if it does get going. He may present it as some kind of beautiful workers' collective, but it'll all be run by people like him, as their spare-time plaything.'

Bernard Day smoothed back his long, already grey hair. 'Ashley's never quite recovered from the abolition of the GLC.'

'I'm sure the railway should never have been closed,' said Fellows, 'but I can say that after all this time. It's like that marvellous plane the Labour government scrapped – the TSR2? You can be nostalgic about it now – but it was costing an absolute fortune back then.'

'It would be a lovely ride,' Jane said, 'but Ashley's talking about running proper services along it again. Whenever I think back to taking a train – I don't do it now – I always remember how slow it was. It would take ages. And then you have to *change* beforehand, and *wait* for the connection . . .'

'What about all the cars here?' said Greg.

'But you don't ask that question when you're setting out on your holidays from, I don't know, Crouch End. Not until you're already here.'

They fell silent, and Greg sensed a communal irritation and shame at having become so deeply engaged by something that oughtn't to concern them, and didn't even exist.

Then Jane looked up from her empty mug. 'The other thing is, the way Ashley rewrites history to suit his romantic dreams. If you read up on the history of Carrock,' she said with practised carelessness, 'you see how the railway was built, and why. Indeed, the way I'd imagine all of them were originally conceived. Standard Victorian capitalism: not some glorious unified state creation like the Health Service.

'The Carrock railway was built by a pure speculator, to make profits. Saw the mines waiting for better transport for their ore; saw the tourism potential in Carrock; raised the cash and built the railway. If he was around now he'd probably do a timeshare development. Then it cost so much to build, with the tunnel and the viaduct and everything, that it was permanently in hock, and it was nationalised like all the others to prevent it closing years before it actually did. So this kind of lost-innocence idea of the town' (Jane fell into a solemnly deep litany) '– that the railway was built back then for the simple good of Carrock, and can be so again: a myth.'

'Whenever you listen to Edwards on his railway,' said Bernard, stretching back in his chair and then standing up to leave, so then they all did, 'you can see that what he's really thinking of is Larkin's "Whitsun Weddings". You know, the "frail travelling coincidence"? The "arrow-shower, somewhere becoming rain"?'

Who were all those people at the meeting then, Greg was thinking on his way down into town on the Friday. If Edwards is just a troublemaker here, and everyone thinks so little of his scheme, why were they all there? Or was Jane pre-judging the town just as much as Edwards?

This time Greg tried a small pub called the Bobcat, in the middle of a terrace of houses at the top of the High Street. He chose it because there was no sign outside for Rombout's Real Coffee, no menu offering lasagne and chilli, and it seemed just too far up the hill for holidaymakers to reach.

The old man Greg had sat next to at the meeting was at a table by the wall, hand still on his stick, regarding his pint with concentration but occasionally turning his head to converse with the barman. Greg took up a stool at the bar by himself, and looked down the pub to watch two men playing darts at the back. The quiet *clock* of the darts, the men's low, grim whistles of appreciation at each other's shots, and the sporadic, mumbled conversation thrown across the room were the only sounds in the nearly-empty pub. Greg fell into imagining Edwards teaching 'The Whitsun Weddings' year after year to his English A-Level students –

1. *Define the meaning of Larkin's final image;*

2. *What is the poet's attitude to the wedding-couples that join the train?*

3. *. . .*

45

– until the metaphors themselves would have come to seem the subject, and the train journey the explication. A copy of the volume always upstairs at the bookshop, perhaps, on automatic repeat order whenever it sold: a book that ordered itself . . .

'This man'll say different, of course.' The wheezing man was pointing at Greg, his eyes still fixed on his drink. Greg frowned in enquiry. 'Nothing to do with the town at all. You probably think it has.'

'This plan to start the railway up again,' said the barman to Greg as he dried a glass.

'I sensed you weren't terribly happy about how that meeting went.'

'No, I'm interested,' the old man replied. 'But it's nothing to do with the town – we don't need it. I haven't been up there since it closed.'

'You could give it some money, Arthur,' said the barman in mock sternness.

'I might. I might take a few shares to help it.'

'Did the fact that the man who's organising it doesn't come from Carrock annoy you?' asked Greg cautiously.

'No. That's fair enough. We've had it for fifteen years and nobody's done anything about it. Took someone from outside.'

The old man's genial, if astringent, disinterest was puzzling. At the meeting he had appeared scandalised by the whole proceedings; his question had been derisive refutation: This Will Not Work.

'You were quite annoyed there,' persisted Greg. It seemed that plain speaking was all right.

'No. I was only saying what he knows as well as I do' – Arthur was still looking at his glass, but obviously meant Edwards, not the barman – 'that nobody'll use it, not to get to Wetherbeck. He wants to do it because he wants to do it. I take my hat off to that.'

'Won't you lose your money, then?' said Greg. 'If you buy some shares?'

'No!' The imputation of disaffection was making the man increasingly irritable. 'There'll be plenty of holidaymakers to go on it for rides.'

'Did you travel on it much when it was open?'

The old man nodded slowly. 'I don't think he ever did, mind. In the winters when Carrock was cut off it used to be the only thing that could get through. But you don't need it for that now there's the big road. Then they used to have summer specials all the way up from London – two locomotives together, the trains were so long. Pretty fast, too. I joined one of them once at Wetherbeck: non-stop all the way here. You didn't see much of the scenery from them. It was the stopping ones that were so slow; boxes and bundles to unload at every station. And here, you could go out of here, say' – Arthur aimed his stick at the door – 'and look over towards the station, and see all the smoke rising above the houses. And there'd be crashing and banging up there half the night where they were shunting. It's a lovely line – especially that viaduct. Going over that is like you're floating on air. Eh, John?'

'Eh.' A dart went *clock*, one man said, 'There,' and the other, 'Played.'

'Is most of the town interested in the idea of restoring the line? Or is it, sort of, suspicious of it?' said Greg.

'I don't know who *the* town is,' said Arthur. 'The people I know think like me. Not too keen on all these Londoners taking over all the shops, but they can have the railway. That's out of the way. You saw how many turned up the other night. We'd all forgotten it was still there. Are you working in one of these climbing shops or something?'

Edwards wasn't a threat to the town then, or rather to people like the old man: not a threat but a curiosity. 'The Youth Hostel.'

'Busy now, I bet,' said the barman.

'The old mine guvnor's house,' the old man said.

'I didn't know,' said Greg in surprise.

'All these things just get forgotten. You only think of it as a youth hostel. That's what you thought it was built for. The reason why it's up at the top of the town – so he could look out over all the miners' cottages down below. There's still a few rows of them left across the west side. The London people tend to take them to do up.'

'I see now why you're interested in the railway restoration,' said Greg. Edwards had been half right in his earnest diagnosis

of the town's need for – how had he put it? – 'a sense of itself'
again. Just to postulate a working railway once again was to
redefine Carrock to someone like Arthur who lived there, who
had himself redefined it as a town without a railway any more.
But when the old man grumblingly maintained again, as Greg
knew he would, 'Nothing to do with me,' he was half right
too.

When Greg went up to his room that night after closing the
reception, Ruth held out a glass of whisky to him. She was lying
full-length on his bed, propped up on the pillows, and had a
glass in her other hand, too.

'I am so *fucking* bored with tungsten,' she said.

'You've been working hard on it all evening, then,' said
Greg.

Ruth assessed her glass carefully.

'How much more have you got to go?'

Ruth looked over at the nearly empty Scotch bottle.

'What do you want to do?'

Ruth returned a defiant smile that said: '*This*'. Her eyes were
glistening bright, Greg saw – she was only drunk enough to be
angry and extra alert. She rubbed the bottom of her glass
tenderly along the fine hairs on her arm.

'And your day, Gregoire?' Ruth enunciated with exaggerated
politeness into her whisky.

'Oh, I met an old man called Arthur in that pub the Bobcat,
and we talked about the railway when it was open.'

'Yes, I saw that membership form for some Preservation
Group on your desk. Why are you doing that when you think
it's such a waste of time?'

'Well, I don't, I –'

'Oh you *do*, Greg! You gave me that big spiel in the tunnel
about it was *such* a huge undertaking, and they didn't know
what they were taking on, and it was all so *pointless* . . . No,'
– Ruth pointed at Greg with her bare foot – 'no, I know why.
You *like* the thought of it all failing. You sat in that tunnel
hating every minute of it because it was all black and cold and
weird, and it made you feel really gloomy and solemn, and you
liked that. I could see you sitting there really loving it –'

'You couldn't see anything.'

'So that's why. You walk up and down the line getting terribly depressed about how it's all gone, and it's all silent now, and then you go and talk to these old codgers in the town who tell you about when the Queen came to Carrock in her Brighton Belle, and then you think that's all gone too, and can never be regained, and then when someone comes along with some pathetic notion of trying to turn the clock back and pretend it never closed, and you can see how daft that is, it makes you even more sad and morose at the thought that it's all gone, but it shouldn't be, and it could all be brought back, but it can't be, because it's all gone, and that makes you enjoy it *even more*.' Ruth swallowed the last of her whisky, rapped the glass down on the bedside table, and relaxed back with her hands behind her head.

'You like the ruins, Greg,' she began again almost immediately, in a helpful-advice manner. 'You like the ruined railway. The morbid fascination, the sad memory of it all: still there, but no longer. The railway will have closed like the mines here did. Finished. Worked out. You can treat it like Tintern Abbey if you want,' – and Ruth let out a squealing peal of laughter.

Greg looked out of the window at the dim black humps of the fells.

'Let's go for a walk,' said Ruth eagerly, swinging her legs on to the floor and stretching out her arm for Greg to pull her up.

Outside, Ruth led the way on from the end of the hostel drive and towards the last houses, drifting across the street away from and back to Greg, running her hands through the air on each side of her, or holding out her full skirt like a dancer. The pavements fell away and grassy banks narrowed in as the road climbed into the fells. They wandered slowly up the hill, taking it gradually enough to retain their breath. Smoky clouds furred the edges of the moon, and a faint breeze lifted up strands of Ruth's hair. Listening to the soft slapping of her flip-flops Greg was aware of his mind peacefully emptying again as it seemed to do in Ruth's company. Ruth started singing under her breath, a keening, undistinguishable song, and broke off as the grassy bank flattened out and they looked down on the lights of Carrock.

'You can't believe there's any sound down there,' she said. 'It looks as silent as up here.'

'I'm not sure if I can hear the main road,' said Greg. 'I thought I could everywhere. You can't see the headlights from here, the fells are in the way. It's funny how you need to see sound to hear it.'

They went on, and Ruth told Greg how the road climbed up to the top of the pass, switching back and back on itself as the incline steepened – the only way over into the next valley. She pointed up to the left and to the right, but Greg could only see the crumbly tarmac before them, brown in the moonlight, and Ruth's long, pale arms fanned out in front of her.

Then Ruth stopped. Greg stopped. There was silence; then a rustling and soft crunching; then silence again. The crunching again – something small treading the wild grass down. Ruth stepped out of her flip-flops and crept over to the hedge. She eased down on her haunches, and a hedgehog climbed deliberately down the narrow verge just beside her and dropped on to the road. It waited, took several steps, waited again. Even in the dimness, standing away from Ruth, Greg could see how agile it was, how much all of it moved. It didn't shuffle or waddle, as he expected, but strode, almost, its whole body tensing and relaxing as its front legs reached forward. The hedgehog walked on, in tinily strong, even strides, its eyes fixed ahead on the opposite verge, and passed Ruth, then Greg; at the other side of the road it pulled itself up into the grass in a single, slow haul, and burrowed on out of sight, although the grass rustled occasionally for a few minutes more.

Ruth stood up and hugged her shoulders. Greg could feel her brimming with pleasure. She skipped over and put her arm through his and led him back down the hill, about-turning them after a few yards to retrieve her flip-flops.

They walked briskly down to the town in a bouncing, elongated step-for-step. Ruth's dreamy preoccupation, which had replaced the querulousness, had now become an exultant animation. 'All by himself!' she proclaimed. 'He didn't know anything was there except him! Nothing mattered except him!' She hugged closer to Greg.

Quickly Greg found they were back at the hostel door, as

Ruth loosened her arm gently from his. While they were creeping up the creaking wooden staircase he wondered how he should say goodnight to Ruth, but he was still wondering as they stopped on the landing under the skylight, and Ruth traced her fingers lightly under his eyes, and pattered away.

Chapter Six

It was the following weekend before Greg could join the working party at the station. The first Sunday he and the Warden had had to fix a leak in the roof over one of the dormitories (Greg had only found out through a casual aside from two junior-school boys as they were calculating how many penny chews to buy). The Warden, diverted from the snooker final by more clearing up, exhaled his cigarette smoke in heavy hisses.

A week later, equipped with the Warden's scythe, secateurs and shears, Greg met Edwards and fifteen others outside the station on a sultry, cloudless morning.

'You want to see the story so far?' confided Edwards proudly. He drew a key from his pocket, unlocked the padlock on the front doors and swung them open on a clean, newly-swept booking hall. There was a half-torn-off poster on the wall which said BRITISH RAILWAYS BOARD: NOTICE OF CLO. Edwards led Greg through a door on the left. 'Booking office,' he announced. It was completely empty except for a large wooden rack next to the old ticket window. 'Used to be full of different tickets,' said Edwards. 'Go anywhere.' Then out through the far doors – already rubbed down to the wood on the inside – on to the platform, which was clear of glass. They walked past the hotel to the end, where Edwards held out his hand in rakish display. For fifty yards the thin dog-walkers' path was now a wide, tuffety corridor. 'You'll need more than secateurs for this,' he said, indicating the sawn-off trunks of young trees protruding from the trackbed.

Greg's track gang was to start work further up the line, while the other resumed near the station. The leader, Les, had been one of the men in blazers at the meeting; here he wore a boiler suit and floppy sunhat and carried a large machete. As he led the way along the path beyond the cleared stretch he introduced Greg to the rest of the gang. Pete was a butcher, Kevin worked in the local branch of Lloyds, Jeremy sold cars, Adrian was co-owner of the Nutbrown healthfoods shop, and Les himself had a building business.

'The plan is to do this every weekend?' said Greg.

'Until we reach Force Road,' said Les. 'It won't be as bad as this all the way. It'll be better when the schools go on holiday in a fortnight – Ashley'll be hitting them soon for work parties. They're all on exams now. We're doing evenings too while it's light late.'

They walked for about a quarter of an hour, and then the path curved to the right. Greg followed it, and Les called, 'Hey – here we are.'

Greg looked back and saw him and the others waiting, it appeared, by the undergrowth at the side of the trackbed.

'We start here,' said Les. 'This is where the line goes.'

Greg regarded the path he had been about to take.

'There's a bridge down ahead. The path leaves the permanent way to get round it.'

Greg hadn't noticed at all when he had come this way with Ruth. If what Les was standing in front of was the old line, it had completely disappeared: here was simply a matted thicket almost too dense to push through.

They spread out across the tall wall of vegetation. Three had saws, and headed for the stoutest trunks at either edge. Les handed Greg a pair of long-handled clippers, and went himself to join Jeremy in hacking a way through the middle.

Greg found he could cut through branches up to an inch thick, and tackled the elderberries and all the other spindly and obviously fast-growing bushes and saplings he could find. Around him there was a constant noise of chopping, slashing and sawing, and the swish and creak as boughs fell or were hurled aside.

The permanent way, thought Greg as he lopped down saplings. How is this line permanent? Here it has become a wood; there is nothing to remember the railway by. If they managed to clear this part of the copse away completely there would be a piece of flat ground you *could* lay a railway track on again – but it was going to be an act just as pioneering as when the line was first built. Greg thought of the great embankment further on that led across the meadows to Scale, and then the tunnel. They were the permanent way, would always be there – had been built only for a railway, and waited only to be used for it again. And then suddenly Greg saw them differently. The embankment was a mound of soil; the tunnel was a cave. Earthworks, and mineworks. All this was digging on the surface of the land – you could label the dents and humps and holes you made however you chose. You couldn't *invest* people in the land: when the people went, the land remained for itself. It was like when you came upon men digging up the road: you looked down into their hole and saw the layer of tarmac, the bedding of hardcore beneath, the uncovered pipes further down – and below them the men had hit the clay or the chalk; had reached the earth. Then you saw how the pedestrians were walking and the cars were driving just on the thin top layer, that people had decided to call this area of ground a street, but that whatever they called it the earth was the same underneath.

Greg brought down branches and leaves all round him, cut and cut and wrestled the jaws of his cutter through the thicker trunks with a squeak. He stopped after an hour, suddenly giddy with the heat and exertion. Les came over with a large flagon of beer.

'Bring a hat next time,' he said as Greg gulped from the flagon. Then Les waded off back into the bushes with his cleaver.

Greg took up his cutter again and attacked another young sycamore, wrenching the handles round to try and slice through the wood. The sap bubbled out over the blades, the small tree canted over, and the grass-green leaves flopped on the ground. He looked around at what they had done so far, and now felt not encouraged but disappointed, futile. In their wake the young wood was becoming a stumpy, shorn wasteground scattered with torn foliage. It was interesting how people had left this piece of land completely alone for fifteen years, thought Greg – had walked round it always, so that it had grown into absolute anonymity – and now all of a sudden they had conceived a design for it and were clearing it away in hours.

Then Greg saw that in an hour the six of them had come less than ten yards, and couldn't guess at how much farther there was to go.

They stopped for lunch and ate their sandwiches sprawled amongst the felled undergrowth. Les chatted desultorily to Greg about the station, which the county surveyor had since looked at. It was safe, except for the platform canopy, which it would probably be cheaper to pull down than repair, but never mind. Needed a new roof; he could fix that. But he wanted to be doing this sort of stuff on the line, really, not more bricks and slates, which he had all week already.

'I sit behind a counter all day,' broke in Kevin, the one who worked in the bank, who was about Greg's age. 'It's good for me to get out at weekends and work here, too.'

Greg wanted to ask him why he didn't choose an easier kind of outdoor exercise. He decided he could find out by enquiring, 'Do you know the fells around here much?'

'No,' Kevin said, half-surprising himself. 'They're on your doorstep so you don't bother: you can always see them. But I never knew this was here. I don't think I remember the railway at all. It looks like it'll be good fun; it feels like a proper day's work.'

They got up to begin again.

'Can I have a go with your machete?' said Greg to Les.

He strode into the thick brush with Kevin, who had taken Jeremy's, and they threw themselves at the tangled screen of branches, trying to propel themselves through it with the swinging momentum of their strokes. They flung whatever they hacked blindly behind them, a haze of wood-dust and the lemony smell of sap around their faces.

The two of them worked close together, Greg cutting on his left, Kevin to the right to keep their blades away from each other. Soon Greg saw that they were only clearing a path as wide as themselves, not a broad swathe – but they had already lost sight of the others. Make some sort of line, he found himself thinking over his machete blows, Make-A-Thin-Line-Through. All the time they were chopping, ripping, flinging, he was peering ahead for gaps in the foliage, and saw only the grey twisted corridors between more stalks and trunks. As the afternoon lengthened it became just his own panting breath, his sweat-shiny arms working by themselves, and the blade in his hand whipping off the thinner branches, biting into the heavier stems. Kevin was right next to him, but somewhere over there, and Greg had no idea how far they had come.

Whatever this was they were doing, Greg now needed to get to the end of it, to make this path they were creating lead somewhere. He wanted to come out on something. Simultaneously (but Kevin was still working almost with his back to Greg) their blows became more extravagant – cutlass slashes. Greg whirled his machete in front of him, smashing into the bushes; Kevin gasped out with every desperate tennis player's lunge. Greg sensed their path straying to the left when he was sweeping through cow parsley while Kevin was having to hack round an elderberry clump. The undergrowth remained high around their legs as they laid about them at waist level. The task contracted to things immediately blocking them, which had to go, immediately. As they started to see sunlight and open sky in small streaks amongst the vegetation ahead they flailed faster, diving on, until they were aiming their swings directly at the patches of blue and gold.

They burst out of the trees and pulled up teetering and dazed, a twenty-foot drop at their toes, on the precipice of the demolished bridge.

The path they had made meandered all over the place, they found as they breasted and stumbled their way back to the others. At one point they were confronted by half-hacked-off, splintered birch boughs hanging limp over beaten-down bramble – but no route through. The two of them exchanged looks of brazen bewilderment and set to again. When they began to hear the others' saws they drew apart to broaden the way – Greg squinting back up it thinking, how wide is a train? They reached Les and the rest once more, and turned to regard their labour. Les pulled the brim of his hat down lower, and Greg and Kevin gazed ahead with him at a wobbly isosceles triangle of clearing that drifted to an apex well over to the left.

Kevin inspected his machete blade innocently for minute nicks. 'That bridge is going to take some work.'

After a final hour of collecting up all the cut-down vegetation into a huge pile it was time for Greg to head back to the hostel for the evening. He stood with the others for a few more minutes watching the great bonfire they had lit settling and sighing, and beyond it through the swimming air he could see what they had done in a day. They had taken perhaps the first ten years of overgrowth off the section of trackbed they had uncovered – it was the last five, when trunks had thickened at their base and roots had spread and pushed up the ground, that remained. About a third of the distance to the bridge had been properly cleared, but now he knew how far the bridge was, even if they had looked across to more woodland past the other parapet. Greg could begin to plan a train service running to the bridge and back: Connection For Minor Road and Woods Beyond. There would soon be the line for it; already you could pick your way through.

The gang met every Sunday over the following weeks, and soon added Saturdays too. Jeremy and Kevin went down the line two or three evenings during the week as well when it was fine. All of them individually acquired their own machetes. A saturnine camaraderie grew amongst the six, conducted entirely in an exclusive slang: now they leered and brandished their Mashers at each other and threatened the vegetation. *Mashed.* Les turned up with a chainsaw to level the tree stumps, and quickly everyone was having a go at Massacring in roaring, frenzied swirls of sawdust. The quest to beat a full way clear to the bridge turned into the Battle of the Blurge, and the Warden studied Greg through his cigarette smoke as he would a small cub scout when Greg accidentally mentioned it on his euphoric return one Sunday evening. At the end of the day they all – except Greg, who had to be back for hostel opening at five – retired to the Duke of Cumberland and, Greg deduced from their subsequent conversations, talked endlessly of weedkillers, drainage and other trackbed matters on which they were rapidly making themselves experts.

The Battle of the Blurge was properly won within a month,

and celebrated with a competition to see who could drop a large elderberry sprig onto the roof of the first car to come up the road beneath them. Then they went back to where they had started out, to scythe the scrubby grass as low as possible, and dig out tree roots so they could flatten the ground. The following week the other track gang reached them, and together they were able to look all the way back to the station site – the confirmation a distant flash from one of the windscreens in the council depot. Greg noticed how the trackbed actually ran between walls of mature oak and beech trees. Now he could imagine the first part of the journey from Carrock: the bumping over the points past the hotel, the houses dropping away behind the screen of poplars at the end of their gardens, and the train easing into the woods, the odd branch flicking the carriage windows. A brief rumble over the bridge . . . but that was as far as they had come. They had cleared a mile of line. Beyond the bridge there was another station to aim for: get to there and you could start to call it a railway. For Greg, casting his mind back over the previous weeks, the experience of track clearing had been completely contrary to his expectations. He had anticipated being an adventurer from the first day, a pioneer reclaiming the land yard by yard from time like cleaning the grime off an old painting from the corner inwards. Yet initially he had found himself simply cutting down trees, destroying a young secluded spinney – nothing to do with trains. It was only now he had a retrospective sense of trailblazing, and for it they had needed to use all the bits they had, to see the thing whole. Join the clearing up with the remains of the bridge, then add to it the previous clearing, make it all uniformly wide and level, and tie it back on to the station. It wasn't until you had cleaned the canvas completely that you could see its brushstrokes formed a picture at all. Now they had all looked back and seen the old line, however, Greg knew that was all it could be.

Edwards, meanwhile, had been leading his crew on the station renovation, and also raising some money. A couple of hundred from the first jumble sale, even more from another a month later. A hundred and fifty from a collection of old newspapers. The town was also saving its glass bottles, used postage stamps and spare half-cans of primer and gloss. His finest inspiration to publicise and equip the sweeping, scrubbing and painting now in progress was a kind of reverse-Kleeneezee-man operation where his volunteers knocked at doors asking for donations of old brushes.

Greg enjoyed walking through the station doors and booking hall on his way to the track-clearing, and each time found something else new: a waiting room floor sanded and sealed; cracked window panes and rotten sills replaced. One day the booking hall was filled with a scaffolding tower, and week by week Greg watched the high ceiling brushed of cobwebs, washed to peeling grey-white, stripped, and repainted in egg-shell.

'Not authentic,' a small man called down sadly in response to Greg's admiring remarks. 'It was a lot of free paint, mind. And you don't look up here for your train, do you?' Greg noticed that with the through doors left open all day as the station gang worked the sour, cheesy smell on his first tour had gone.

'Where does "essential renovation" stop, or whatever the council man said they allowed?' asked Greg one Sunday morning as Edwards was on his knees painting a skirting board.

'Doesn't,' replied Edwards immediately. 'If I could get that canopy fixed and the other platform back up before they come to take a look I would.'

'Even though we haven't leased it yet?'

'We carry on as if we've had a lease for years. Then they'll wonder why they haven't already given us one.'

'But what happens if, say, the canopy falls down while we're trying to mend it?'

'Save them a job,' said Edwards, his eyes following his long, caressing brush-stroke.

It is just a shell, though, thought Greg as he wandered round. Indeed, opening the station up and clearing it out had made conspicuous how thoroughly gutted the whole place was. The rooms in the building – whether Edwards denoted them 'waiting room' or 'station master' – were all identically bare, clattering cells. The first school party had arrived with a smart collection of garden spades, rakes and weedkiller sprays apparently lent by enthusiastic parents oblivious of the punishing use they were destined for, and had transformed the area beyond the platform where the tracks had been (the knobby football pitch Greg had seen on his second day in Carrock) into a flat, scorched – space. That was the only word which occurred to Greg when he saw it: space for something; space created by the removal of something. He began to understand and share some of Edwards's tension – to see why he appeared to want the whole station rebuilt in two weeks. If the council came and looked now, what would they think? It seemed to Greg that in working to restore a railway station the gangs were only helping the council to see lucrative alternatives: a sturdy Victorian building with empty rooms now ready for fitting out as offices with spotlights and filing cabinets; a broad, even plot of raked earth awaiting the foundation trenches to begin a cul-de-sac of bungalows, or perhaps all-over asphalt and white grid-markings for another car park. What Greg had felt at the start of the track-clearing, he knew someone from the council could feel contemplating the station: they could both stand on the edge of the platform and see something else, and the only difference would be Greg lamely thinking to himself, But this is supposed to be a station.

Increasingly he was becoming uncertain as to where the inspiration of the project actually inhered. Did you look at these broken physical relics and still see ungainsayably the implication of a railway? Or was it the power of the volunteers' collective fantasy of a railway over the contrary implication of all the overgrowth and dereliction that it was no more? Or was it perhaps only an individual fantasy – Edwards's – tolerated by default? The other volunteers, it seemed to Greg, turned out mainly for the exercise, the open air, the new companions, an undefined but galvanising sense of purpose, and the chance to play with large knives. All this was made possible by, and perhaps in return legitimised, Edwards's maverick private charade?

Soon Edwards forced the question. Greg dropped in at the station one morning and found the small, elderly man who had been up the scaffolding tower carefully painting on each newly-finished deep-plum door a name in bold cream letters. On a trestle at his side a book was open containing period photos of railway station interiors. He had done WAITING ROOM and STATION MA.

'He certainly makes it clear when he wants something done,' said the man meekly. 'Never leaves off.' His tongue enacted the slow curve of his brush round the bottom of the S.

'Haven't done this for years,' he went on. 'Used to be with the dairy. Fitter, really, but did the signwriting on all the floats too.'

Greg said it was going to look very nice and left him on the final R.

'All got to be done this week,' the man called back. 'For some reason. Big list of them.'

On the Sunday morning Edwards accosted Greg at the entrance doors, which now had C.W.R.C. across them. 'If you want everyone to know it's a railway station,' he said with the expansiveness of an impresario, 'write Railway Station all over it!'

The ticket window had TICKETS arched above; the inside of the entrance doors said WAY OUT. There was a PRIVATE STAFF ONLY on the booking office door, and on the doors to the platform, TO THE TRAINS.

'Starting to look like we mean business?' said Edwards as they stood at the edge of PLATFORM I (a sign hung from the canopy).

Greg regarded the empty expanse of ground before them. As other volunteers arrived and came through TO THE TRAINS on to the platform Greg could hear Les calling across from his ladder to each of them, 'You've just missed it.'

The two of them turned round to watch the new arrivals' reactions. Initial surprise and interest gave way to dubious embarrassment, and finished either in huge amusement or faintly threatened exclusion. Everyone read the signs with intense scrutiny, as if trying to make out what they said. 'Very nice,' they remarked, in reference to the skill of the signwriting. On the signwriting man's face pride fluctuated with shame, and both gave way to efficient engaged-elsewhereness.

'Better?' said Edwards to Greg at last. 'Worse?' – offendedly facing out Greg's ungrateful silence. 'No different?' he ventured hopefully.

'No idea.'

'I fail to see,' said Edwards in exasperation, 'why writing Railway Station on a railway station should cause an advanced crisis of structuralist signification.'

'But there aren't any trains here,' said Greg humbly.

'I *know* there aren't! The council will know there aren't. But we want the council to think that we know there soon will be, so *we* can know they'll think there soon will be too. Trains,' Edwards added.

'Won't they think that we know there aren't, and that we know they know there aren't, and that we've put the signs up to pretend we don't know?'

Edwards's frown showed he was still unravelling Greg's logic, but he was shaking his head dismissively.

'It's pre-empting things,' persevered Greg. 'You can only go as fast as you can. You can't tell people you're something when they can see you're not. These volunteers know how much they've done and how much there is to do. It won't encourage them, this – it just looks as if you've got designs on their labour by pretending you're so far away into the future from what they know needs doing now.'

'If we don't get into the way of thinking that this thing's going to be finished tomorrow, it never will be,' said Edwards. 'I know what I'm doing.'

'But you've got to leave everyone else to know what they're doing as well,' said Greg.

This conversation had gone too deep too quickly. Greg felt that both of them were beginning to reveal more of their assumptions about each other than they had intended, and realised that he had been cast as the bovine reactionary to Edwards's mercurial progressive. He left the last word to Edwards, who muttered, 'It's only a few stupid signs.'

Chapter Seven

Greg never saw Ruth. They no longer even had the silent morning car ride out to Scale Fell together – soon after the hedgehog walk Ruth had announced in a distant tone of recalling the hazy past that she had 'concluded that part of the research'. Now when Greg bumped into her around the hostel she was only ever carrying a battered and hugely-swollen paperback of *The Seven Pillars of Wisdom*. His enquiry one day as to how she was finding it elicited merely, 'Oh, he must have looked hunky on his motorbike,' and left Greg, as after all his attempts to initiate simple conversation with her, feeling at once humiliated and reluctantly superior. All conventional overtures for her company his intuition rejected as facile and irrelevant. It wasn't simply that coming from him they would – shall we, *he-hem*, go for a drink – sound unbearably gauche: they weren't necessary, because Greg didn't need to see Ruth. Somehow she lived in his head all the time, and she lived in her own as well somewhere else, and they were in the same building all day and never saw each other, and Greg didn't mind. Occasionally he granted interviews to an imaginary reporter and tried answering in surprised truth, 'Yes, I think so, beautiful indeed.' But such an affirmation immediately seemed to assert a possessiveness that required its withdrawal.

Yet while Greg was beginning to rely on Ruth to be in his mind, she relied upon him for all sorts of things, and principally his socks. Ruth never had any clean pairs, and gradually acquired most of Greg's, skidding around in stockinged feet with them long and floppy at the toes. His room, too – where these days she presumably read T. E. Lawrence in the evenings, and in which she now placed jam jars of wild flowers on the windowsill, and also seemed to use his toothpaste a lot, but not, so far as Greg could tell, his toothbrush.

And every so often Ruth made her night visits to Greg's room, languorous and intense, on no apparent pretext – or was it simply to snuggle up for a while at the foot of his soft bed? Once she came to tell him – or Greg only remembered from the night – that she had found out the Warden's name, had heard him talking to someone on the phone: it was Tim or John or something. Another night she wanted to know if she should give up her thesis, she was so tired of it – and Greg, who this time had actually been asleep when Ruth entered, and fought to focus his eyes on her throughout her monologue, couldn't tell whether Ruth really only wanted an audience for her rhetorical thoughts, or if that was all he was then capable of being. And once – very late – Greg had woken wide awake as the Anglepoise flooded on and Ruth was stooping over him, her face tinged a dull fawn under the skin. He held out his hand to shade his eyes from the light and Ruth interlaced her fingers with his.

'Greg. I've thrown up everything. *Everything*.' The front of her nightshirt sagged low and unbuttoned. She pushed her hair out of her eyes with her other hand and waited for him to say something.

'Do you still feel sick now?'

Ruth shook her head. 'Feel better.'

'Not sleepy?'

'It's so disgusting,' said Ruth, sinking down on her knees beside him and shivering. 'To think all that hideous stuff is actually inside you. That stinking *mess*. Just *rancid* inside . . . I get really horrified when I think of it all pouring out of me.' She stared at Greg meekly with wide eyes, and a vein was pulsing underneath the left one.

Greg said she should go and try and get some sleep, and Ruth said she couldn't possibly – couldn't stop thinking about herself. She held on to his hand for a few more minutes, then got up to fetch his dressing-gown from the door, and curled up under it on the bottom of his bed. Greg watched her back rising in deep breaths, switched out the light and took a long while to get to sleep in the foetal position.

Such encounters seemed afterwards to bear no connection with the rest of Greg's existence, including the Ruth whose path he crossed every day, but at the same time to embody the central, unusable truth of his relationship with her: he and she, being essentially themselves, were this together. Formulated further, Greg knew, it would have to be always, 'Ruth doing —, and Greg . . .' – Greg, in fact, witnessing, accompanying. This was why, with the recollection of any of these uncategorisable night-collisions, it seemed they had only taken place in his mind. Greg had no memory of a single willed action of his to confirm he had actually been part of them, and in any case found each time that he was only participating – responding to Ruth, telling her firmly what she should best do – after the event, and mentally. Sometimes it seemed to Greg that he came close to Ruth, and she to him, only through his possessions: his dressing gown left in a rumpled heap at his feet that morning when he woke up, the Gibbs SR tube squeezed flat in the middle. And even these relics were like the diggings you find in the morning by the nocturnal animal you never see, just trite analogies for Ruth, just more for the mind.

But one morning – this was already the end of August – Greg was seeing off the last hostellers, and routinely asking them where they were going today, and they said they were going walking in the fells south of the lake, and afterwards he decided he would too. It was the one day off he had during the week, and this time suddenly he didn't want to go up to the station. The frantic communal activity there, all the sweeping and washing down and tidying up, it had begun to feel like the youth hostel. He sat on the bottom of the stairs to look at the Warden's Wainwright and map; since he and Ruth had looked down on the town by night he had not been out into the hills at all. Ruth came down, squatted behind his shoulder, said, 'Walking? Yes!' and sprang back upstairs, reappearing with a boot on each hand to say, 'I know where.'

They drove into town and out the other side, and the road dropped down to run beside the lake, which they could see only as silver swaying tinsel among the trees fringing the shore. A line of mobile homes and cars with mounded roof-racks ground on slowly in front of them, until eventually Ruth directed Greg into a small parking area of pits and roots under the trees. They were at the foot of the lake. 'We go round the lake away from the road,' she explained, now having taken over the Wainwright, 'and then up.'

Even on the path through the trees Greg felt the weight of the sun, could see the sky between them in streamers of almost turquoise blue. As they climbed up into the woods the shouts of children and excited barks of dogs died away quickly, and while all sight of the lake had vanished, the knowledge that it was there behind them, together with the surrounding subaqueous gloom, made it feel to Greg as if the water met the margin of the trees in a solid buttress even as high as he was now. Then the wood stopped, a ladder stile took them over a dry-stone wall, and they were out on the fellside, beginning a long steep trudge uphill.

'Was it this hot when you came here before?' said Greg to Ruth's back.

'Never have,' Ruth said ahead of her. 'I could see this ridge from the window on the landing. It goes along level above the lake, and then round in a horseshoe. The summit's called The Knott. There's an old cobalt mine somewhere down in the valley I'm supposed to know all about.'

'How did you know which way to bring us, then?'

'Worked it out in the car,' she said, turning round in surprise at his obtuseness.

When they reached the ridge, gasping after the climb, they flopped down in the grass and lay spreadeagled a few yards apart looking at the sky. Shortly Greg felt Ruth sit up, and in his mind saw through her eyes the coppery sheet of water below. He could hear only the snipping sound of her pulling stalks of grass. Then it was joined by a whine as of a current switched on. Immediately it was a tearing and an air-shrieking, and he jerked up in terror and strained his eyes backwards to glimpse an RAF fighter plane slam past just above them.

'Jesus,' Greg said eventually. 'I could do without that.' He slumped back, listening to his voice momentarily break the silence. The silence returned once more and remained. Greg turned his head and saw Ruth was smiling.

'I knew you'd say that.'

'You like low-flying jets up here on a beautiful quiet day like this?'

Ruth shrugged. 'It's there.'

Greg paused. 'It needn't be. It could fly over the sea.'

Ruth threw a piece of grass in front of her. 'I can't stop it. We're here and so's it.'

'Do you like it, though? Do you like the thought – the experience – of it here?'

'Quite. Yes. I should think it must be brilliant fun to fly one of them. But then you're going to say, so I *approve* of them being here because I think they're all right. Whereas you *disapprove*, because you don't.' Ruth held up her hands carelessly. 'How does it change anything to sit and think you disapprove and it shouldn't be there? We just saw it.'

They walked on. Along the top, out of the lee, the grass darkened and lightened in scuttling waves as the wind raised it, smoothed it. The ridge went southwards, and they were heading away from Carrock, leaving the lake behind as if funnelled into the river at its end.

'Ruth,' said Greg, 'does all your geology knowledge help you when you're out walking like this, when you're looking at the fells and the lakes? Or does it get in the way?'

'You mean, I can't just see a cutesy valley, I have to see some, morainic glacial erosion shit?' Ruth considered, then shook her head. 'When I think of Pleistocene ice ages I think of ring binders and library books. The more I . . . don't do this thesis the less what I'm supposed to be writing seems to have to do with what I'm writing about.'

'Because all this around here seems too infinite to reduce to geological formulations?' asked Greg after a while.

Ruth looked at him forgivingly. 'It just seems,' she went on, 'simply *physically* different activities. I'm walking on a hillside, looking at rocks, get rained on . . . and then I'm sitting in a room writing on pieces of paper and reading data in books. There's absolutely no connection I can see.'

The ridge was bending left around the head of the valley, and rising gradually. Now they were picking their way between outcrops of rock as the path wound up to a peak.

Greg tried again. 'You don't even enjoy your research because . . . it helps you to understand what you see around you?' Why did everything he said come out sounding like Carl Sagan?

'Understand what? I don't have a problem with it. What sort of therapy are you thinking of?' Ruth dropped her haversack at her feet as they pulled up to the summit cairn, and they sat down with their backs against it to stare at each other, and then down the valley at the lake, and the town, and the Thunacar range in the bright haze beyond both.

'Is that your cobalt mine?' Greg was looking down at a cluster of corrugated iron roofs amongst a tangle of dirt tracks and earth heaps.

'Closed in 1960,' said Ruth. 'And see through there, between those two fells,' – she was pointing eastwards – 'that amazing light-grey splodge? That's the old slate quarry at Force.'

'Horrible. What a mess.'

'There's your problem.'

'You see,' said Greg slowly, 'I don't know how to look at all this. The fells, the lake, the tourists, the old factories, the mines . . . I don't know what sort of idea to have of the Lake District.'

'What sort of idea do you want to have?' said Ruth. '*That*,' – she swept her arm out to gather in the whole valley – 'isn't an idea. But you can have any idea for yourself if you want.'

'No, look, I'm just interested. In a disinterested kind of way. I thought when I first came to the Lakes that it was going to be, oh, mountains and lakes, which I could explore. But from day one I actually found myself thinking all the time about railways, and then unemployment in the region. And now, supersonic jet fighters at two hundred feet. And when I look at those mines and quarries I wonder if we should think, they've mutilated a landscape that should be untouched, or, they're small blemishes left by something that used to provide a lot of work. You see – what is this place? How should people treat it, including me? I don't know. I'm new here. That's why I was curious what you thought.'

'All this place is this place,' said Ruth, 'but that doesn't get you anywhere. The quarry over there was good business for the railway. You're not going to dislike the railway now because it's associated with that?'

'So where do you stop? You can see everything from up here. Do you pick anything out and say "Don't want it"? If nobody did that, wouldn't the whole place be ruined very quickly by huge roads and holiday homes everywhere?'

'*Ruined. Ruined.* The Ruined Cottage. The Ruined Abbey. Everything must be perfect or ruined. I can't answer you. I don't know why you have to get your mind straight on everything before you can do anything. I just like going for a walk. I just . . . like it.'

'It's land,' said Greg. 'It's nothing to do with us – it's not us. But everything we do has to do with it. That's all.'

The breeze had dropped, the sun was high above them, and the heat stilled and softened them. Ruth eased back against the cairn into shadow and closed her eyes. Greg sat with hands clasped round his knees and gazed at the trembling dazzle of the lake way below. Why think, he thought. The lake is there. It is all it is. The beauty in these mountains is not their shape or scale, but their passivity: we come up into them because they will leave us be. Was it any better when he and Ruth talked than when they didn't?

The sun heaped itself on his back.

At last Ruth said quietly, 'Greg, we have a long walk left.' Greg lingered by the cairn for a last look about him, and could only see it all there, away from him: an entire landscape, whatever that meant. They stumbled down the other side of the summit, bleary with the sun, and followed the long-curving, slowly-descending spine round the valley.

It was late afternoon as they crossed the road to the car, now solitary under the trees, but Ruth skirted the car park and set off again on the path they had taken first thing. 'There'll be a way down somewhere,' she was saying.

Then the trees and the heat were behind them, and here was the water: level and hard off afar, rocking and rippling at the narrow, gritty shore. Ruth was already pulling off her socks and jeans; she stretched up on joyous tiptoe, and ran crashing

TRAIN, TRAIN

in. Greg watched with one boot in his hand as she rose in solemn slow-motion in her T-shirt out there, streaming and runnelled, hair frayed across her face, an unconscious parody of titillation, out there.

Chapter Eight

The rest of the summer sped by, and there were only weeks left before the hostel closed for the year. The sunlight turned orange – or was the orange only in the trees and heathers it illuminated? If the lights hadn't been switched on by the time Greg was serving the evening meal the hostel's interior was grey and murky.

Ruth was back on her thesis: the last chance to catch up on the summer's work before the end of September and the forthcoming meeting with the tutor – but the initiative had come from Lawrence of Arabia. Suddenly he became unspeakably boring, and the disintegrating wad of Penguin an unreadable sheaf of loose leaves, and Ruth had nothing to do again. The resentful taciturnity which descended on her during September seemed directed more at Lawrence's perfidious dreariness than simply the obligation to work again, and she brooded frequently and with intensity to Greg on how it was 'such a *stupid* book'. She spent all day in Greg's room (he was forced to read in the common room), and when he went up in the evening thinking to cheer her up she would gather her files quickly and hurry out, rebuffing him with, 'No, you really don't want to talk to me now – I'm just too horrible.'

Greg knew by now that there would never be whole sight of Ruth. However many times they met their knowledge of each other would not accrue. Whether this was because she didn't expect it to – wouldn't of anyone – or whether he was constantly learning more about her, but it was an infinitely linear more, never confirmation of the same, he didn't know. At least she never held your ideas against you – mainly because in a sense she didn't listen to them in the first place. Greg mooned away out of reach of Ruth's sullenness, and found himself galvanised by the railway again.

The view from the peak above the lake had stayed with him, or rather its unco-ordinated blur had. Recollecting it, which Greg did often, he found he had seen nothing. Going as high as they could, able to survey everything from above, he had been able only to look here and there – here old mine buildings, there a town. He had found no perspectives, no imperatives, that the whole sight was no sight: the land only reflected man and his works, reflected him back at himself, didn't sort him. When Greg thought of the view from the cairn he couldn't think what to do: his mind inevitably moved on to coming down again, and Ruth at the water, diving straight in.

But there was the railway, which had selected itself out of the landscape on his first day without looking for it, and which now seemed to Greg to break down into gradations of ever smaller, ever more tangible components: a green road that became a small wood, which was trees, which people cut down, who were Les and Kevin and Jeremy, who needed saws and choppers. It was something that linked the town and the country – Greg visualised the juxtaposition as standing on the platform at Carrock and walking along the embankment by the meadow. It was at once compact and limited – a railway ride for the town from under the canopy to the bridge – and also, when you added on the tunnel, and the navvies' graves, the distance to them, and then on to something like the viaduct he'd only seen in the here-and-there from the top of Thunacar, and on from there . . . uncomprehendably vast. It was small enough, and large enough. It was recalled to Greg one evening when he answered the phone in reception and Edwards's quietly quizzical voice said, 'Got the lease . . .'

The council had met and approved letting Carrock Station and the trackbed as far as Force Road to the railway for a peppercorn rent – but only for a year at first, and providing it was to a limited company. For the time being they were retaining the rest of the line, but postponing the plan for a footpath along it. No steam trains were to be allowed at the station pending further discussions with the hotel, no activity at all there after sunset, no car parking in the forecourt (Edwards was reciting in a brisk nasal drone), no trespassing in the adjoining service vehicle depot, no disturbance of the existing tenant of Force Road Station, which was now a private residence, no trackside fires, no dumping, no animals.

There was a month, at most, of the holiday season left, and Edwards reeled off the urgent plan of campaign: station open to the public before all the holidaymakers left, share issue for the railway company, Light Railway Order for a service to Force Road. They'd have a prospectus under way for the issue, inserts in all the railway magazines, leaflets and posters for the tourist information and the shops in town; they'd be putting some track down in the station, and there'd be an exhibition about the history of the line in the old waiting room, and Edwards was delegating this to Greg to make a start on. 'You are now the railway's archivist,' he concluded benevolently, as if confirming a long-standing request of Greg's.

Greg had three weeks, a grey postcard, and a large rusted lamp.

The lamp had been found, a brittle carcass, by Jeremy one day during track clearing: grasses and brambles had completely grown over it. No one was quite sure what it would have been used for. Some said it was a platelayer's lamp, to mark him out to train drivers when walking the line on foggy mornings. Others that it was a coupler's lamp, for him to see what he was doing when he was underneath carriages connecting them up to each other. (That it should end up a mile out of Carrock Station at the track side further glamorised the mystery.) Les maintained it was not a railway lamp at all: it was a miner's lamp, from the tungsten mine on Scale Fell – underneath the crusty flakes of rust you could just make out, there, see, the corroded initials S.M.C., which must stand for Scale Mining Company. In any case it was an old lamp, found on the line, and it made everyone think of the old railway.

The postcard had come from the signwriting man. It showed a monochrome panorama of mountains and valleys, and in the middle a feather of steam rising from an invisible train. The caption underneath said merely, 'Carrock'. The signwriting man said as far as he could remember he had always had it, and he thought it would have been taken around 1925. Greg asked him why, but he only scrutinised the card impassively. When? Where? By whom? For what? The card told Greg nothing about itself except, banally, that once upon a time there had been steam trains on the Carrock Railway, which he knew, and now could at least see. But it spun in his mind a portentous, riddling essay of speculation in which the story of the line, of Carrock, even of a hundred years of history was entirely conjectured, while at the same time entirely eluding his grasp. When the essay posed the question: *Can we even be sure of calling this a picture of a train?* (or had the passing locomotive unexpectedly defaced the deserted prospect of hills with a white blot?) the heavy carapace of imponderability overbalanced its gangling, crablike legs, and the card was once again an inert relic like the lamp. Not a key for a lock you had to find, but a one-way glass from the past to the now, with the see-through side for the past: for Greg's purpose, simply a stage prop.

Greg needed as many for the exhibition as possible – but what was going to be the script? He dropped a short letter to the local paper requesting information, mementoes and recollections from readers, and found a more satisfactory refuge from Ruth's unsociability in the public library.

He started by reading the Carrock Official Town Guide, and when he came to the couple of paragraphs dealing with the building of the railway he found them in some way familiar. Then it clicked. The Jane-woman in the tea-shop: this was the history of the town she had been reading up on. He noted down three subjects touched on in the potted résumé to investigate further, and showed the list to the librarian, a man in his sixties who seemed delighted at such a vague brief:

1. 'much controversy' over building of line

2. Henry Hilman: founder rly co.

3. modern-day town 'virtually creation of rly'??

The librarian handed over the desk to a woman who had been filling shelves and was gone a long while. Eventually he returned empty-handed. 'You'd better come with me,' he said, and led Greg back through the Private door and down a flight of stone stairs into a large yellow-lit room full of tall shelf-stacks and wide dark-varnished chests-of-drawers. The librarian pulled open drawers to disclose old maps, drew his fingers *snickersnicker* along rows of gold-blocked spines, pointed out leather-bound volumes containing indexes for the *Cumbrian Star and Chronicle*, and peered round into an adjacent room that appeared to contain nothing but bundles of old newspapers the colour of burnt milk. His features settled into a beatific smile.

Greg spent three days there, reading in the basement, while next door the librarian – neither of them introduced themselves – thumped bundles around grunting at his rheumatism, or sat on them carefully peeling apart the damp, fluted pages of a paper and perusing them serenely. When Greg put his head round a door to ask how he was doing the librarian held up his hands to warn, Back! Not yet! So Greg found a kettle and cups at one end of his table and supplied the librarian with coffee, which he accepted with a nod as if Greg were his permanent assistant there. At lunchtimes the librarian took out his sandwich box and hovered at the desk Greg was using, and Greg went out for an hour. On the third afternoon the librarian emerged from the newspaper-store with an armful of papers, drew up a chair on the other side of the desk to face Greg like an interviewer and, newly businesslike, said, 'Tell me what you have.'

'I've been reading all about the protests when the line was originally planned. No one seemed to want it.'

'It would appear so,' said the librarian contemplatively, pulling out the first paper. 'August 1864. Just when work was about to start.' The front page was yellow and crackly, but when he opened the paper the middle sheets were a chalky, moist white, like skin under a plaster. 'Collection of letters all expressing opposition: against the floods of riff-raff the railway would bring in from the cities, against the noise and the industries, against the spoiling of the meadows . . . "we the undersigned" . . . blah blah . . . "desecration and drear uniformity . . ."' The librarian hunted for another paper and scanned it so intently it was as though he was reading not the lines of type but the grain of the newsprint. 'Viaduct? You know, that man in the bookshop who goes on as if it's Ely Cathedral?' He pushed the open spread across to Greg, and there was a scratchy photograph of the viaduct being built, the unevenly rising arches

– almost luminously pale and new – like a huge stone clotheshorse standing across the valley. The editorial was headlined A DISGRACEFUL EYESORE, and began, 'If we are to have railways, so be it. The latest erection of the Carrock and Wetherbeck Railway Company, however, will but discourage even their most ardent proponents . . .'

'Apparently it took the promoter ten years to get his railway bill through,' said Greg. 'They didn't want it because they thought it was going to change everything, and it did.'

'Do you see now what the guide means? There wasn't a town here before the railway came.' The librarian went and pulled two maps out of the drawers. '1860. And 1890.' On 1890 he traced the hatched black and white line of the railway from the junction with the main line across to Carrock. Then they looked across at 1860.

'Just a little hamlet, I suppose,' said Greg, pointing out the sprinkling of black dots that was Carrock.

'Railway developed the mines. Then the foundry and the factories started up – transport for them. Then it brought the holidaymakers in. Guest houses and hotels for them, shops, houses for everyone else.' The librarian's finger circled the 1890 Carrock, now a grey-shaded area as big as a postage stamp. 'Then you needed a town council, and that's when they built the library . . .' He dumped another pile of papers before Greg.

'Look at Wetherbeck,' mused Greg. 'There isn't one in 1860.'

'Grew up around the railway junction, then,' said the librarian. 'Station itself – I remember that – used to be a big place, with buffets and porters and everything. The Station Hotel, few rows of cottages, enough for a village. There's the original Wether Beck.' The blue letters caterpillared round the wavy blue line of a stream. 'I'll do you photocopies of all the bits in the papers. Do you have all you need on Hilman?'

'Yes,' replied Greg briskly, to match the librarian's efficiently sweeping-up tone.

'I'll also send this away to be copied: photograph of the opening ceremony. There's Hilman.' A tall man in a frock coat and top hat stood in front of a large crowd under the platform canopy, holding his arm out rigidly with a flag in his hand, his face set in serious pride. The engine driver, just in view at the right-hand edge of the picture, was scowling back – or perhaps he was frowning in concentration, or alarm at a carriage door not being closed. ALL ABOARD! HUNDREDS THRONG STATION TO GIVE INAUGURAL TRAIN SEND-OFF.

The librarian was waiting. Greg said all this would do him nicely, but his profuse thanks came out stiff and halting. The librarian smiled a thin, collusive smile in acknowledgement of having been able to spend so much time going through all this. As they ascended the ringing stairs Greg had the sense, despite all he had just learnt, that the librarian had absorbed immeasurably more from his exploration of the old papers than he could offer to Greg. His three days' engrossed reading down there in the yellow-lit basement looked out of him like Hilman staring out of the photograph, but at the same time most of it had settled to the bottom of his mind, oblivious to its own usefulness and incapable of access. They came out into the fluorescent light of the main library and Greg dropped his voice. 'When you look at all that we've found it seems amazing the railway ever closed . . .'

'Oh, no,' murmured the librarian confidentially. 'Good riddance. Those diesel trains were disgusting things. Stank to high heaven and you couldn't hear yourself think. I never used it.'

Henry Hilman's ineffaceable self-possession – that ramrod arm flagging off his first train into the future – appeared to have won over posterity. One of the local histories Greg had read, perceiving how instrumental the railway had been in the growth of the town, had gone so far as to dub him, with apologetic tendentiousness, 'the "founder" of Carrock'. His achievements so obviously transcended him as to exalt him. He was far-sighted: he had recognised the possibility and viability of a railway to Carrock. He had persisted, convinced of his eventual triumph, in the face of protracted opposition. He had commissioned great works of civil engineering to carry its route. He had seen the whole design where others had merely carped at individual parts. Above all, railway promotion – the Carrock line being only one of seven he had initiated – was itself only one facet of his sagacity: he was also, among other things, a notable lepidopterist. He commanded his history, like the photograph of the opening ceremony, from centre stage.

Greg, however, along with the train driver, found himself scowling surreptitiously askance. Was he really so great? Hilman's story was scattered with asides and by-the-ways: he had, *as a matter of fact*, no knowledge about railways, was entirely reliant on his subcontractors. His principal motive in proposing the railway – *it must be said* – was personal financial gain. When work on the viaduct over-ran schedule and budget by three times owing to the difficulty of stabilising the foundations over a bog (a problem finally solved by lining it with thousands of sheepskins), Hilman, *ironically*, suspected only slackness and incompetence, and dismissed the chief engineer. As to the campaign against despoliation of the landscape, *he is said to have declared audaciously*: 'If the mountains were somewhere else there would be no need of a viaduct, and my pockets would still be full.' When, with completion of the line already two years overdue because of the tunnel and the viaduct, the subcontractor went bust and the navvies out at Scale tunnel mess were left with no money, Hilman was abroad for a year on business, *having temporarily lost faith that his railway would ever be finished*. His obsession with building the line was altogether too much just that: a dabbling, a toy, a whole railway to be built for him. He was an amateur, then, whom other people's works, and their perdurability, had professionalised. How gawky and unfamiliar in his hand, even, the flag he was waving at the first train, which someone else was driving away . . .

Jane was right, in fact. If Hilman were around now he'd be into timeshares, and he'd want to build them right in the middle of the prettiest valley for the best view. But if you could judge him for then, how did you judge his works for afterwards? Hilman's history also said to Greg that our intentions have no necessary fulfilment in their effects, which may unfairly aggrandise their instigator at the same time as they fortunately rescue those on whom his carelessness would otherwise have been visited. Even if the railway's conception had not been philanthropic, its function (or so said hindsight since its demise) was: it had brought work, for and through which it had planted

and fed a whole community. When you looked down at Carrock
by night, as Greg and Ruth had done, and could see it switched
on as a pool of orange from the streetlights, you were looking
at the moment at which the existence of a town had been
confirmed; even the librarian could look around at his library
and see the railway behind it. Somewhere along the way the
issue of Hilman's self-absorbed caprice had become fundament-
ally civic. Moreover, his cavalier unconcern with defiling the
scenery had in a sense been vindicated. The railway had actually
saved the landscape for a long while from the worse desecration
that eventually forced its closure and outlived it; the viaduct
was no longer a defacement but a monument to itself.

Then Greg got tired of thinking about Hilman, partly because
there was nothing you could do with him – except decide to
leave him back in then – and partly because he had begun to
get responses to his letter in the local paper. There were a lot –
around fifty – and at first he was embarrassed and disappointed
by them. He read mawkish recollections of meeting girlfriends
off the train at Carrock Station, of arriving back there after the
war in the new demob suit. Or there were vague hearsay tales,
from several sources, of an escaped mental patient who had
jumped out of a carriage on the viaduct and the bits had only
washed up ten days later and seventy miles down river. People
were unspecifically sentimental and sorrowful about the line's
closure. Someone else supplied, in tiny handwritten capitals,
justified left and right, what he claimed was a complete list of
all the locomotives ever to have worked the line, 'in so far as
their actual appearance has been documented.' All of the letters
were hesitant and apologetic, fearing that their contributions
would be of no interest at all, and Greg, who searched vainly
in most of them for any point, even any proper ending, felt
inclined to agree. It would all, however, like Hilman, be good
copy for the exhibition; a diverting display. But Greg's cynicism
nagged at him, and he asked himself why he felt let down: what
had he expected? These people's attenuated impressions of the
railway did not fit in with any pattern of history, but only with
their own lives. All of the writers would be taking the history
for granted, had no cause to be grateful to the railway for a
town that had been there as long as they had and long before;

if the reminiscences were pointless, yet they had been important enough to remember and now to write down. Perhaps you could say no more about them than that they were just like the passengers on a train: when you looked for the single collective journey you found instead everyone making their own. It was preferable for that image to supersede the hectoring Hilman, instinctively assuming he could and should drag all and everyone along behind him.

Another letter had a more interesting result. It invited Greg to borrow for the exhibition a poster advertising the railway from just before the war – its owner had been six when he had been given it by the Carrock stationmaster the day his father had taken him to see the trains. He dropped it in at the hostel and it turned out to be a magnificent rakish design: CARROCK AND THE LAKES BY THE LAKELAND EXPRESS. A long, sleek maroon locomotive and innumerable Pullman coaches flashed beneath steepling emerald fells and past an azure blue lake with white-sailed yachts, and the driver, fireman, and all the passengers crowded the windows grinning euphorically. The whole thing called out Speed! and Size! This must have been the zenith of the railway's fortunes, when it had rivalled the mountains and been grand enough for its viaduct and filled its terminal station.

After the man had left, the Warden went and rummaged in his office and came out holding a small white fold of paper delicately between his fingers. 'Another Exhibit,' he said doubtfully. 'I never threw it out because there wasn't a new one to replace it.' His demeanour seemed to be saying alternately, If these bits and bobs are *really* what you're looking for . . . and, Tell me that this is actually quite important to you. But he didn't stay to scrutinise Greg's reaction.

It was the train timetable for the line for May to September 1972: the last one, then. Greg squinted at the close black columns of numbers; by now he was formulating captions for the exhibition as soon as any new piece of evidence came his way:

THE FINAL SUMMER

When the end came there was little left to cut. Services had already been reduced to a handful of trains a day – and a mere two on Sundays. There were no through trains to the cities, and connections often involved long waits. The timetable reminded passengers to buy their tickets from the guard since all the stations were now unstaffed. Passengers complained bitterly about the uncomfortable and shabby trains that latterly worked the line.

Greg typed labels and captions out on the hostel typewriter, and got Peter Fellows to typeset some large title signs for him. Les built some wooden display boards, and gave Greg his photos of The Last Train. The Carrock platform, duskily lit by the gas lamps, was full of people with cameras standing around anxiously. More heads and zoom lenses poked out of the windows of the little two-coach train. The driver waited beside it with his hands in his pockets.

THE END

Although only a trickle of passengers had used the trains during the final weeks, several hundred turned out on Saturday 30 September 1972 to see the last train off: the 2135 to Wetherbeck. Enthusiasts placed detonators on the rails, someone attached a wreath to the front of the train, and the chairman of the town council shook hands with the driver. In a deafening volley of bangs and the blinding glare of camera flashes, and fourteen minutes late, the last train pulled away into the night.

This, to Greg, was the strangest thing: why all these people suddenly got so upset, for one day, when the railway closed, after having not used it for years, and prior to immediately forgetting about it again once it had gone. Was it merely ambulance-chasing? But why had all those people written him those plangent, even lachrymose letters of regret – not at its passing, but at its having passed? Greg found to his surprise that, in a way like all the attenuated anecdotes he had read through, he had no sense of an ending either. He thought back to the public meeting: all those speakers there, who had gone on as if they were somehow personally, not officially, implicated in the closure; as if something other than a railway had been lost, something in their sense of themselves, and shouldn't have been. What, when Carrock's blithe ignoring of the railway had said clearly, It's only a *train*, did people suddenly get so *serious* about?

Greg asked Les, and Les said, 'Well, you thought it was always going to be there, for everyone to use. I know they didn't, but . . .'

He asked Edwards, who said with oracular certainty, 'People feel just a little less civilised. They feel cut off, you know, from the main stream of things.'

Greg wondered if it was because, even after closure, the railway *was* still there. The town led up to the station, the final train left the station behind. At the last, although people had virtually forgotten the purpose of the railway, perhaps they did remember the history, while they didn't recognise it as such. Perhaps the closure had seemed like the streetlights going out.

But Ruth took a look at the photo and said it was another case of people thinking they were doing something, when in fact they were only thinking it, and also it reminded her of when Elvis Presley died, even though he was fat and horrible and she'd never listened to him anyway.

So Greg spent a whole day setting up his exhibition, and afterwards an hour strolling around it on his own, hands behind his back as an official visitor, whom he himself then guided round with suppressed pride:

A RAILWAY FOR CARROCK

The long decline . . .

. . . and the chance of a new beginning.

The last phrase was a little long – it was originally going to be just 'The new beginning' – but Greg had finally decided he needed to pop in 'chance' in the middle, and the more he looked at it now the more he liked its new contingency, its *slight* hesitation.

The next day Edwards came for the inaugural viewing. He slapped Greg on the back when he arrived, and went in rubbing his hands, but within five minutes he became very quiet, and

soon Greg sidled away to leave him alone, and waited for half
an hour outside in the forecourt until he re-emerged. When
Edwards spoke it was as someone who had gone through shock
and amazement and anger, and then on to understanding and
exoneration, and was now able to offer consolation to the
hapless scorer of the own goal. 'You've put in an enormous
amount of work,' he said with sympathetic kindness, 'but it'll
have to be redone.' As Greg drew in breath to reply Edwards
held up his hand. 'It's an excellent piece of work, but we can't
have it like this.' He steered Greg back into the waiting room.

Edwards went round the room rapping Peter Fellows's smart
section headings with the back of his knuckles as he spoke, as
if in front of a blackboard. 'You've got some good stuff here – all
the early stuff. VANGUARD OF PROGRESS . . . INDUSTRIAL
CATALYST . . . TOURISTS' GATEWAY, fine, fine . . . BUSY
MAIN LINE, yep. Like that poster, all the old newspaper stuff,
like all the old town plans. Done that well.' Now indignation
overcame benevolence. 'It's all this' – rap – 'when we get on to
the sixties and after. SLEEPY COUNTRY BRANCH . . . mm
. . . well OK . . . LAME-DUCK ANACHRONISM . . .
DEVOURER OF SUBSIDY! NATURE TRAIL question mark?'

'They're not necessarily *my* views,' said Greg. 'They're what
people have said about the railway . . .'

'And do we want to repeat all that garbage?' exclaimed
Edwards. 'We want to reopen the thing, not hold another wake.
All those people are just wrong, anyway.' He was on to the
photographs now. 'All these pictures of decay and junk – station
falling down, these bushes and trees and weeds and stuff – this
isn't the railway. Who took these?'

'I know it isn't,' said Greg. 'Exactly. I did.'

'THE OVERGROWN WILDERNESS?' sang Edwards in a
flouncy voice.

'Perhaps that is, a little strong. But you didn't have to clear
it.'

'*Recently twenty-three different species of wild flower have
been recorded growing on the old track-bed*! Where did you get
that?'

'Geography teacher. Field trip at the hostel.'

'*Who cares?*' Edwards stopped himself for a moment so Greg

could see the main point was coming. 'There're so many good things here about the railway – a great history. But it's obscured by all this other bullshit, which'll only depress people and is of no importance anyway.'

Greg shook his head. 'It's *all* the railway. What's happened to the line since it closed is one of the most interesting things.'

'We're trying to get people to support it, to join in and help us –'

'They will. *I* am.'

'– and therefore you don't tell them all this about the rise of the private car, and the new road, and how slow the trains were.'

'It happened! You're always going on about the traffic!'

'There's a wonderful history there –'

'It's here in the exhibition.'

'– and if you're doing an exhibition about it *now*, at this moment, you can show how it's all been leading up to this: the re-opening of the line so it can be as valuable as it always was. How it was in the sixties was how it shouldn't be, and deserves to be forgotten.'

'I'm sorry, but if you look at the whole history – I've spent three weeks finding out about this – you see it's all been leading down to this. I could have put in lots more about the navvies who got killed building the tunnel – even that was an appalling muddle. You have to draw your conclusions from the whole thing.'

'And what is your conclusion?' sneered Edwards.

'We're bolting the door way after the horse has gone. It was a compromise in the beginning, and a long decline at the end, and we're trying to salvage a little too late. And we should, and we are.'

They surveyed the exhibition gloomily together.

'Are you really going to redo it all?' asked Greg tentatively. 'Don't call on me again if you are.'

'There's no time,' said Edwards, which wasn't really an answer. 'I want the station opened at the weekend. Posters and things going out at the moment.'

They walked out on to the platform, and Edwards stood on the edge looking down past the hotel, as if he was waiting for the sight of a train, or perhaps watching one disappear. Without turning round he said sadly, 'I never knew that even the last train was a quarter of an hour late. Why did you put that in?'

'I'm sure it wouldn't have mattered. They wouldn't have lynched the driver. People don't mind that sort of thing.'

'That's the whole trouble with this country!' Edwards burst out. 'People don't mind!'

Chapter Nine

On the following Tuesday the railway stopped the traffic in Carrock.

Greg was in Dorothy's with Peter Fellows, who had just said, 'So he's still laying down plans for a radiant past, then,' when they noticed that the metal snake of cars outside had been at a standstill for some while.

'Something's jamming up the one-way system,' said Fellows, craning round to peer under the flowery canopy that hung low over the pavement. 'Just tell him, if you want something badly enough, if you really *really* believe in it – it definitely won't happen. There, they're moving.' The cars inched past the café window, but the normally continuous procession ended as a last car disappeared to the right, and the road was empty. Then a police motorcycle went by, red lights flashing, the window-pane began to buzz, and Greg could feel the rumbling vibration pressing up through the sole of his shoes.

'Awful great monster,' said Fellows as they watched the wheels of an enormous articulated lowloader grind by at walking pace. 'That should destabilise the foundations of all the shops nicely.'

It was taking minutes for the full length of the trailer to pass the window. Greg and Fellows got up and went outside to see what it was carrying.

It was carrying a large, rust-smothered steam engine. You could just see that once it had been painted black; there was a small British Railways crest on the driver's cab, and daubed in rough white letters along the side of the boiler was E.S.G. RESERVED.

'No doubt Ashley'll have a Vision of how to get that into the station yard,' said Fellows to Greg as a second red-flashing police bike brought up the rear. He darted back inside the café, and Greg saw him dump some coins on their table and call over to the woman at the counter. Shutting the door behind him again he strode off up the High Street. 'I want to see this,' he said gleefully as Greg trotted to catch him up.

Greg was quite impressed, as they walked along beside the transporter, by Edwards's latest coup – and by his inspirational gift of attracting derision. Confronted together all the London exiles seemed embarrassed by Edwards, almost preferring not to talk about him unless asked, and then only to make it clear, defensively, that he was Not One Of Them; on his own now, however, Fellows was enjoying himself. Greg had only been saying to him how Edwards had 'whacked our display signs and informed me . . .'

Then the low-loader had come past and Greg hadn't got on to telling how by the time the station had opened at the weekend Edwards had forgotten all about the exhibition: their acrimonious conversation represented his only response to it. At the opening ceremony his speech hadn't actually mentioned the renovation of the station at all. It had been entirely about the *next* stage: the exciting prospect of tracklaying and goods yard rides and then, very soon, the resumption of services.

Would all this have mollified Fellows, or only encouraged him? Greg couldn't decide, because he didn't know how he felt about it either. It would have been nice to have had some proper thanks for all their work in reopening the station, and not felt so blithely taken for granted. On the other hand, given that Edwards's conception of the railway often seemed utterly at odds with everyone else's, his undivertable forward vision was quite useful: because his imagination was always a week to six months to years ahead of reality, the actual tasks in hand got left to the others to tackle as they wished. Between the twin autocracies of his indistinctly-located version of the past and his pressing vision of the immediate future, an odd democracy-by-default was left for the present. You could never lock horns conclusively with Edwards: he was too soon charging on to the next battle. But if his casual departure seemed insultingly to imply that not only your stand but the whole argument was worthless, at least the ground was conceded to you in any case.

Greg's exhibition stood, with its wild flowers and its wilderness. Meanwhile all the volunteers were now booming, 'To The Trains', through imaginary megaphones whenever they went out on to the platform.

As for the station itself, a huge amount of work over the last few weeks had ultimately little to show for it – perhaps this was why Edwards's attention had skimmed on ahead. All the efforts to make the building finally structurally safe – even the platform canopy had now been secured and had its glass panes replaced – only made the reality consonant with the appearance, as Edwards seemed sanguinely to expect that it should be or assume it was. Visitors, and Edwards, could not stop to admire stability, and so far there were few attractions. Principal was Greg's exhibition, and otherwise there was only a small bookstall of railway books which Edwards stocked up, and someone on duty to give out leaflets and answer people's questions about the preservation project.

And yet the opening had been a good day, simply because it had brought people to the station. About two hundred had come and gone during the afternoon – Les reckoned half were locals and half tourists – and the best moment had come when, with everyone gathered outside in the forecourt, and Edwards's stentorian speech over, it was time to unlock the doors. People shuffled in wearing hunted expressions, eager not to see anything in particular, but just to stand where they couldn't have stood before, to enter what had been for so long closed. They paced the platform deliberately along its full length, slapped the door-frames, scrutinised the old track area long and minutely – and only then, with a dutiful obedience, made for the exhibition. It all showed, Greg thought, how unnecessary Edwards's frantically functional approach was: you didn't need to hustle this whole project into perfect, finished railwayness before anyone would be at all interested. People didn't know what they wanted; they let themselves be amused by what they got; they enjoyed the notknowing. Unlike everyone there, milling and pottering and poking around, Edwards was, in both senses of the word, a very uncurious person.

But now some essential, solid, heavy railwayness was creeping up the steep incline of Station Road. What were they going to do with it at the top? Greg and Fellows, having overtaken the transporter as it slowed to below their walking pace, reached the forecourt to see the manager of the hotel already in his porch looking back past them, his rigidly folded arms asking the same question, and the line of seven blue council trucks parked in front of the hotel almost to obscure his view suggesting part of the answer.

By the council depot gates a small cluster of men nudged each other and whooped as the convoy hove into sight. Fellows strolled over to them. 'Is this your baby?'

The group nodded conspiratorially, and a man with crooked spectacles taped together on one side said with an emotional grin, 'Coming back home at last. Actually she didn't work on this branch *itself*, but she was up at Carlisle. Rostered for the coast route, mostly, push-pull work, freight diagrams.'

'Only one of her kind left,' added a teenager in a Motorhead T-shirt. 'Been at Barry since '67, all this time. We've been raising the money for her for five years.'

'So who are you?' asked Fellows with absorbed interest.

'Enfield Steam Group,' replied the teenager, pointing to the white letters on the side of the locomotive. 'Came up yesterday.'

'That's rather a long way. Why don't you keep it down there?' said Fellows.

'We were going to restore it on the Kent and East Sussex.' The man adjusted his glasses and the yellow knot of sellotape gave slightly to leave them more askew. 'But then the Carrock started up and that was the answer to our prayers.' He *means* prayers, thought Greg. 'It wouldn't have been authentic in Kent.'

The transporter was manoeuvring painstakingly, its engine bellowing, until it was straight with the depot gateway. The Steam Group scattered suddenly and pelted into the yard as though flying after a child that had run into the road, so Greg and Fellows went in pursuit. The long load inched between the two sheds, through a newly-dug gap where the earth bank and the hydrangea bushes had been, and then slowly backed up level with the platform, alongside which, Greg could see, a short section of track, steam engine length, had been laid on grey stones. Greg and Fellows watched as the Group unlashed the engine from the trailer, hitched it up to a Land Rover, and with strained, violent yelps of 'Yes!', 'No . . . No!' and 'More, more, *more!*' hauled the great piece of metal down onto the rails.

Fellows pointed out across the track area. 'Our hardworking master of ceremonies.' Edwards was standing over on the far side almost by the screen of poplars, a stiffly amused smile on his face. It was difficult to tell if he had been banished there by the Steam Group, anxious not to have their tricky unloading interfered with or the glory of their delivery diluted by outside participants – or if, conversely, this was impresarial Edwards surveying at an appropriate distance his new act against the backdrop of his theatre. Then Greg thought, Edwards could make it both.

The lowloader was bumping off back through the depot, Edwards was striding over with hands on hips, and the Group were standing around in aimless anticlimax. Edwards passed them with a quick nod and came up to Greg and Fellows saying, 'Can you imagine this belting through Scale Tunnel, then?'

Fellows had become quiet and edgy and was leaving the other half of any conversation to Greg, who said, 'This must be the best bit so far. A real steam engine here. You never told us this was coming.'

'Will be when it's running,' said Edwards. And then under his breath, 'Awful people, these trainspotters. Can't think further than rivets and wheel flanges. Just warning you.'

'They'll need to be quite keen on all that. It's in quite a state. Why didn't you tell everyone else this was going to be arriving? We just saw it by chance in the High Street.'

'They're welcome,' said Edwards, again answering Greg's points in order, but only as far as the first one. He smiled magnanimously. 'I was just pleased to get hold of this for the line. People in the town'll like it.' He clapped them both on the arm. 'Have to go – local paper's over there wanting a word. Just wanted to see what you thought.' Edwards went to join a man on the platform putting away his camera, the hotel manager hurried up to them both, and soon it appeared that Edwards and the reporter were each uneasily conducting two different interviews.

Greg and Fellows wandered round the locomotive for a proper look. It was there, at last: a railway engine for what was going to be a railway. Now you could come through the platform doors to a train. Greg wished the other volunteers had been there to see it arrive, and not been unconscious victims of Edwards's divide-and-rule tactics – partly because he would have liked to see what they made of it. Curiously, now that it was there and the odd, illicit thrill of its gigantic progress through the town was over, there was nothing to feel about it. The Group had the monopoly of love and gratitude for the safety of their charge: Greg was happy to leave them that. It was a parodically obvious symbol of a railway – it was the thing you saw on the road sign at a level crossing, he remembered; it was not unexpected. It wasn't because he didn't know anything about steam engines, either: this didn't make him want to know. It wasn't that it was rusted and derelict and out-of-order: a vague mystery could be found in where it had been for so long to get like that. It was that it was so purely utilitarian – a huge iron boiler on wheels to drag a line of carriages along with a cab at the back for someone to drive it from. To make any sense of it you had to imagine the carriages full of people, or even the whole lives of the members of the Group, whose patterns would be altered by the interludes of restoring a steam engine. 'What do you think?' he asked Fellows.

'I think if it took them five years to buy it, it should take them about twenty to do it up.'

Greg sensed in Fellows's balefulness his disappointment that the engine had been successfully shoe-horned into the station after all, which could only have been partly mitigated by Edwards having had no hand in it. They watched the animated triangular conversation over on the platform. 'Presumably that's what he's telling the man from the hotel. The council specifically said no to steam engines for the time being.'

'While he's assuring the newspaper man it'll be running in six months.'

Greg wondered what Edwards was telling the journalist. The idea of a steam railway for tourists had been a mere expediency, so Edwards had implied back at that meeting, bringing in cash to support the full service. What was the story, then, about this new relic which they couldn't even use?

By now the hotel manager had fallen silent.

'Look at him talking their heads off,' said Fellows.

'He must be convincing them both,' added Greg, not sure whether he wanted Edwards to.

'That he's a pain in the bloody arse,' said Fellows.

As he walked back to the hostel Greg suddenly felt taken unawares by Edwards. How does he want to help this town? he thought. By giving it a medicine it won't know it needs because he has invented it. Why were Greg and the other volunteers helping Edwards to reopen the railway? Because Edwards needed the use of them. Where was the social spirit of Edwards's vaunted scheme in not informing the hotel manager, or any of the volunteers, about the railway engine coming, and in the nonchalantly dismissive scorn towards the people who had actually brought it? The railway wasn't the town's lost democracy: it was Edwards's private secret.

Then Greg felt annoyed because Edwards was making him annoyed, when it was only a railway, which Edwards was consistently taking too seriously or too lightly, which made you do so too, only the other way round, so that it was either a large chunk of rusted metal or a manifesto for congregation and nothing in between, and with an onrush of intensified exasperation Greg realised Edwards was *still* taking him unawares! Leave us alone! he raged. I know you do – but don't!

And now Ruth was going back. On the Friday she was travelling home to Ipswich, and then on to Southampton on Sunday for the new term and a meeting with her tutor the following morning. The last days of her stay at the hostel had been subdued and strained. She was still toiling to complete her summer's studies – there was a 10,000 word paper she had to have ready for Monday, she confided to Greg in glum terror at the beginning of the week, which she was only starting that day. All the previous reclusive evenings had been 'preparatory work'. The scratchy temper had given way to a blanched, taut ponderousness that made her swallow a lot and forget to wash any of her clothes, so that now in addition to the Wee Willie Winkie socks trailing from her feet Greg's shirt tails hung out over her jeans.

Also she had upset the Warden, who had caught her in his office peeking through his papers – and she hadn't been able to explain to him, of course, that she was only trying to check on his name for when she said goodbye. So she and Greg still didn't know; it was extraordinary how even when Greg heard the Warden on the phone to someone he obviously knew, he always spoke as if he was taking messages for somebody else. The Warden's considerable umbrage at Ruth's trespass, which seemed to contain both a baffled hurt and the final confirmation of all his suspicions, made Ruth sulky and obstructive in like manner, since she had only been trying to be polite to him anyway, and it summed up utterly how right from the start he had treated her like a tiny schoolgirl.

The oncoming autumn had turned the mornings, now, as well as the evenings. The hostel woke to windows streaming with condensation, the lawn was crackly with the first frost, and the sun, when it appeared, seemed to take half the morning to rise into the sky. The Warden grudgingly agreed to do the breakfast by himself on Friday, so that Greg could run Ruth to Wetherbeck first thing for her train, but implied extra disappointment that Greg too was thereby complicit in Ruth's irresponsible mischief. These days the hostel itself was usually half-empty, so the Warden could easily cope. Nevertheless, while there was less work for them all the place also had begun to seem worn and shabby and a bigger chore than in earlier months when it had been full. Greg was starting to resent the persistent trickle of hostellers: always someone every night, even if only one, wanting dinner and breakfast and packets of crisps. He realised he was waiting for the hostel to close for the year.

No chance of going out with Ruth on her last evening: not only would it have been as factitious and gawky as all the other planned dates they hadn't been out on, but Ruth had remembered that her paper had to be typed, and there was no way she could do it over the weekend once she was home.

'Can't you give your tutor some excuse? said Greg.'

Ruth shook her head. 'He's like him,' she said, waving towards the Warden's office.

After dinner Greg took the hostel typewriter up to his room (how was Ruth planning to type it otherwise, he wondered), and installed Ruth there to pick away at it for the evening while he ran things downstairs.

Towards eleven she came down as he was closing things up for the night, and lingered. 'Is he around?'

Greg went and put his head round into the Warden's sitting room. 'Um, Ruth just wanted to say goodbye, in case we don't see you in the morning.'

The Warden shuffled stiffly out into the doorway, and Ruth stood in front of him nervously chewing her hair and with her feet together, and said her thanks and goodbye solemnly and correctly like a small schoolgirl reciting a poem.

The Warden wiped his hands on his trousers in embarrassment, gave her an uneasy briefing about all the hard work he hoped she'd do at college, and they shook hands for a long time until all three of them sensed that each was waiting for the other to let go.

Ruth hopped and skipped thoughtfully up the stairs in front of Greg, and back in his bedroom he saw – Ruth was rearranging pages of writing all over his bed – that she had typed one paragraph of her essay.

'As soon as I came to type it up I found it all needed rewriting.' She added doubtfully, 'The first half's quite good now.'

'This is going to take you all night!'

Ruth bit her fingernails.

So Greg sat down at the typewriter with the first instalment of crumpled, heavily-amended sheets and began to learn about the geological difficulties of mining in the Lake Counties, and Ruth sat cross-legged on his bed scribbling and crossing out and periodically dropping another page from the pile on her lap on to the pile beside her. As the night wore on Greg watched the tails of Ruth's g's and y's spear down deeper into the words below; at half past one the two of them found they had just argued for a quarter of an hour on the use of semicolons; and by four o'clock – Ruth said they were near the end, but Greg still had a sheaf of pages at his side – they had retreated into their separate worlds of weariness, and found a fragile, formal delicacy with each other whenever they had to speak. At quarter past five, Ruth standing behind him with her hands on the back of his chair, Greg typed the last words, and after several long moments she leaned her head against his as he sat staring ahead of him.

Thus Greg and Ruth had ended up spending the night together. Greg thought if he stood up he would fall over, and if he tried to kiss Ruth (his scoured consciousness distantly posited this extra difficulty of mining in Lakeland) he would probably miss her lips like a drunk bringing his glass up to his nose. His awareness shrank to her temple beating warm on his own, and now her arms were around him too.

'I have to pack, Greg. I'll wake you in time for when we have to leave.'

Ruth gone, his mind offered him the small speech that was meant for her but not to be said to her. *I did this for you, although I didn't know at the time.*

Then Ruth was rocking him awake in his chair. 'Quarter to seven.' It was still dark outside when she pulled back the curtains.

By the time they were ready to set off it was muddily light: a bitter, hazy morning that made them feel alert but act slowly. The car was covered in white rime. Soon after they had left Carrock behind, Ruth's head flopped over to rest against the seat, draped by her hair. Greg concentrated on being able to tell himself constantly that he was driving the car and not the car him. As the dotted white line to his right endured minute by minute there seemed no room in his brain for the possibility that they would reach Wetherbeck and Ruth wouldn't be softly asleep next to him any longer.

When the train slid in Greg said to Ruth, 'I want to keep on knowing you,' which was the truest thing he could find to say. (He had silently rehearsed it while they had been waiting on the platform.)

Ruth said, 'You looked after me this summer,' which struck him as a surprisingly cloying thing for her to say.

Suddenly it felt – he knew they both felt – that a proper goodbye had already been said some unspecific time before. Ruth clambered into the carriage and Greg turned back towards his car, already fearing that what he had said wasn't true at all – he hardly knew her, except when she was asleep – and wondering whether he had nevertheless touched the tiniest part of her, or whether the closer you got to someone, the more you saw how people are entirely protected from your knowing by their mind not being yours. Who'd have expected Ruth to be so vaguely sentimental just then? As the last coach pulled away a nearly-empty tube of Gibbs S R hit him on the shoulder.

Two weeks later Greg stamped the last three hostellers' cards with the smudgy black image of a sunlit lake, and the hostel was closed for the year.

Greg had no plans – which meant going back to London. The Warden hadn't enquired about them, however; it seemed to Greg that the grim relaxation with which, from inside his office, he had watched the last rucksacks jostle out of the front door, would be consolidated when Greg followed them. Why don't you go and become a Traffic Warden, thought Greg.

They spent the rest of that day, and all of the next, clearing up the hostel, Greg silently depressed by how bare and tatty it suddenly looked, the Warden expostulatingly angry at the amount of 'gratuitous damage' committed over the summer; Greg was irritated by the Warden's hysteria, the Warden annoyed by Greg's complacency; Greg once venturing – not caring if he was being equable or wheedling – that 'You have to expect this sort of thing,' the Warden high-mindedly rounding on him, as Greg knew he would, 'Unfortunately yes, Mr Craven.' By lunchtime on the second day, as the rain began spidering down the window panes, Greg had decided he was leaving the next morning. He rang Edwards at the bookshop to see if they might meet for a drink that evening. Edwards was crisp, cavalier, and distracted.

'Have you got a customer?' said Greg. 'Shall I ring back?'

'No, no. But I'm driving over to Millom tonight. Rotary Club gig spreading the word.' A momentary pause. 'So, when you come back we'll have a proper railway for you to work on. You'll see the changes in the town by then. Give me your address in London and I'll send you all the bumf for the share issue.'

'I don't exactly know what my plans are,' Greg protested lamely.

'You don't want to stay in London. No one should live there.'

Then Edwards said that Greg would be silly to stay away from the railway for long, because they were just getting to the best bit. Greg found himself thanking Edwards for all his help.

Greg went and found the Warden and mentioned that he thought he would, make a move tomorrow, if that was about it here? The Warden tapped his unlighted cigarette contemplatively on the packet and nodded, and they spent the afternoon scouring blackened pans. By nightfall they seemed to have done everything, and stared nervously at each other, fearful in case the other was going to suggest some kind of leave-taking sociability, and knowing that if the one didn't the other would have to. The Warden muttered that he must just attend to a bit of paperwork, and Greg remembered theatrically that he hadn't checked his oil or tyres yet.

Half an hour later their paths converged again in the hall, and the Warden, as if now there was nothing else for it, mumbled hesitantly, 'Have I ever shown you my collection?'

'You haven't,' said Greg in surprise.

The Warden led the way into his sitting room, shuffled round behind the door, and unlocked an old mahogany cabinet to reveal several shelves full of books. He selected three and passed them to Greg, and waited for him to peruse them.

They were three editions of Kipling's *Kim*: one musty and leatherbound; one in faded red cloth with large uncut pages, and a trim, modern olive-green volume from a book club.

'I've got three complete Collected Editions,' the Warden confided, 'and I pick up as many different editions of the best books as I can find.' He spread his hand in front of the array in the cupboard.

Greg knelt down next to the Warden to peer inside. 'You like to collect all the different kinds of binding, all the various illustrators, then?'

'Of course, Kipling's own are the best,' said the Warden. 'So sharp, clean. I take a look at all these new-fangled painting efforts, though.' He pulled out a Folio Society edition of the *Just So Stories* in an ivory-coloured slipcase, and traced the lines of gold blocking on the cover. 'I like to see him done in an appropriate form.'

'What is it about Kipling, then?' said Greg carefully.

The Warden's disconcerted look suggested that this was a question he had never had to address. 'Well, I came across him first when I was in the army – read all his poems when I was

97

out in Aden. "If you can keep your head when all around are losing theirs . . ." I still go along with that.'

'Ye-es.'

'Now I just tend to read the kid's stuff, though,' the Warden continued apologetically. '*Jungle Books, Kim*, these . . .' He was flicking through the *Just So Stories*; then he stopped, and paged back to the silhouette of the Cat That Walked By Himself leaving his coal-nugget footprints in the snow. The Warden regarded it. 'Young Ruth,' he said after a while.

'So what are your favourite bits?' said Greg. 'I only read *The Jungle Book* when I was very small.'

The Warden was turning the pages again. 'I like that bit when the monkeys all run helter-skelter through the tops of the trees . . .' He smiled uncertainly at Greg. 'You know, they pick up Mowgli and escape as fast as they can, absolutely pell-mell, right across the top of the jungle. I read that a lot.' He nodded slowly, sagely now, and then shut the book with a snap. 'That's all I can say, anyway,' he concluded in huffy dignity, as though all this was evidence he had had to give under duress.

'I did go to Bateman's quite recently,' said Greg. 'I thought his wild garden was great. I suppose you could see from that why he wrote things like *The Jungle Book*.'

'I *didn't* like that,' said the Warden with distaste. 'I couldn't for the life of me see why they had left it like that.'

Greg tried again. 'Of course, Kim wouldn't be the kind of kid you'd want in a youth hostel! I mean *one* wouldn't . . .'

The Warden stared hard in front of him. 'I suppose not, no,' he answered quietly in chastened puzzlement.

They went out for a drink because both knew it would be too impolite not to. The Warden suggested they drive out to a pub in a village over the fell where he sometimes had lunch when he was out walking.

The evening turned into a long, relaxed and businesslike discussion about the future policies of the Youth Hostels Association: hostels likely to be closed, to be improved, the relative merits of certain refurbishments; the economics of providing meals; the politics, according to the Warden, of the local volunteer management committee. The two of them were determinedly pessimistic, slightly wistful, and agreed that things could certainly be better. Throughout, Greg had the feeling that, in different ways, neither of them quite believed a word they were saying. But he kept noticing anew that they were actually sitting there side by side gazing at the log fire, and already the Warden was on his third pint of Guinness, his moustache matted with foam. The ruminative formalities sat between them, and gave them sentences to offer each other, which in turn clocked up time spent together, it seemed for its own sake. As Greg's Mini juddered back up the hills into the pale tunnel of its headlights, it appeared to him as if they were together in a tiny cramped space capsule, had come miles, miles, away into nowhere. Four months to get as far as this – or was it rather, four months wasted, and then in a mere few hours . . .? Whatever, it was as far as they were going to get, or needed to, even if Greg hadn't been leaving in the morning. By now the Kipling-interlude seemed an uncomfortable intrusion, as well as Greg's only fragmentary sight of the person whose official title was the Warden. Greg felt he shouldn't have needed to see that – when the formality between them had momentarily faltered just then it should have been shored up, not conceded. As far as he was concerned, the Warden was all there was, the monkeys' flight through the treetops too little basis for speculation, and too much.

As Greg drove towards the motorway and London on the wide white road, the old railway line wound and skimmed along away to his right. He could glimpse it in stretches, and now counted off to himself the bits he knew. There was the embankment; that belt of trees would be hiding Scale, the church, the cutting; the hump of Scale Fell was almost lost in the mist this morning; beyond that would be the old viaduct. He still hadn't seen the viaduct, except from the top of Thunacar. He had only heard all about The Viaduct.

On an impulse – leave London until after this – Greg took the next right, and skated his car around the narrow lanes. Eventually he reached an old barn that according to the map was as near as he could drive to the bridge. He walked round the edge of a steep field, his trainers soon sodden from the long wet grass, and the scattered sheep transfixed in mid-chew by his approach. Up, and further on up, and finally on to the brow of the hill – and there, in front of him, the great brick span spread across the gorge. The grassy road led on to it on this side, even continued across it, he saw, perhaps two hundred yards . . . and then on. Twenty slender arches that went down, and down, and far down the water boiled around the feet of the middle pillars. Two hillsides meeting in this deserted valley, a river along the bottom – and this! thought Greg: way out here near a few sheep: so many thousands of bricks in the thing.

The way on to it was blocked by a close-barred, spiked iron fence taller than Greg, but, as at the tunnel, there was still an entrance. One of the bars was gone and you could squeeze through. Greg found himself treading lightly, tentatively, over the furry grey-green carpet of moss and grass. The floor wasn't hard like brick; there was soft earth under his feet. Here and there tall wind-straggled thorn bushes had seeded themselves.

Greg leaned over the parapet. You were so far up you couldn't see the pillars below in the water: the sides of the viaduct seemed to cut back underneath you. When Greg peered down it felt as if the whole structure was gently easing over in slow motion, a rectangle reclining into a parallelogram, and would soon . . . languorously to the end . . . *crash*!

Again, as Greg had discovered on that first walk with Ruth along the embankment, perspective changed and changed again around him. A massive bridge clamped over this small river; a thin, stalky bridge tied like a cobweb inside a vast-spread valley. The viaduct the best viewpoint from which to regard the high hills; the viaduct the focal point of the entire dale. It can't just be, thought Greg. It is to be used for something.

What was it for – this empty viaduct?

What were these four months in the Lakes for? The hostel? The Warden, Ruth? The railway? The Lake District itself? Greg knew there ought to be answers, because now he had been able to ask the questions.

Start with the youth hostel. What had he done there? What was it for? The youth hostel wasn't *for* anything, if you meant for anything other than itself – not for shareholders, not for margins, for an owner. It just was: there for people to pass through it.

Could you remake the railway in that way? Was that what Edwards said he wanted – even if he seemed to be planning the opposite?

Something that wasn't *for* anything. Greg wondered if this was why he had been confused when he had looked at the landscape with Ruth. All those contradictory signs he had read as claiming what the Lake District was for: for lead mining, for cobalt mining, for caravans, for timeshares. And then Ruth had seemed to say that it could be for all of them, which was right except it didn't acknowledge the possibility that one of them could supervene and *make* the whole place for itself. The Lake District was not a lead mine, as the Rhondda Valley was a coal mine: here you could still see all those things, and you could still see the Lake District as well around them. Greg was thinking, It's only while you can still see the land and recognise it as such, and not anything else, that you can truly accommodate all thoughts and decisions about what people should do. The way this viaduct delicately high-straddled the river valley as if not wanting to touch it . . .

Was all this partly just a way of asking himself if he was going to come back? Whether he would see Ruth again? All that had been started, which would have to have some sort of ending . . . Everything here seemed more provisional, but more possible. All that Greg had unexpectedly assisted in constructing during the summer just gone – the recovering of the railway, the halting acquaintance with the Warden, every encounter with Ruth. It was as though he had been surrounded by a mass of land, great spaces – so much left untouched, all around. In each case so little so far accomplished, such smallnesses, and the consolation which could equally be an admonition – that the empty openness remained. Nothing had been ruled out.

WINTER

Chapter Ten

Greg was with several hundred tightly-crammed people, in London's morning rush hour, and it was as quiet as the Lake District.

He had stood with them on the platform at Lewisham, where they had waited separately, edgily, watching their white breath, and shuffled forward as the rails began to quiver and rumble. The doors clunked shut behind them, they had found seats, or not, and after the train had creaked and jerked away, they waited. They waited quietly, reading their newspapers, their library books, their typewritten reports, or sunk into a hot, huddled doze, while the train stopped, started off again every so often, and each time more people shuffled on and clutched at luggage-racks to sway where they stood. And now they were all waiting while the train was waiting. Distantly an invisible train rushed down another line. The windows misted up. On one side a child's tricycle upended in the scrubby garden below disappeared; so did the car breaker's yard on the other. Still the people were quiet, sheltering from each other. The train jolted on again towards London Bridge. Travelling was waiting.

There were unexpected quietnesses in London too, Greg was noticing for the first time, at the other times of day. As he went up the escalator at quarter to nine to the sports department of the large store where he had found a job, the whole place was silent. There were other staff ascending with him, talking amongst themselves — but the vast empty floors around them registered the surrounding quiet and not the scatterings of conversations. Even during the day, Greg found (he was thinking back to the clangour and bustle of the hostel in the early morning and evening: pans, tins, crockery, boots, packs, yells), sudden pools of calm were left as the only customer in the department drifted out. Or there had been the exultant madness of the track-clearing expeditions: the bellowing of the chainsaw, the smashing and thunking of the machetes next to that, their own bawling above both. In the big store everyone spoke in a measured undertone, speaking against the weight of the labyrinthine building around them. Feet padded on the carpets, doors hissed pneumatically to; it was never loud in there.

This was it: in the Lakes you heard quiet when no one was around – when the hostel was closed, or on top of the viaduct – and when there were people there, you heard them, being as loud as people are. In London you couldn't rely on that: how could you hear so little when you could see so many people? All the real noise, indeed, seemed as if it was piped, turned on for a quick blast by some distant functionary – not just the blare of music from an open boutique frontage, but even the sudden roar of a bus and its thick-chugging exhaust. Slam up the volume – and then as quickly down again. But the people, being or made quiet, were all deferring to something. It wasn't that everyone was reticent because constantly aware of others; rather that no one seemed to notice their own self. During the journey to work in the morning you put yourself on hold, as you would, say, while leafing through a magazine in a waiting room, and it was the same in the evening darkness on the way back. In between, in the big store, you were *in* waiting, and therefore you *refrained*: you walked slowly, spoke calmly, hovered discreetly, backed off unobtrusively. The customers did too. You had to be as noiseless, neat, and apparently stationary as the building and its fittings. Whichever side of the counter you were, behind your every action stood the tacit, nervous question: What would the store like me to do? At the training sessions Greg had attended when he started, the teachers had habitually accorded the place the third person singular: '. . . doesn't think that –' . . . didn't want Greg to ring up a £9.99 pair of goalkeeper's gloves one day as £999. After the trickling sweat and the succession of seniors' countersignatures, however, Greg felt a weak thrill of creation, augmented by the silently complicit admiration of his colleagues. The store could not make this mistake, but *Greg* could.

It was also – this not noticing yourself in London – that there was so much standing in the way of seeing anything. Down here the sky, when you could look at it at all, was a strip between the tops of streets. There was no horizon. In front of you everywhere was a building. Across Green Park, where Greg walked once on his afternoon off, you could see rooftops and towers beyond, and even as you picked them out the park shortened. In the store, there were departments every side of you: above you, further above you, underneath you, even below ground level holding up the rest. You couldn't seem to look out of it, either, for Greg never found any windows. The only light of his day was the unsteady, gathering daylight of the wait on the station soon after dawn, when all commuters shifted from foot to foot and explored the platform in frail paces. Then the daylight was shut out by the white haze on the carriage windows, then you walked under the black awning that swept over the station concourse at London Bridge, then you hurried down into the tube. By the time you came out of the store in the evening it was dark.

Greg had grown used to large perspectives, to there being land enough around to leave him alone. Back here he now felt occasionally helpless, babyish and maudlin. Let some more light in! he silently beseeched, annoyed at how obvious his plea was, and how pressing. But everyone else was waiting, too: they couldn't see further than the next street, the next wall, the next identical cube of artifical light. They stared hard, out in the street, but they weren't looking. Everything, in London, was near. So people waited for distance, waited for emptiness, for the chance to choose to be nothing if they wanted, and waited for everyone else, who in their turn was waiting.

After Greg had been working at the big store for three weeks, he began walking over London Bridge itself with the hundreds striding towards the City, and caught the tube at Monument instead. That way you could think you were actually entering London of your own accord, and see the city framed and limited by the sky. And every day you crossed a vast gap right through London and out both sides, that even London couldn't fill. Occasionally this dogged obeisance to the grey Thames seemed to Greg melodramatic and meretricious – a wanting to think well of himself. At other times, as the multitudes thrust past him in their blue overcoats, oblivious of the wide water around them, he felt melodramatic and defiant, wanting to stop one of them and say, *I come from a place* . . .

Just as Greg had stood on the platform at Carrock looking at the flat expanse of earth in front of him, and tried to think it into activity, so now he found himself awaiting the train at Lewisham, closing down the station in his imagination, and clearing most of it away. Pull up the rails and their rusty brown sleepers to leave a line of sockets stretching away in the ballast, then . . . But that was all you needed to do, he realised; there was nothing else here worth noticing. He couldn't be bothered to speculate or work out how many bridges they went over on the way up to London, or where the tunnels were. The only point of this railway, its dirty, peeling buildings and the oil-spattered track, was to get hundreds of passengers in to work each day. Take them away, and you might as well build houses on the space left behind.

So why not on the old Carrock railway? No passengers there, which was why it closed. What other reasons, then, for all that massive programme of work to try, as they were doing, to rebuild it? It must be more than wanting to preserve and use again some great physical relics like the tunnel and the embankment, something other than that there was a fine view along the way, compared to the approach to London Bridge past the Huntley and Palmer's factory and Millwall football ground. If you tried asking not, 'Why are we doing it?' but, 'What will we have done by doing it' . . .? One day somewhere along the blur of his morning train ride – Greg couldn't tell where they were – the words came to him: *It will have set something in motion.* The restoration project itself was a kind of travel; from the opening of the station doors at Carrock to let people walk inside, to beating a path to the bridge with Kevin, they were discovering things themselves and offering those new spaces on to others. More than that, they were setting up a journey they knew could be there, but wouldn't be so until they had built it – like writing a book, when you knew what the plot was and how long it would be, but the story would only be there once you had written it out in that number of pages. That was how you set the journey in motion: you made another larger, infinitely slow, unrepeatable journey along it yourself, in order by so doing to construct a story of stations and fields and bridges and hills and woods, whose curves and straights were fixed and permanent in space and time – there for anyone to discover, and to be continually travelled.

To travel, in fact, rather than just to wait, you had to put your self on the journey – so that, in a sense, the journey travelled you. Travelling, on the Carrock line currently being relaid and extended to its end, in Greg's mind, was a feeling of history. For the rebuilders, every day would take them nearer to something, become part of a narrative you could rerun backwards from the present. Even for the carriageloads of holidaymakers whiling away an hour or two, who would most likely be the railway's main passengers, a journey down the line would add a period of time to their lives, and not, as with this transitional vacuum of slumped, stifled people between Lewisham and London, subtract it.

And here was Greg not having even seen the whole line. He'd been as far as Scale – three miles – and he'd deviated from the main road to go and stand on the viaduct, and that was all. What was at the other end of the tunnel? What about the other twelve miles? How about Wetherbeck, the junction with the main line, which he had only tapped with his finger on the librarian's map? There, indeed, when he had only been back in London a month, was one reason on offer to him for going back to the Lakes: what was along the rest of the way? To do the whole journey himself, if only by walking it. After that, as well, he could properly think it.

In the middle of November Greg came home one evening to find a bulky manila envelope on the mat, and a card advising him that the postman had been unable to deliver a large parcel that morning, which was now awaiting collection at the sorting office.

The envelope contained the railway's share issue prospectus, the Autumn newsletter of the Preservation Group, and a scribbled comp. slip from Edwards.

Town behind this in big way! Now we'll see real democracy
in action! Advise y to get y cheque in quick if y want some
shs.

Greg dropped the comp. slip in the bin and sat down to read
the prospectus.

It was a cool, clean production: a silky, coated paper, wide
margins, headings picked out in pastel pink, and tables and
figures in boxes in grey. They were going for £125,000, for
starters – they, not just Edwards, for now there was a Carrock
and Wetherbeck Railway Company (1987) Ltd, whose board
of six directors included L. Tait (that was Les), A. Shillingworth
(Adrian of Nutbrown Healthfoods), and V. Senior, who was
Victor Senior the accountant (Greg had heard about but never
met him, though he must have been one of those on the stage
back at the public meeting). Services to Force Road, the prospectus confirmed, were due to start the following summer if, 'as
initial inquiries indicate is likely, a substantial Manpower Services Commission grant is forthcoming following a successful
share issue, to provide essential labour to assist the major task
of tracklaying'. Edwards had also enclosed a leaflet advertising
the issue, on which he had scrawled, '200,000 of these in every
rly mag & Lake Dist pubcn libraries banks p/offices etc.' A
pound a share, and you had to buy at least fifty.

The prospectus emphasised that this was a unique opportunity to invest in 'Britain's most scenic railway', as well as,
architecturally, its most impressive: once reopened, it would
boast the largest viaduct and the longest tunnel of any private
line in the country. Then there were the company's longer-term
plans. It would run sumptuous Pullman excursions from London
– 'The Lakeland Belle' – tapping the luxury leisure market so
successfully identified and exploited by the rejuvenated Orient
Express, and providing the very highest standards of comfort.
For the growing interest in industrial archaeology it proposed
special 'History Train' tours, to view the relics of Lakeland's
industrial heritage from a classroom-carriage equipped with a
qualified guide who would contribute lectures and commentary.
Above all, this rolling classroom would figure in a wider promotion to all secondary schools and places of further education

that offered a complete package of extended field trip study facilities, for geography, geology or botanical excursions. The self-contained study-fleet was to be completed with sleeper accommodation and dining car, and the whole project to be marketed as 'Training for Tomorrow'. There was no longer any mention of freight trains, as Greg remembered from the handout Edwards had given him on their first meeting. But if you were taking people to see how all the mines and industry had closed down you couldn't also run trains to pick up ore and slate from them.

The measured, impersonal assertions of the prospectus made use of the word 'leisure' a lot; 'work' not at all. Either Edwards had had little hand in the writing of it, or he was content to tell capitalism what he knew capitalists wanted to be told, in order to get their money. The railway, the prospectus implied, was going to be an even more sophisticated purveyor of leisure activity than Greg had expected: not simply offering joy rides – fake train journeys – but giving people *working* holidays. Indeed, providing for those who worked at finding for themselves the subtlest, most detailed, and most expensive kinds of luxury, a newly engrossing experience of pleasure. On the one hand Edwards was offering Carrock's townspeople shares in their local line at a quid a time; on the other the Railway Company (1987) Ltd was proposing to avail *QE2* cruise passengers of a plush, upholstered glimpse of Lakeland.

Whether the directors believed in such projections, or which of them were the market-led realists to Edwards's romantic democratists? Whether, if they didn't, one ought to risk such hostages to fortune? Whether they deemed such upmarket plans as fully compatible with, or perhaps useful subsidy for, the proper railway, whatever that was . . .? When you turned to the Preservation Group newsletter such worries seemed distant and academic. It chatted on confidentially over four typed and duplicated sheets of bright green A4, a hand-drawn steam engine on the front for its logo. The loan of a working tank engine had been promised for when services began. The imminent arrival was expected of a diesel shunter, a sleeper carriage to accommodate volunteers ('but don't expect too many hot baths!'), and a steam crane. T-shirts and sweat shirts were now available from

Edwards's bookshop and the station that read, I'M PUTTING CARROCK BACK ON THE RAILS! Don't forget the *Bygone Days of the LNER* slide-show on the 20th, another collection of secondhand books planned for a fortnight's time, still need as many old rags as possible for the loco restoration work – "Isn't it about time you had some new kitchen curtains anyway?!" The newsletter was as intimate as the prospectus was monolithic: 'Bill's painting programme', 'Jim and Dean in the signalling department', 'Rose and the girls in the cafeteria' – each volunteer's name cited conferred a proprietorial importance on its owner. And yet, 'Simon's track gang'? The whole group was a gang. Negotiations with the management of the Carrock Grange Hotel, the newsletter confided, were simply 'continuing'. Progress, its overall import didn't say, was steady, sensible, and small. A mile and a bit of railway to relay completely, including a new bridge, before any of it would be there at all. There was less than a year to do it in, and if they managed it it would have taken them nearly a year. It was an 'ambitious' project: that was the other keyword Greg took away from the prospectus. What did 'ambitious' mean?

By the end of the following week, when Greg finally got around to calling in at the sorting office, he was still toying with the idea of sending Edwards a cheque for £25, by return post.

When he handed his card over, the clerk smirked to his colleague, and came back with a large polythene bag full of laundry.

'Not the sturdiest piece a packin' I ever seen,' he said, fishing a scrap of thin brown paper out of the bag. 'They was all over the van when they come in. Bit with the address on only turned up the next day.' He plumped the bundle of shirts, socks and jumpers into Greg's arms, and Greg fell over a pushchair behind him in his hasty exit.

Ruth! Had she really borrowed all these clothes from him?

But in fact, when Greg went through the contents of the bag, there was still at least one shirt apparently unaccounted for. Keep it, he thought sentimentally, whether you know it's mine or not. Then it occurred to him that it might well be lying in some goods van in Swindon. Greg hadn't been able to decide how to ask Ruth if she still had some of his clothes; you couldn't write to her just on that pretext, and every time he had tried to draft in his mind the paragraph to precede and prepare for that bit there always seemed to be another paragraph that needed to go before *that*, and then another before . . .

There was no note from her to go with his clothes. Had there been one, or had that disappeared like the shirt, if that had? Anyhow, a month and a half after finishing her essay, Ruth had finally got around to doing her washing. Greg made a euphoric resolution to write to her as soon as possible, but not to mention anything about the state of the parcel when it had arrived, since when he imagined her reading about it, or remembered the looks of the post office clerk and the people in the queue, it seemed as though he had sent it like that.

Over the following days, as Greg began to plan when to prepare to start his letter, Ruth filled his musings more and more. Every fortuitous interposition, or so it seemed, of a banal thing between the two of them – so that instead of Ruth he got an all-night essay on lead mining, or a bundle of old clothes, or a hedgehog – only left more to know, to the extent that, the slighter the conjunction, the greater Greg's unconscious, habitual conviction that he could know it without seeing Ruth at all. He dreamed through days in the sports department, therefore, of being with her all the time, living with her even, in some unspecific place – Ruth being dizzy and solemn and contemplative and chewing her hair a lot. It seemed as if they could say anything to each other, though he could not frame one pair of sentences they might actually exchange. They never disagreed. Once or twice as he rode the escalator down to the street in the evening, walking his fingers speculatively down the rubber handrail at his side, it seemed to Greg as if they were already together. But then he came out into the damp orange glare of Oxford Street and had to leave her oblivious in Southampton while he went to catch the tube.

When he sat down to write his letter, of course, words failed him utterly: he knew how to shelter in a tunnel with Ruth, or how to climb a mountain, but had no idea how to just speak to her. The letter went through drafts of what seemed to Greg abject self-confession, a businesslike and boringly thorough résumé of recent events, and a catastrophic attempt at explaining ironically how he hadn't the first idea what to say. In the end it turned out to read as if a friend had written to Ruth to report on what Greg had been up to, and then changed the 'he's to 'I's. Greg sent the letter off hoping it would get lost in the post, weeks went by, and he heard nothing.

The year moved into December, and the store got busier. It now opened for an extra hour in the evenings. The trains and tubes were crammed more tightly as Christmas shoppers joined commuters. Oily rain seemed to lie in the streets most days; crumpled-up paper bags and newspapers scuttered around people's hurrying feet in wet balls. The department filled up with stock, spacious displays of new sportswear ranges giving way to simple piles of goods: a pyramid of tennis balls, bags of golf clubs huddled together like corn stooks, large bins heaped high with junior football team outfits in cellophane packs. At lunchtimes the staff canteen was full and noisy with the newly-swelled Christmas staff. Several school leavers joined the sports department for December, and as trade increased and the enlarged team got to know one another, working there took on a rampageous, flurried air. They united in silent conspiracy against any customer evidently desirous and capable of spending a large amount of money, to ensure with implacable collective courtesy that he bought anything they put in front of him. They compared their own extravagant Christmas shopping purchases in the store, each smugly celebrating their 25% staff discount and confident that it was only their colleagues who were thereby induced to spend twice as much. They scrambled out after the store closed to stand jostled together for hours in a crowded pub round the corner, hooting and shrieking out their gossip and banter at each other after the murmuring and constraint of the day. With the rest of them Greg was caught up and surged along in this omnipresent, physically pressing ebb and flow of people, from the train in the morning uninterrupted, it felt, until the train the next morning.

One December night he shambled and sniggered his way home very late after a long evening and many pints with his sports department friends, and fell through his front door to find the phone was ringing. He dived for the receiver and sank creased and rumpled into a chair, to hear Ruth's distant, swirling voice say, 'Greg?'

'Yes . . . Ruth! How are you? How's the term been? When does it finish?'

There was silence at the other end. Amongst the rushing winds sweeping the line he thought he could hear choking, shuddering breaths.

'Ruth?'

Eventually she said, 'I'm so glad I've reached you. This is the most awful . . . I've just done the most terrible thing . . .' Some of her words sounded slurred and drunkenly laboured, but the line was coming and going.

'Are you in a phone box? Give me your number.'

'I just feel so lonely. There's no one here I can speak to. It won't take incoming calls . . .'

Another silence. Greg started to say, 'Will you tell me what's —'

'I'm so *stupid* sometimes . . .' she continued, and then the pips went. Greg hunched forward in his chair, then heard Ruth sob out, 'Oh fuck this phone', and the dialling tone cut in.

Greg paced swayingly round the flat for two hours waiting for her to ring back. Two days later, when he still hadn't heard from her, he called her home address to see if she was there, and her father, who didn't seem to know of him, told him she'd just left for France to go Inter-railing till Christmas.

Chapter Eleven

Greg couldn't go to his parents for Christmas, because his parents were going to Gibraltar on a cruise. However, Greg's mother's eldest sister Biddy had rung her and said that their only daughter and her husband were not coming to them this year, so they were going to be on their own.

It was to be Christmas in Totnes then – a long, late drive down to Devon on Christmas Eve after the store closed, but it would be out of London, well out. The only alternative Greg could imagine was to lie cocooned in his bed throughout the holiday, ringing Dial-a-Pizza whenever necessary. The disadvantage of this was the complex and doomed evasion called for on his parents' return. ('*Promise* me you won't just . . .' his mother had said with censorious concern, as though he might sidle off with a Tesco's carrier clanking with bottles of cheap sherry, which was indeed how such luxuriant hibernation in Lewisham would feel.) Greg calculated that it was about seven years since he had last seen his aunt and uncle, and as with all such older relatives his memory and opinion of them, when he searched for both, seemed frozen from his first encounters with them as an infant: they were people who gave him chocolate teddy bears and birthday cards with racing cars on.

The night before Christmas Eve the Sports Department gave themselves a reckless and occasionally frightening party in the pub round the corner, and on Christmas Eve itself were quiet, extravagantly steady, tetchy, and privately wondrous. The last day was a matter of selling people what they had waited too late only to have to spend too much on, and of doing it as determinedly and remorselessly as possible in order to get them out of the shop. On the minute the store closed Greg sold the

last lime-green tennis ball and two sheeny Lycra bikinis to a
gentleman thrusting a £50 note at him in mortified resignation,
and made for the tube.

Among the scattering of Christmas cards on the mat when
he got in was one postmarked Carrock, and signed simply

from Thos. Hines

So there it was. But there was also a note enclosed, a small
sheet of the careful, jerking fountain-pen script Greg had seen
in the admissions book every day over the summer:

Dear Greg,

Have decided to leave the YHA. I think a younger man is
needed to run the hostel, though I shall miss the Lakes. But I
felt I could not reopen it for another season. It has been a
good few years, 22 in fact. Am moving to a flat in Stockport,
address below. Please consider yourself welcome to call.
Thank you for your help this summer and my good wishes.

Yours ever

T. H.

Only when Greg reached the smooth, glitter-shot darkness of
the motorway did the accumulated frenzy of the day and his
preparations to get away relent, and the Warden's letter stand
alone for what it was. Greg was certain that this was a sudden,
recent decision; he was sure, on no evidence he could adduce,
that when he had left the hostel in October the Warden had
only been thinking of how to repair all the damage for next
year. And now this news. It would have been an instant, cold
apprehension, Greg suspected for some reason, of nothing, of
pettiness and waste: a decision made not serenely in front of
the snooker, but before a cracked washbasin hanging off the
wall: a decision to abandon, not put back, not to tidy up once
again – something, all of a sudden, you could not bear yourself
to do ever again, because you could imagine yourself doing it
so well.

A flat in Stockport: the Warden would be near the Peak
District, but if Greg could see this new home as a liberation, it
was only in the sense of seeing the Warden going away from

you. Stockport Greg remembered, from having changed coaches there once, as large precincts and a pullulating bus station full of bright orange buses; all you could say, perhaps, was that, for good and bad, the Warden would be insulated there by his own separateness. How much choice had he had – or worse, how much had he allowed himself? But for the small chance of one day passing along the Warden's street, Greg knew he would never see him. It felt as though an enormous effort would be necessary in order to be trivial and relaxed with the Warden, unless you took each other by surprise, and to try too hard would only make the distance greater. But perhaps all this, it depressed Greg to admit, was only what you thought when you didn't like someone enough. Indeed, while the Warden might invite a visit, Greg sensed how he might be embarrassed, even humiliated, if you actually made one. You couldn't do it *for* him. You had to let him go, see each diminishing in the other's eyes as it happened, watch him trudge up the hill he set constantly before him, on his own.

'There's one of those little railways down here, dear,' said Greg's aunt. 'The Dart Valley – it goes up to Buckfastleigh. We went on it a couple of years ago; nice ride. There's one down at Paignton as well. Didn't you say you saw one in Somerset, Jerry?'

'Minehead,' said Uncle Jeremy. 'That's a long one, Greg. Goes nearly all the way to Taunton. I was looking at possible holiday cottages around the Quantocks' (Uncle Jeremy had recently sold up his chain of estate agencies) 'and I kept on driving under it, over it, past it. Must be more than twenty miles. I take my hat off to them.'

Immobile after Christmas dinner, which at five o'clock they had just finished, the three of them sat round the television, watching *Disney Time* with the sound turned down. Greg had discovered since *The Queen Speaks to the Nation* at three that Uncle Jeremy was now the proud and active secretary of the local Conservative association, retirement enabling him to make it a fulltime occupation, and had managed to deflect another peroration by belatedly answering Auntie Biddy's enquiry as to what *else* he had been doing in the Lakes. The news that Greg had been working in a youth hostel his uncle had received with, 'There's not a lot of money in that, is there?'

'I salute them,' Uncle Jeremy was now affirming. 'It shows you can run railways at a profit if you get rid of all the layabouts and spongers. Someone's seen a good business opportunity, and I bet now they've got a nice little earner. All power to them, I say.'

'I shouldn't think they're doing it for the money,' said Greg with careful affability. 'It isn't the point of the one up at Carrock.'

'You're going for all these Development Grants then, are you? Handouts from all sorts of Regional Boards and Planning Committees? If you do, you'll only get it once. You rely on that – once it's gone, it's gone.

'Maggie's always said she had no time for the railways. Huge bottomless pit to pour money into. Never takes the train anywhere. Are you seriously saying that if a line can't be made to run profitably it should *still* be kept open? If it's losing money it means everyone who lives along it has got a car: don't need a railway as well. I tell you, Greg, these union bosses, these far-lefties and anarchists you get on the railways, they're not interested in running trains. All they want is revolution. You haven't got any of them on your railway, have you?'

Greg ate a chocolate.

Eventually, opting for placation over counter-attack, he said, 'These people, if we say they exist at all, are completely harmless. They're only encouraged by how much they see they can wind you up.'

'Who's this "we"? We're talking about normal, reasonable men and women, Greg – if *they* wanted revolution they'd vote for it. And the more strikes and go-slows, the less they'll want it.'

'There aren't any strikes nowadays. Unions get their assets seized if they strike.'

'Exactly. The Iron Lady, Greg! Thank God she's putting the country back on the right track. Some firm values at last – someone who knows where she's going. You'll see, one day. You'll see.' Uncle Jeremy smiled benevolently.

'Maybe if Mrs Thatcher made sure the people who run

industries like the railways got paid decently and had decent working conditions, if she made even a *token* gesture towards fairness, instead of making things worse by starving the whole system of cash —'

'You can't pay yourself what you don't earn, young man,' said Uncle Jeremy patiently. 'Where's the money going to come from? Let me admit to you something that may surprise you: I hear these people talking —'

'You *imagine* these people!'

'I hear these characters talking in that way — these activists — and I get worried, Greg. I get worried about this' — Uncle Jeremy spread his hands — 'our cottage here; about the bit of money I've got from the business — everything I've worked for and built up over the years; and my daughter and her husband and their new home which they've just finished furnishing themselves, and their first car; I get worried for us all. They'd take it from us, Greg. They would! Why should any of this be taken away from us? Is that what you're advocating? Why shouldn't we look after what we've got?'

Remember to say 'we', Greg told himself; include yourself with them. 'We are sitting pretty,' he began. 'Down here we have absolutely nothing to fear, any more than America need expect to be invaded next week by communists. As long as we sit comfortably, we'll be able to carry on sitting comfortably. It will probably get better for us, in fact. But, Uncle Jeremy, it isn't really the point, any more than closing the entire railway network is because it isn't making a profit like a bank. The trouble is that the only thing that happens to you — the more you congratulate yourself on what you've got, and the more impregnable you make yourself against the imaginary communist invasion — is the more paranoid you become that they must be after you. The more you amass, the more there is for *them* to take from you. When, if you actually *listen* — here, now — you'll hear nothing, because these people, whoever they are, have given up shouting, because they know that even if they don't, you'll still hear them, and then still do nothing. They don't want what you've got, anyway, but they don't want nothing either.'

Auntie Biddy was turning up the television.

Oh God! What pious, lofty, sanctimonious . . . And the way it had whined through into his voice! And he had slipped into 'you'. Greg waited for the thunder to break.

Uncle Jeremy slapped his hands down on the arms of his chair and turned on them both an impermeable, contented grin. 'I think it's about time for all our presents, Bid.'

Greg had Boxing Day to endure before he could properly get away, but on Christmas Day evening, as they stared at James Bond, he prepared his passage by saying casually and apropos of nothing, 'Yes, I thought I'd take a look at that Dart Valley Railway – day after tomorrow,' and added, 'and then up to Somerset, perhaps . . .' in case Buckfastleigh was too near to sound a convincing escape. His aunt and uncle had been generous and solicitous towards him, and were obviously pleased to have company, but even though Greg wondered if the sole, unquestioning audience of Auntie Biddy was half the explanation of his uncle's orations, he felt annoyed with himself for having to suffer them amiably; any dissent he did express, indeed, was treated as quaint whimsy. Politics for his uncle was an indulgence like a one-sided village cricket match: you slogged away all afternoon, certain that the other side were enjoying as much as you what was just a game, to be played in the best spirit, and if they wanted to watch each successive six-hit carefully enough, they'd eventually learn how to do it themselves.

On Boxing Day Uncle Jeremy opened the batting again at breakfast with, 'Take Beeching, since we were talking about railways. A man there who had the courage of his convictions – someone who was prepared to close down a *third of all the lines in the country* to turn British Railways round. I suppose you'd say he ought to have given them all a pay rise?'

At lunch he said, 'If you're looking for a steady career, Greg, you could do a lot worse than estate agency. I've never regretted my time for one moment.'

At tea, as they were watching *Bob's Full House*, Uncle Jeremy thought the prizes, 'A bit stingy. Couldn't they do better than that for Christmas – a sandwich toaster? Give some of that licence fee to a good cause instead of paying for Labour Party propaganda.'

TRAIN, TRAIN

As he was going off to bed he stopped in the lounge doorway and tapped his pipe softly in the air at Greg with a subtle look of leaving him something to think on for the night. 'If, as you maintain, profit and money-grabbing are so evil and despicable, how come all these workers keep putting in for massive wage increases?'

'*Exactly*,' pleaded Greg.

Uncle Jeremy regarded him with satisfied, jowled knowing, as though to say, so you deny that too?

A Santa Special meant your Mummy and Daddy took you for a ride on the steam train to meet Father Christmas at the other end. Such had been the popularity of these trains this year, said the blackboard propped up outside Totnes Station, that extra Specials would run on the 27th and 28th. On cue, snow had begun to sprinkle the platform, which was thronged with small children in large woolly hats, and parents saying 'You want to go nearer the engine, do you?' and 'Sandra, you've got your wellingtons on the wrong feet!' Greg got in the rearmost and emptiest carriage, a youthful guard – he looked about sixteen – wafted a flag the size of a towel, and the train jogged off up the Dart Valley.

Greg looked out over mounded sweeps of pasture, at cows shuffled together under trees. In the early afternoon both ground and sky were already tinged with mauve, and the snow silted slowly down, burying the soft gradations of the landscape so that only knife-edges and dark slabs stood out in the white: a wire fence across a field, a black box of a barn. The train seemed to contain all its sounds within itself; not the children's loud, earnest questions ('Do we have to come all the way back after we've got our presents?'), not even the distant thump of the steam engine ahead, would be heard outside its snow-spotted windows. The train was not part of the snowfall or its silence: it owned only its narrow corridor, and lost each last iron-solid segment of the adjacent world as it left it.

The train made a brief, wheezing stop at Staverton, where no one got on or off and up in the signalbox a pinched, huddled signalman peered out at them, and in another ten minutes crept into Buckfastleigh, where carols were trilling thinly from the public address tannoy. By now the snow was dropping densely; it seemed the sole source of light. The train was due to wait for an hour and a half while all the children queued to meet Santa. Greg had planned to walk over to Buckfast Abbey – there would be time – but now it looked as if in half an hour it would be dark, and he would see nothing and risk losing his way back. He stood under the platform awning and watched the loco-motive, its sides glistening and grimy, pushing its column of steam up into the falling snow. The schoolboy guard came over, nudging his peaked cap back on his brow.

'Lost your kids?'

'No, no. No. I was just sheltering out of the snow.'

'Uh-huh. You looked like you'd lost something. You just come for the ride?'

'Yes. I've been helping to restore the old railway up at Carrock, in the Lake District, so when I heard about this one I thought I'd come and see.'

'I haven't heard of that one. It must be very new. So many nowadays. This one's been open a long while.'

'How long did it take you to relay all this track? It must be, five or six miles?'

'Oh, we didn't have to,' said the guard. 'Took it straight over from BR when Beeching closed it. The bypass they built up there chopped the top of the branch off, so we preserved this bit. If you look at all these other new lines starting up where they're having to put down track again after twenty years, it's jolly slow. The Swanage ... Llangollen ... Yorkshire Dales ... Great Central ... Mind you, they've all got running lines and they're all extending. How long's the Carrock line going to be?'

'Fifteen miles. It's supposed to be the most scenic railway in the country. There's a huge viaduct on it.'

'That is a job, then. Every preserved line says it's the most scenic. We're lucky we haven't got any big bridges or things to look after.'

'It sounds as if there are quite a few restored railways,' said Greg. 'All those you just mentioned – I'd only heard of the Bluebell, and that one in Wales, the Festiniog?'

'Dozens and dozens. Loads in Wales. More all the time, all over the place. In fact, of all the locos that went to Barry Island for scrap at the end of steam – hundreds of them – they've all gone. Last ones left there just been bought for preservation.'

'Ah. I wondered,' said Greg. 'So that's what Barry is.'

'The older steam lines are always moaning that there won't be enough volunteers to go round if these new schemes keep starting up, but they all seem to find people. During the school holidays I work here every week.'

'How long have you been doing this?'

'Year and a half,' said the boy. 'My ambition is to be the booking clerk. I'm afraid I have to go and eat my sandwiches now.'

The guard now hunched up on a bench with his lunchbox and Thermos on his knees, and Greg wandered down the platform to the bookstall. He had always found the selection of books Edwards had put on sale at Carrock Station puzzling and uninteresting: they were either picture books containing hundreds of photos of identical locomotives, entitled *Maunsell 4-6-2* or *Southern Double-headed Steam*, or indignant political manifestos called *Not the End of the Line: Railways and Rationalisation in Monetarist Britain*. Again, they left Greg thinking, What is in the middle? What he wanted to know was, how did you nail a piece of rail to a sleeper, or, now, what did having enthusiastic schoolboys as guards say about running a preserved railway? But here on the Buckfastleigh bookstall Greg found, and immediately bought, a thick guidebook called *Preserved Railways in Great Britain*, and took it into the steamy station buffet to read.

It was a directory, simply, of all the restored lines: potted history of the British Railways years; circumstances of closure; story of preservation effort and reopening; length of line now open; catalogue of rolling stock; a picture or two – altogether only a couple of pages on each line. But there was a whole book-full. Greg read of standard-gauge lines, narrow-gauge lines, standard-gauge reopened as narrow-gauge, lines reopened twenty years ago, lines reopened last year, lines eighteen miles long, lines half a mile long, lines in the Scottish Highlands, lines in the Kent Marshes, once grand main lines now quietly restored for a small part of their original length, once debt-ridden, unsuccessful mineral lines now carrying hundreds of thousands of tourists, lines that employed twenty fulltime staff, lines that had computerised ticket systems, lines that had twenty working steam engines, lines that had one small diesel, lines that had as many mainline diesels as steam engines, the Bluebell Line, the Watercress Line, the Poppy Line, the Lavender Line, the Dart Valley, the Severn Valley, the Nene Valley, the Colne Valley, the North Norfolk, the South Tynedale, the East Lancashire and the West Somerset. Britain was covered in private railways.

Here was a second Railway Age – a century after the brief era when all Britain's railways were built, when everywhere in Britain had to have its railway, when at any time there was a new line opening somewhere. A century later, everyone was building railways again! Everyone was building new lines, which were the old lines being built again. Moreover, although there had been a regular succession of reopenings during the sixties and early seventies, as the late seventies became the early eighties the whole process appeared to have speeded up. Between 1960 and 1975 had started perhaps a dozen. In the eighties there seemed to have been several every year. And while all the older ones, like the Dart Valley, had simply stepped in after Beeching had closed a line down, and carried it on, all the new ones were prepared to re-lay track, rebuild demolished stations, re-erect bridges. The Carrock project, Greg saw very quickly, wasn't special: it was utterly typical. There seemed to be dozens setting out like it was, and dozens that were already miles and years ahead. Until now, whenever he had asked himself, Why – why were they trying to reopen the railway? – he had seen the answer as the viaduct, or the tunnel, or the station: something whose enduring disuse begged the question. Or he had seen the answer as Edwards, or Les, Julian and Kevin of the track gang: individuals who just wanted to do it. But while you could no doubt find the same particular answers legitimately for each particular project, what was making them all happen at the same time? Why was everybody deciding now, after so many years, to use all the old stations and embankments and the engines at Barry? And why – as it became clear to Greg, reading of yet another line restored and reopened after decades of abandonment and decay – was everyone so good at it?

The buffet was nearly empty, the gaslit platform outside

was clamorous, the carriages were being shunted slowly back alongside. An authentically muffled voice over the tannoy was saying, 'The four forty to Totnes, calling also at Staverton . . .' It was leaving in five minutes. Greg hurried out into the snow.

The journey back, as the train swayed through darkness that seemed to float just above the distant, phosphorescent-white landscape, the children withdrawn and still after their treat, felt different also for another reason. Whereas on the way there Greg had been looking out at the view, thinking of *this* railway for *this* place – a train to go up the Dart Valley – now he felt as if he was travelling on a kind of alternative British Rail. A collective, disparate, national institution – Preserved Rail. A far-flung and growing network of railways, in business to run not football specials but Santa Specials, to ferry not commuters but holiday trippers, to make its stations and trains look as old as possible, to lay on a train service so that schoolboys could be guards on it, and wear uniforms because they didn't have to, and bank clerks and healthfood shop owners could clear its track. Its customers, in a sense, were its volunteer staff; it took you, not to somewhere, but to itself. This was what the Carrock line was going to be, it seemed, whatever it was – although Edwards had his completely different idea, and for as long as it was still unbuilt you could hope and want it to be like that too. Next to all these other lines Greg now knew about, the Carrock railway looked both less and more interesting. There they were only trying to do what everyone else was doing, or had already done – yet at the same time what they were doing was not something just of the Lake District and them, but something of England. Or rather, something at large in England seemed to be doing it.

Chapter Twelve

'Where are the women, Greg?'

This was London again, and rain, and Ruth.

A Christmas card had arrived the day after New Year, postmarked the 28th, a World Wildlife Fund card with a huge, blankly-staring panda filling the front cover, that came with 'All my love, Ruth.' Also inside was written 'Grrreg In London till 4th parnets will know where.' Greg phoned Ruth's parnets, and this time her father was genially apologetic about his previous ignorance of Greg – knew now how well Ruth and Greg had got on last summer, even in spite of all that confusion over his name. Greg caught up with Ruth in Islington, where she was staying with a friend, and they arranged to meet on the evening of the 4th before she went back to Ipswich on the train.

At Leicester Square tube a sharp, blustery wind was sweeping rain across the street. Ruth was standing at the top of the steps, legs wide apart in mid stride, intently watching the evening newspaper seller out on the pavement.

'Hi Greg,' she called distractedly as he joined her, as if he were sliding in to a film that had already started.

The man shrugged deeper into his overcoat and growled again. 'Yerp! Ep!' Impassively he pocketed coins with one hand and thrust a paper back with the other. 'Yerp! Ep!'

'Presumably,' said Ruth deliberately, eyes still fixed ahead, 'one day a *very* long time ago he was saying "*Standard*". That's what he's selling. *The Evening Standard*.' She waited, engrossed again. *Yerp*! *Ep*! 'If you could have studied him over the years, and taped him say every six months, and interviewed him as well each time to see what he thought of his job just then . . . And you could have related the two . . . And you could have plotted a graph of how what he shouted changed . . .' Ruth turned to look at Greg, her face softening in the surprise evoked by someone who has arrived that instant, and they set out into the rain, neither asking the other where, but up towards St Giles' Circus. They branched off along Long Acre, because Ruth said she was starving, but she rejected all the restaurants they passed because she didn't like that kind of food. As they strode through the wet towards the Strand, taking turns to hump along Ruth's very large holdall, she continued her breathless speculations on the newspaper vendor. 'You'd have to go into all the linguistics of it, like why has he shortened *Standard* in *that* particular way, and how far does he still *think* he's saying *"Standard"*, or is he aware he's just going "Ep!"?' (Ruth gave it the hollow, sepulchral resonance of a last glug of water down a plughole.) 'It's his *job*, in fact! His *entire* job is just to say that word.' The Lyceum was on their left. '*That* is a subject for a thesis, Greg,' Ruth said crossly, 'not all this mining crap. A whole thesis about one syllable, and a man's whole life! That would be something useful – and *amazing*.'

'Who to?'

Their strides quickened in the gusting rain.

'Me, I suppose!' Ruth said brightly.

They about-heeled back down the Strand towards Charing Cross, and finally dived out of the wet into a McDonald's by the station. When they got to the head of the queue Ruth only wanted a small chips and a banana milkshake and said she wasn't hungry after all. They perched against the sloping wall seats and Ruth picked at her chips and drank half her milkshake in contemplative silence, her sodden hair sprawled over the table in leaking, fibrous tentacles. There was no need to ask this girl about that desperate phone call – or no way to – because this was a new Ruth, today's Ruth. What kind of Ruth Greg would work out properly, of course, once they had said goodbye. Already this evening there had been the hedgehog-walk Ruth, ardent and enraptured, and now here was the Ruth who became as a child, the Ruth who had been sick in the night, who had said her meek goodbye to the Warden: you took her into McDonald's and sat over her protectively like a father while she quietly consumed her chips. The Ruth out of her depth in some adult deep-end had been on the other end of a crackling phone, unseen, soon disconnected.

In a crowded and smoky pub down Villiers Street, where the noise of the jukebox was rising steadily above the commotion, Greg told Ruth that the Warden had left the hostel suddenly to go and live in Stockport, and that his name was Thos. Hines.

'That means I can go back there this June and finish the map stuff,' said Ruth disinterestedly, as though she had expected the Warden to do nothing less, and for no other reason. 'Are you going back too?'

'I don't know. I haven't thought about it enough. Perhaps yes, if I can. They haven't asked me yet. But it would be nice anyway to see if the railway manages to reopen in the summer as it plans. I'd like to help with that.' He told Ruth about the mile and a half to Force Road, and the share issue, and the board of directors, and the news in the newsletter, and Edwards and Les and Julian and Kevin, and the guard on the Dart Valley . . .

When he had finished Ruth stared back at him. 'Where are the women, Greg?' She drained her lager and spread her arms in appeal to the moiling pub behind him. 'Where are the women in all this?'

Greg considered a moment. 'Um . . . they do the tea room.' Then he added, doubtfully, 'But you wouldn't want to be a booking office clerk, would you?'

Ruth came back with two more pints. 'The whole thing's just so male, Greg! I'm not saying half the blokes who volunteer to paint steam engines should stand down so women can take their place. But what does it *say* about you lot?'

'It's not just men playing with big trainsets,' said Greg hotly.

'But supposing it is – what does *that* say? Their wives are their mothers who send them out in the morning with their sandwiches to play, and their mothers in the cafeteria give them their tea in the afternoon, and they come home in the evening for their supper and give their mothers their muddy clothes to wash.'

Thinking Yes, Ruth, Greg said, 'No, Ruth. Some of the people – the guys who look after their own steam engines, or the kids who like to dress up as guards and punch tickets – it's a kind of toy thing, yes, a kind of playing at doing something real. But that's just their hobby. A rugby team's all male. So what?'

'Greg, when you tell me about this railway, I don't know what to say. You describe it as if it's some new social movement, some watershed in British history – but it doesn't have anything to do with me at all. In fact it sounds no different from the history I have to read about the mines in Carrock in the nineteenth century; it's just a lot of guys deciding amongst themselves what to build for each other. It's a private thing. It's a male thing.'

'Are you saying the mountains are male? Or a tunnel and a viaduct – bricks are male? Is a transport service male?'

'The people who write poems about them are, and the people who build them are, and the people who run it are.'

'OK, I know why women haven't done any of these things – but how would it be different if they did?'

Ruth frowned. 'Can you get me another drink? It is disgustingly stuffy in here. I'm getting rather pissed on all this Kronenbourg – a Scotch?'

When Greg had squeezed his way back through the throng to the corner where they were sitting, Ruth was holding out long hanks of her hair in decisive conclusion. 'All the conquering, Greg. All the grandness behind it. That's what would go –'

Greg set her whisky before her. 'He seems to have made it a double.'

'– The huge viaduct that has to conquer the valley. The tunnel that has to conquer the hill. All these poems that have to say what *he* feels about the mountains, as if that's what they were put there for. Massive great deafening steam engines. All this *asserting* yourself: you've built a railway therefore you're wonderful.'

'A viaduct has to be big and tall enough to take the line across on the level! The valley's that deep. A locomotive has to be big and powerful enough to haul a load of coaches!'

'I know, Greg, I know. It's the *kicks* you all get from them being that big. It *is* just what you have to build to cross a valley, and what you have to build to pull your train. But everyone treats them as these huge triumphs of man's will, as if he decided to build them that way when he could have built them smaller, just to show how great he was. It's the hill that's the big thing, the valley that's the big thing: you all use them to congratulate and swell yourselves.'

Their foreheads were almost touching in the effort to hear each other over the churning, thumping jukebox. Greg called across at Ruth's eyes inches from his, 'So how does it harm you, Ruth? I can see it does, but how?'

'Oh, it doesn't,' Ruth called back. 'Or, all this drink seems to think it doesn't. I just wish you'd admit what you're doing – realise you're only men. It's not only the ones who run railways, who like punching tickets, it's all of you. I just wish you'd be humble and see that you're doing something exclusively man-nish, and that you like it because it's mannish, and because it's making you more mannish. All these things that are supposed to be out there, for all of us – they're only for you. Or only you want them. It's a rugby team that thinks it's a "transport service", or the other way round. I can't understand why you all need any of it, but I suppose I wouldn't.'

'If women wouldn't want to do it anyway, Ruth, but it's there for the doing, how are men to avoid being men, and encouraging more men-ness in each other, when they're forced to do it on their own?'

'Just by noticing all the time they're doing something really weird, something that is all men.'

'I see what you mean, I think. You're saying men are not *necessarily* macho or any of those boring things – just solipsistic. Or that being self-absorbed *is* being macho. That fits in with the guy who's running the project, actually.'

'The bookshop bloke? The one who sent you all that stock-market stuff? He does sound a complete prick,' Ruth declared – but apart from this Greg had never mentioned him – and tossed back her whisky.

In the taxi to Liverpool Street Greg said, 'What would your alternative be, Ruth? To the toughs' train service?'

'I don't know,' Ruth said dreamily into the holdall she was cuddled round, her eyes closed, her feet in Greg's lap. 'This is quite nice.' After a while she continued, 'I didn't say you shouldn't do it. I wasn't criticising. You always assume there must be a completely right way of doing things. I can see you fitting this entire conversation into your world picture. I was just saying . . . all sorts of stuff . . . I mean I wouldn't want to ride camels and sleep in the sand and get beaten up in torture cells . . . although he seemed to enjoy that . . .'

'What?'

'*Seven Pillars of Boredom* . . .' came Ruth's muffled voice, '. . . or whatever that pathetic book was called . . .'

A pause.

'But nor would I,' said Greg.

'I know,' yawned Ruth.

Ruth was becoming – or Greg, with a directionless irritation, was coming to see her as – reliably unpredictable. If you couldn't anticipate where her thoughts would be, you could work out how far: how far from where you'd thought they were, and how far into them she was. And Greg was getting used to how far they would get, or wouldn't get, in their conversations – although this could have been because whenever they came in contact they drank too much, or talked too late, or the place was too hot or smoky or loud, or because he was simply proving Ruth right by wanting things to be profoundly perfect. *Don't worry about me* seemed the subtext of everything she had ever said: it made Greg worry all the time. *You're you, and I'm me* was her tacit assurance – but for Greg it was an oblivious challenge, a benign threat: are you the one who's odd, or am I?

Sometimes, therefore, Greg found himself more perplexed by Ruth's ideas than she seemed to be. How could you not try and accommodate the viaduct that conquered the valley, the railway that asserted the wonderfulness of men, into your picture of Carrock and the Lakes, and then into your picture of everything? What did it all, as Ruth had asked, *say*? For her a question was answered by the diversion of posing it – the only diversion, since things were as they were. For Greg every line cast into the water presupposed a fish destined for its hook, and each time you hauled one to the surface you had to ask yourself why you hadn't caught a dog. This one was either a big question or a big red herring.

It set Greg thinking about Carrock. Who took *responsibility* for the town being what it was? You could see it as the sum of its parts: a haphazard agglomeration of people servicing tourism, people deserted by industry, recent London escapees, people still farming the fells and dales, people who lived there in their holiday cottages for a few weeks a year — you could see it as the successive social movements that had shaped it. But somehow, and in several ways, while you saw people in social groups you felt them as individuals. When you looked at human achievements, even if you saw their construction and implementation as communal, you felt the initiative, the vision, as an act of will: a necessarily individual will, a single psychology. A social development appeared to happen between people, among them, but once it was done, became a completed action, it seemed to have been done by someone. Carrock's foundry, its ball-bearings factory: both would have closed down owing to declining orders, a changing market, new competition, maybe, outdated plant, inadequate investment, perhaps even bad industrial relations. All sorts of reasons. But the psychological shape of each such closure was singular: it was as if one person had taken one comprehensive decision, and against each employee in turn. You wanted there to be one person, so you could execrate them and also because to believe such things could happen as a concatenation of contingencies was too desolate.

The viaduct: millions of bricks in the thing, laid together by hundreds of men. But laid to one design. Everything came together in twenty simple, regular arches: at the end you saw a single design, that one person could have drawn.

The railway: the fixed track: the straight, equidistant, continuous rails, *leading you on*: again there was a shape to things. With a road, by contrast — with all its individual cars, caravans, lorries jockeying for position, overtaking one another — there seemed no design. Everyone was free to drive too fast, to crash, to be indeed unaware of what they were doing at all relative to anyone else. On the railway everyone could make the same journey; the rails would always be there like that.

And yet, there was a paradox. You saw people as social groups, but you felt them as individuals. Even the harmony, the successful communality, you saw as if it were the work of a single person, an egocentric exemplum, instead of something that belonged to and was sustained by everyone. Someone was responsible for such designs: you made them be – even some Hilman, some Edwards, perhaps. Perhaps it had been truly their initiative, or perhaps their ego aspired to aggrandise itself with the whole achievement – howsoever, individuals, with their caprices, their self-absorption, their controlling themness, their will, interposed themselves.

This sense that, if something was there, someone must consciously have done it; that you either did something, or you didn't – here was an essentially masculine sense? That you were what you did, not what you were: for good and bad, possibly, but for too much, almost certainly. Was this anywhere near what Ruth had been saying? Don't try to prove yourself constantly, because most things don't prove anything; look for proof, and mostly you'll find only the exercise of will. People needed to be both individual and social – not neither, as in the city, but rather both at once. It was this potential human reticence, made actual by distance and separation, that had baffled Greg on the summit of The Knott. Of what he had been looking for, there had been nothing to see. There was nothing to sort people; it was why you went up into the hills. There was the shining sheet of the water, and the heavy stillness of great past displacements of the land, and the you was simply you regarding them. No one, and nothing, was looking at you. The male need to do something to prove you were there: there was nothing to do. So you came down from the mountain and laid railway tracks to run along, not only for everyone, but also for you.

Where *were* the women? Greg thought until he realised he didn't have to think at all: just ring the YHA. The woman was already going back in the summer.

Yes please, said the YHA, they had been about to ask him anyway. Mr Hines's sudden resignation had caught them unawares, but a new warden had now been appointed who had lots of exciting plans and, unlike Mr Hines, who had preferred to manage on his own until June, actually wanted a fulltime assistant from Easter. They'd ask him – Melvin Asmussen, the new warden – to get in touch.

Greg had gone back to the big store for the January sales, where he found large posters in the staff canteen announcing record takings for the Christmas period – 'Our Very Best Christmas Ever!' The train up to London in the mornings was still as crowded now as during the Christmas rush: when you opened the carriage door people tripped out onto you in order to climb back and pull the door to again to hold themselves in. In the local newspaper a spokesman for Network South East explained that the new Capitalcard tickets had unfortunately become too successful, since cash limits left them no money to run longer trains. On the radio Greg heard that fares were to be increased on 'over-used' Intercity services to reduce demand.

The hordes had poured in on the first day of the Sale. They observed a dignified gait that every few steps broke into an apologetic run, peered round the large cardboard boxes they carried off electrical goods in, and slapped credit cards down on the counter in front of Greg with their eyes lifted away in reckless defiance. Greg sold exercise bicycles, carbon-fibre tennis rackets, fluorescent skis, cashmere golf sweaters, skateboards, croquet sets. Everyone had spent all their money and bought everything before Christmas; everyone spent all their money and bought everything again. Greg trooped out of the staff entrance in the evening past new posters: the best first day of the Sale ever; beyond expectations; thanks to all involved for a magnificent effort.

In the evening paper Greg read that the city banks, owing to losses incurred since the Big Bang, were having to cut the salaries of their top dealers by up to £30,000, down to £120,000. The Lewisham Hospital announced that, to cut expenditure by a further £100,000 a year, another surgical ward was having to be closed for three months. On the radio the Social Services minister talked of lotteries.

The mornings got lighter; the evenings got lighter. The sale crowds thinned, Greg stayed on, and after two weeks the store was quiet and respectful and timorous and closing at 5.30 again. The staff association joined an appeal to buy a body scanner for the nearby Middlesex Hospital. You put your change into a tin at the checkout when you bought your lunch in the canteen; there were sponsored walks; five dispatch staff in the basement had their heads shaved. In a month £1,000 was raised.

Mel Asmussen rang – an Australian accent – and suggested

that Greg come up to Carrock at the end of March, two weeks before the hostel opened. 'Slap as much paint around as we can,' he said. 'Get some bright colours in the place. You got any posters we can cover these godawful green walls with?'

In February the share certificates for the £50 Greg had finally sent to the Carrock Railway issue came in the post, with a smug, or maybe just blithe, Edwards comp. slip that said simply, 'Fully subscribed. If you wait long you'll miss the opening!'

Near the end of March Greg noticed that the bowed, shuffling Italian who looked after the gents' toilets next to the sports department had disappeared. Since Christmas Greg had twice seen him rebuked for walking through the department. Ancillary staff, with their brown overalls and cowed demeanour and smell of disinfectant, were supposed to keep to the back stairs.

SECOND SUMMER

Chapter Thirteen

A bright-eyed squirrel, perky and luxuriantly-tailed, wearing a clomping pair of boots. Mel Asmussen pressed the stamp down on the corner of his *Guardian* and assessed the orange-inked image. 'Squirrel Nut-you,' he said.

'Better than the old one,' said Greg. 'That lake used to look like the puddle of oil you get underneath your car.'

'That blinding black sun. Imagine stamping Hiroshima on every hosteller's card.'

Carrock hostel: new and light and Mel's. The piles of heavy, hairy blankets in the dormitories had been replaced by flowery duvets, which matched the new flowery curtains. All the Warden's typewritten notices – at once severe and unnoticeable – reading HOSTELLERS ARE REMINDED TO SWITCH OUT ALL LIGHTS ON VACATING THIS ROOM or LEAVE THE KITCHEN AS YOU FOUND IT, PLEASE had come down. Mel said, 'We're not a nursery school.' Up went posters for CND, the centre for Alternative Technology in Machynlleth, and the League against Cruel Sports. Over reception was a sign saying YOUR HOSTEL MANAGER IS MEL. 'Wardens are for wildlife reserves,' said Mel. The place now seemed twice as big. This was what a week's painting by the two of them, using yellows and bright greens, pillarbox reds and brilliant whites, had done.

Mel himself had long blond hair that receded from his forehead and curled back down on to his shoulders, sometimes gathered within a plaid headband, sometimes bulging beneath a baseball cap with the peak turned to the rear. He clopped around the hostel in clogs, wearing a sleeveless T-shirt and shorts, his drooping Zapata moustache snaggling his hoarse words. 'You heard of Woody Guthrie?' he once asked suddenly as he and Greg were perched on stepladders painting a ceiling

– but although Greg gave an uncertain yes this turned out to be all Mel wanted to say.

Now he and Greg were sitting at the breakfast table – the squirrel stamp had come in the post – and Mel was telling Greg of his plans. 'We're competing with Ibiza, man. Is this a monastery?' Wholefood menus for the meals, then; glasses of wine on sale in the evenings; real coffee afterwards. Visiting folksingers, bonfires and barbecues, a telescope to study the night sky. Adventure holidays: sailing on the lake, rock climbing, birdwatching, orienteering. Build a field study centre on to the back of the building. Access for the disabled. Conservation volunteer programmes with the National Trust to rebuild over-used footpaths . . . 'There's also a bunch of guys coming to stay here for a few weeks when we're slack after Easter,' Mel finished up. 'Some Manpower Services project to do up the old railway.'

'Really? What are they going to be doing?'

'I don't know,' said Mel. 'Getting paid five quid more than dole money for fifty hours' hard labour. You know, this guy Tom did bugger-all while he was here. Did he just sit around all the time?'

'No, he worked very hard, Mel.' He worked all the time, Greg thought, until there was nothing to show for it. 'It was very hard work for the rest of us too last summer.'

'I bet. You know he didn't even open the place up at Christmas? Hung about here all by himself, I suppose, the miserable bastard.'

But it had only taken them a week to paint out the Warden, a week to improve drastically on twenty years. The previous autumn Greg had felt his own departure from the hostel as an escape: the Warden had been staying put and he was glad to go. Now you found that, apart from the navy blue paint and the notices, which you got rid of quickly, the Warden had left nothing else. He went away very easily, had all the time been making nothing, only holding things at bay. Just as he had seemed to expect people not to like him, so in the defiant darkness and grimness of the hostel had been the assumption that people would only tolerate it, no more. This was already Mel's hostel; it hadn't ever been the Warden's.

'He just stood still,' Mel was saying, 'thought this place could just stand still. I mean, didn't he *notice* that not everyone over here drinks tea all the time now? It drives me crazy sometimes, this country – as if everyone's under orders to be old-fashioned.'

'I think he did his best,' said Greg, not meaning to be sentimental.

'He should have been in British India,' said Mel. 'Maybe he was.' He coloured in the squirrel's boots with his biro. 'He sounds so English, Greg. Stays on too long, almost congratulating himself on how dedicated and self-denying he's being, even though he's hating every minute, and when he goes, he finds all these rules he upheld and bowed to – *he made*! Someone who can't . . . *imagine* himself, either endures, or vanishes . . . I don't know. I never met the guy . . .' Mel fell to giving the squirrel a tumultuous bouffant hairdo and a piously frowning brow.

'I wouldn't be surprised if lots of people object when they find all the changes here.'

'*Greg*! I'm sure they will. Because they'll actually notice something here for the first time. And I shall be *amazingly* sanguine. Irrepressibly, implacably, sanguine. And once they realise that you've only switched the points, but they're still on the rails – that these are the new rules they have to obey – we're away. Wasn't that Britain's major legacy to India, apart from the Civil Service? You see, there we are again.'

'What was?'

'Railways. Covering the subcontinent with railways. The iron road. Train services . . . service industries. That's what you're all so damn good at – or what you like doing, anyway. I'm in favour – but do something else as well.' He added a raptor's-beak nose and a handbag to his drawing, and held up the newspaper for Greg's opinion. 'The Blue Squirrel,' he said. 'The hoarder. The saver. Teaching us how to line our own snug little nests.'

'Tail up at the moment.'

'The trouble is – I don't know why everyone says the British are complacent: you're appallingly conscientious. Or maybe just conscientious about being complacent. The trouble is, when someone suggests at last that Britain shouldn't or can't just be one huge service industry, then you go and appoint her. You kind of work hard at your lack of interest and your sense of duty.' *Plunk*. His throw found the bin. 'Gone off that stamp.'

'Actually,' (Greg had suddenly wondered why his role always seemed to be to listen to people telling him things, and whether this just showed how English he was), 'I'm sort of involved with restoring the railway here.'

'Oh Christ,' said Mel.

Later in the morning they walked down into the town: Mel wanted Greg to give him a guided tour. Greg had said he didn't think he knew Carrock very well. Mel said, 'What don't you know?' Greg said he didn't know. Mel decided they should go and find out what it was, if it was.

'So what's this Casey Jones thing?' demanded Mel as they came down towards the market square.

'Well, I was just helping . . . It's to connect Carrock back to the main line, if possible. That's the ultimate aim. But you can only open a bit at a time, so for a while it'll only be little steam train rides for tourists. The whole line is fifteen miles long, you see. It'll take years to restore.'

Momentarily Mel looked shrewdly uncomprehending, then he shouted with laughter. 'This is great! Did you ever see that Monty Python with the mountaineering expedition to climb the High Street? Have you ever been to India?'

Greg stared humbly back.

'Fifteen miles, mm? Twenty minutes' drive down the main road? You're going to spend years rebuilding a railway that just takes you someplace down the road?'

'And where does India come in?'

'The railways in *India*, yes. Thousands of miles long. An amazing achievement. The only way from A to B, except flying, which no one could afford anyway. You build a railway there, you really have opened up some territory. Took me five days, even on the train, to get from north to south.'

'It's more for the scenery, this one, Mel,' explained Greg. 'It's a magnificent ride, or it would be, or must have been. You'd see if you walked along the old trackbed.'

Mel was deliberating. 'So you take a walk along the old trackbed . . . You're laying down railway track to run trains on

142

– for people to ride in – to view the mountains – when they can walk the line right now?'

'OK,' said Greg, 'people have got by without the railway. They still could now if nobody was bothering to try and reopen it. But Mel, it's not just what you *need* . . .'

Mel stopped. 'You're right, man,' he said in surprise, walking on. 'You're right.' He was silent for a while. 'Yes, that's actually good,' he began again. 'You know, in the States, everyone has all this stupid shit they don't need – phones that look like parrots that sit on your shoulder while it looks like you're speaking up their ass and such crud. They just want to have it hanging around. They redefine themselves every time they haul in some new piece of junk. But over here, you go in for pointless things which *involve* you in all sorts of stuff, which is kind of ludicrous, but good for you. I mean, if you did it in Australia . . . I was at Mankinholes hostel last summer – first one I ran over here – you know, Todmorden way. And you hear before you get there that people in Lancashire spend all their time breeding pigeons and growing huge leeks, and you think it's all cobblers. But you get there and they do! It isn't quaint or dumb: they're bloody pros at it. God knows why. And yet then when I try and think back to taking a road train across Australia . . . brain can't cope with both things at once. You can't use one to get at the other, though you keep thinking you ought to.'

'This is a rather small country, I suppose.'

'Rabbit-turd of a place. No one here thinks it is – I don't mean everyone thinks Britain's still a great world power, although they do. But you don't think it's small, Greg, or you wouldn't be talking about taking years to go fifteen miles. I mean, no one thinks further than their own back garden: if it'll fit into that, they can handle it. You take your tiny back garden – and you try and grow a giant leek in it! You take a few miles of mountains, and try and build the Trans-Siberian Railway through them. No wonder everyone's got their eyes too close to the ground to notice who's governing the country.'

'Why is all this good, then?' said Greg. 'You said it was good.'

Mel considered. 'I think it probably is. I just like the way no one's trying to prove anything to anyone else. You don't say, "I'm wonderful because I can make my telephone calls up a parrot's ass, which I was able to acquire through my, oh, cable-TV, toll-free, instant video-shopping channel." You just grow leeks, and if yours is the biggest the *leek* wins first prize. No one minds what anyone else thinks of what they're doing. They don't want everyone else to do it too to reassure them that it's hip: they just like doing it themselves. You let people be. All I've done this morning is bend your ear about who you are — you could have just told me to get fucked.'

They came to a halt and Mel gazed around. 'Where the hell are we? This looks like Slough.' They were outside a brand new development of light industrial units and prefabricated warehouses: honey-yellow bricks, crimson plastic guttering, and silver roller-shutters. A British Telecom van stood in front.

'I can't remember what was here before. I wasn't looking where we were going,' said Greg. 'But this wasn't. This isn't what I didn't know. Even this road's new. The kerbstones were fleshy white; the asphalt was rich and black and still scattered with sand.

'"Carrock Dale Business Park",' read Mel. 'I love it. Business *Park*. Twig in a plant pot.'

'Carrock Dale's made up,' said Greg. 'This isn't a dale. Carrock's Carrock.'

'Park means the spaces for all these cars.'

Greg pointed up at the sign along the side of one of the units. 'I know him.'

'Who?'

'ROMAN TIMES PHOTOSETTING. Peter Fellows. Shall we go and say hello?'

They found Fellows under small brilliant spotlights, gently holding up a long strip of glossy bromide paper as it oozed out of a grey cabinet the size of a wardrobe on its side. Around him in the large, empty-looking room figures flickered on green screens, more grey and beige boxes hummed thinly and clunked and blipped. Neat white slabs of manuscript lay on tables; there were only three other people at scattered desks.

Fellows looked up, then sagaciously around at his new surroundings, and bowed. 'Moved in a week ago.' He eased the end of the galley out of the machine and hung it up on the wall. 'You just come back, Greg? At the hostel again?'

Greg introduced Mel, and Fellows found plastic cups of coffee for them. 'We're all set up now,' he said. 'Everything we need. Business is *very* good.' He took them round the unit – it was too big for a room, thought Greg, it was a 'unit'. The fax machine – proofs anywhere in the country in seconds, or overseas, if you like, and back again just as fast. The Modem: they could put their typesetting out for keystroking if they were full up in-house and it would be sent back down the line – there was a chap in Durham who wrote a whole wargames magazine every month all by himself on his Apple, and phoned it through to Fellows to run out as finished copy. *Very* fast processor, eight pages a minute, automatic pagination, full page make-up, disk reader, cope with any language, hundred and fifty typefaces, graphics on screen . . . 'Jane has half a unit just along from us for her cheese cold store: doing very well too, expanding.'

'What was here before?' asked Greg.

'This was where the foundry was. The council bought the site soon after it closed, shilly-shallied for ages about what to do with it. Playing fields, some kind of industrial heritage museum, all sorts of ideas, couldn't decide. Then last autumn they suddenly got their act together. Foundry came down in November, trading estate announced in December and I reserved this, work started after Christmas, and here we are. About time, really: that's a year the foundry's been closed now, or it was till they demolished it. It had to be used for something. I think the council kept trying to think of something that would sort of substitute for the foundry. *Compensate* for it. But you've got to let new people use their own initiative.'

'How many people have you got working for you now?'

'Six,' said Fellows. 'Two more setters just moved up from London to join us. You can't really find people round here qualified in all this stuff. Taken on a local girl to answer the phone and do the post and things.' He darted off suddenly to press odd keys at irregular intervals beneath a bleeping screen.

As Greg and Mel left the business park – Greg now knew where he was, though he hadn't been down this end of the town before – and went back up the hill towards the High Street, Mel said, 'Good man, that. Knows what he's doing: got a smart business going there. I suppose even those yellow and red sheds are an improvement on an old foundry.'

'Mm-mm.'

'That's polite for no?'

'It just occurred to me ... how you could raze a whole foundry in a few days after it's been there for, I don't know, a hundred years or something, and a few months later you've built over it as if it never existed.'

'Oh, come *on*. It shut, yeah? Everyone there out of a job. Do they want it left standing to remind them all the time? Clear it away and hide it so people can *forget* about it.'

'I'm sorry,' said Greg, 'I suppose I was thinking of the railway.'

They dropped into Dorothy's. 'Hell of a job,' said Mel. 'Smacking a table with a hammer to make it look old.'

'Actually, there's an interesting thing I've just thought of,' Greg remarked, finishing his coffee. (Mel had said nothing else since entering, drained his mug instantly, and been sitting with hands clapped on thighs, waiting to leave.) 'The foundry's down there – or was – at the bottom of the town. And the station's up there at the top. There's no siding or old goods line from one to the other. They couldn't have transported the iron ore on the railway, then, or they would have had to take it across town by lorry first.'

'That's kind of common over here, isn't it? Station's miles away from the village or whatever it's supposed to serve? The foundry would have to be down by the river, anyway, for the water.'

'And the railway was built for the mines,' continued Greg, 'which are up on the hill. And the line would have come in on the level, too.'

'So the foundry must have been opened after the railway, and they must have been bloody glad when someone finally invented the artic.' Mel got up and took their empty mugs back over to the counter to the white-haired man in his late fifties who cleared away and washed the dishes, and who was now thanking Mel for the thought. The man had been there from the first time Greg had called in; after a few visits the two of them exchanged a gruff nod whenever he came over to wipe Greg's table, and

Greg noticed that Fellows and a few others said, 'Morning, Alec'. But already Mel and Alec were in grim conversation and exchanging rueful smiles.

Greg sat and thought about the foundry. Heavy lorries roaring through the town's streets; the buzzing dual carriageway main road; the decline of the railway – it was simple, he had assumed. A problem was a policy, solutions consisted in degree – fewer lorries, more trains. Now he began to see how social problems weren't necessarily caused *by* people, but could fall between them. Everything in the town might be compatible, but it had been fitted together at different times. Such history was like a relay race in which each new runner started away without quite grasping the baton.

'I know it's what you're supposed to do, man, but, *shit*,' exclaimed Mel as they continued on from Dorothy's through the market square. 'All this fucking on-your-bike stuff. You feel so made for him! But he must have done that already – you can't be mad for ever.' To Greg's enquiring look he went on, 'That guy used to be a foreman at the factory here – shut last year, apparently: did thirty-five years. And this is all he's been able to get since. Wife works in one of the hotels, he tops up her money and he says they just get by. Isn't he the kind of guy we're all to *congratulate* nowadays for his *self-respect* and his *dignity* and *determination*' (Mel had caught the pained, confidential, husky elocution), 'that he's prepared at least to *take* a job . . . One should, Greg! One really should, actually – him *doing* that, putting up with that, at his age. It's no solution. But . . . I don't know, just think of him washing up that pathetic Cotswold crockery every day. Who is that *for*? What the hell is that earthenware heritage kitsch meant to remind you of?'

'Does he mind? I know he probably couldn't say in there.'

'Has no opinion on it, as far as I could see,' said Mel. 'Not entitled to one, anyway, if that's all there is, are you? And if you did have one and work there it'd only make you mad again.' Mel looked at Greg. 'I was full of shit back there at your typeface friend's place.' He stopped and regarded Dorothy's. 'You go there regularly,' he pronounced.

'I have, yes, seen that man Alec in there before. But we never seemed to get around to talking . . .'

TRAIN, TRAIN

They hunched into their anoraks against the swirling, stony March morning and trudged about, Mel wondering aloud at how, apart from a few trips to the supermarket and lots to the DIY store since he'd arrived, he knew nothing about the place, and Greg suspecting that in two weeks Mel's easy buttonholing camaraderie had already brought him more acquaintances than Greg had made in nine months. I've just got off a plane from down under, Mel didn't say but managed ingenuously to imply, you're the one who lives here. Far around them the fells were lost in a stained mist; back down steep streets they glimpsed the lake as dull bakelite; the buffeting wind seemed one instant to blow all the air away and leave the streets clean with cold like an absence, the next to rush and smother as though you were jostling through streets overgrown with blind, tousled bushes of cold.

Hauling themselves up to the bleak estate at the top of the High Street (the door of Edwards's bookshop along the way had been closed for lunch), they had halted outside a grocer's with its windows whitewashed out, to look across at a crescent of dirty lime-green council houses and a rusted wheel-less car propped on piles of bricks. Greg had remarked proprietorially that this was old Carrock – all the housing built for the mines and the factory – and over there, spreading down from the station in those broad, tree-lined avenues, was guest-houses-and-hotels Carrock, new Carrock, with that new holiday flats development just going up, reaching right down to the lakeside.

'This isn't very old, Greg,' Mel pointed out as Greg came to the same realisation. 'Over there's older. That's Victorian, all those big guest houses; most of this is probably twenties or so. It just looks beaten up. You mean stopped Carrock as opposed to still going.' Of course tourism and industry had come to Carrock together, Greg was thinking. By old he meant out-of-date, in need of repair.

Just then the wind dropped, and in the distance the mist slid sideways to bring some of the hills in around them: at that moment it was as if the town were emptied of everything you could ever feel about it, everything except its physical self. Suddenly Greg saw – and knew Mel must know too – how small it was, cupped here amongst the mountains; even the railway had had to build its way out. How little space the town had, how tiny its capacity – how much could you manufacture here in how much of a factory? Come and visit us, Carrock seemed to be saying, over the vastness around, come and stay here, please, bring your work here, bring your holiday if that's all you have. If it had ever once thought of itself as big, it never would again. The only direction it could look to was outside.

'*Titfield Thunderbolt*,' said Mel after a while, looking across towards the station. 'I've been trying to think what that film was called.'

'Not like that.' Greg shook his head firmly. 'The Carrock railway is not like that.'

'I liked the bit where the bishop shows up to shovel the coal in,' added Mel. 'Rest was crap.'

'You ought to meet Ashley Edwards, the bloke who's behind it all. He hates that whole quaint side of trains. He sees the railway here as . . . potentially a way of rejuvenating the town. A new sense of community. I don't know if I can – it's such a huge project. But I'd like to. Something's got to be done.' Greg included the whole estate in the sweep of his arm. 'It needs it. Make *everything* needed again. Not just little bits.'

'That sounds extremely quaint,' said Mel. 'With an old railway?' He set off down the hill, then stopped and smiled at Greg. 'Cat Stevens, Greg, Cat Stevens, it sounds to me,' his tone saying, remember him? He broke into a jaunty shamble, his moustache twitching its own dance as he sang:

'Now I've been happy lately, thinkin' about the, good
    things to come,
And I believe it could be, something good has begun.
I've been smilin' lately, dreamin' about the world as one,
And I believe it could be, something good's bound to come.'

Mel waved his hand dismissively. 'I don't know, I never met the guy.' He swaggered on, singing with finicking, moon-eyed radiance, as Greg was forced into a faltering run to keep up with him.

TRAIN, TRAIN

'For out on the edge of darkness, there rides a Peace Train,
Peace Train take me searching, come take me home again.
Peace Train sounding louder, ride on the Peace Train,
Ooh – aah – eeh – ah – ooh – ah, come on the Peace
   Train . . .'

Chapter Fourteen

Carrock Station, when Greg went up there at the weekend, was now a station: a diesel shunting locomotive stood idling at the platform, heading a long train. Behind the diesel came low flat wagons piled high with lengths of track attached to sleepers – something from a giant Hornby train set – then linked to them were several deep trucks full of pale grey ballast, and then one full of men in boiler suits with shovels and picks slung over their shoulders like troops on their way to the front, and finally a guard's van with Kevin from the bank leaning out to blow a whistle. The diesel's greasy green sides shivered and drummed, its engine burbled and throbbed, and a shaft of dirty exhaust spurted from the pipe in front of the cab. The train bucked, making all the trucks clank together on their couplings, and slowly it eased away down the line into the trees.

Tracklaying! Rails on their way towards Force Road; rails already, as well, covering most of the football pitch beyond the platform. On the furthermost track was a chocolate-and-cream-painted sleeper carriage with faded checked curtains at its windows and a line of washing from its roof to a nearby telegraph pole. Alongside was the ESG steam engine; as the tarpaulin stretched over it flapped in the wind Greg could see paintwork underneath that shone new and black, but also that the drooping hollow in the canvas was explained by a pink-rusted boiler resting on trestles to the rear. Over on the far side of the railway's land, in the lee of the poplar trees, was an encampment of several bright orange and blue tents. The blackened circle of a fire, still curling with wisps of smoke, was surrounded by a haphazard ring of sleepers obviously hauled up as seats. The front of one of the tents was being unzipped, and an emerging hand – apparently clasping a beer bottle – became a bare arm, which was followed by a dazed face that blinked out a seraphic smile into the sun. The face became visibly aware of the watch on the end of the arm, aligned itself precariously, took in for a heavy moment the fact of midday, and all collapsed back inside.

Greg found Edwards in the Stationmaster's office, which was now full of shelves and box files and stained coffee mugs, reclining with his feet up on his desk and talking into a portable phone. 'Yeah, it was OK last week,' he was saying, 'and last night, but we could do with an extra floodlight. Tonight looks like being a clear one, but just in case there isn't much moon again . . .' As he noticed Greg his face spread into a surprisingly unknowing grin. 'Right, we'll come and pick it up,' he finished, and tossed the handset into a tray of papers. He tipped himself onto his feet and seized Greg's hand. 'My friend! I heard you'd been spotted in town. Good to have you back!'

How disconcerting. This was the first time since Greg had met Edwards that he hadn't been given the feeling of breaking into someone else's meeting.

'You didn't tell us you were coming. Have you been up at the hostel?'

'Redecorating it all the way through,' explained Greg. 'We had to get that done before I had time to come up here. It looks as if everything's happening.'

Edwards slumped back into his chair and scoured his eyes with his knuckles before gazing up at Greg. 'It's a big party. I'm glad you've come back for it.' His arms sagged down to the ground. 'We've just started this twenty-four-hour tracklaying over the weekends. We're past all the houses now, so they don't get disturbed. Three alternating shifts, beginning Friday evening, finishing Sunday evening. Going really well.' His smile became wan. 'It's the hours round the campfire afterwards . . . and before. Les gets all these crates of cheap beer from somewhere. The shift that's just come off seems to join in with the one waiting to go on. That's the problem, Greg . . . the hotel.' Edwards's chin came to rest on his chest – and then his eyes scrutinised Greg again. 'This is, Saturday morning, right?'

'Just turning into afternoon.'

Edwards hobbled off to pick through the litter of mugs and rejected each with a grimace.

'Can I join one of the tracklaying shifts?' said Greg.

'That's really specialised stuff. There's a team of guys from the Mid Hants who're coming up each week to show us how. You can go and have a look. You *could* join the gang preparing the trackbed just ahead of them. And you can join in the fear and loathing.' He was jabbing at his phone. 'I'd better see how the shop's doing – I've got a school-leaver holding the fort. Oh, *hi-ii* . . .'

Greg held his hand up as goodbye. The last thing he heard as he went out onto the platform was, 'You are doing *very, very, very* well . . . in fact, you are doing the very *wellest* . . .' Greg thought of a grandmother standing in the bookshop waiting to pay for a Beatrix Potter.

There was a new red sign at the far end of the platform that said CROSS LINE HERE, and a pathway of sleepers level with it leading across the tracks. Greg looked carefully both ways, listened, and nothing disturbed the somnolent bright desertion, so he jumped down and picked his way across towards the dumpy tent that had briefly put out its blind feelers to the sun.

The flap had been zipped up again. 'Excuse me,' Greg called from a couple of yards away with uncertain forthrightness, 'would you be from the, Mid Hants tracklaying party? I wondered what time the night shift began so . . . I wanted to come along and see.'

'You fucking idiot,' croaked a muffled voice deep within. There was a long silence. Eventually, 'Eight': the word collapsed into a sigh, and the prospect thereby acknowledged rendered the inhabitant terminally speechless. But then, just as Greg was turning his back, the voice called out urgently, 'Hey, can you come and wake me up?'

But there was no carousing when Greg turned up at seven. The day was going grey, and three men were squatted down on the sleepers slowly stirring the ashes of the fire with their pick handles, and not talking. Greg sat down and his presence was not acknowledged until one of them said deep into his collar,

'You can still wake me up.' Then another said, 'You haven't brought any booze, have you?', and Greg said, 'No, I'm afraid not,' and the other nodded gratefully, and after this only a police car siren broke the quiet.

Over the next hour half a dozen others came out of the darkening gloom – the flaring basket of a Tilley lamp bouncing towards them from the platform, a torch switched on inside one of the vanishing tents to irradiate a glowing orange igloo out of the night. Les and Jeremy thumped Greg on the back and set Thermos flasks down in front of them. There was the rasp of tyres skidding into the station forecourt. Les leaned on his pick and said solemnly, 'Henry the Fifth. Eve of Harfleur,' and then explained, 'Did it at school.' Then the whole gathering was transfixed in the blinding incandescence of a floodlight leaping across at them from the station, and Kevin's voice shouted, 'Yo!' As the blazing beam approached them, now swung skywards to rake the empty heavens for slow-droning bomber squadrons, the putter of the diesel came on the wind, and deepened, and soon the tracklaying train rolled out of the trees and was shuddering to a halt in the platform. Its men climbed out with winks and no words and stumbled away, the new shift loaded in all the telescopic stands for the extra floodlight, the locomotive shunted a new wagon full of ballast on to the front of the train, and then they were drawing out of the station again.

They rumbled through the darkness for perhaps five minutes; whenever the gurgling revs of the engine fell for a moment you could hear the swishing of the trees. Greg only had time to realise that they were probably going more slowly than it appeared (just as a tube train at thirty or forty seems to shriek and career through its black tunnels), that the train was creeping carefully and evenly along this new track, before they were pulling up, braking, and stopping in a broad, bleached arena of white light, a giant rail-borne crane standing ahead at the limit of the new rails.

Now all weariness was gone: these people were at work. Half the men (Greg joined them – what was the point of watching?) set to shovelling ballast from the truck into barrows, and trundling them beyond the crane to the trackbed. The rest were fastening lines from the jib of the crane to a section of track on the long wagon. Each section was about thirty feet long; the carpet of ballast on which it was to be laid had to be thick and level. Greg lost count of how many times he returned to the truck to refill his barrow. His arms jarred and trembled from pitching his shovel into the heavy heap of stones; his knees jolted against his barrow. Eventually he came to feel strangely weightless, and when they broke off finally, two hours after they had arrived, to watch the track section swaying down on to the ballast, the weightlessness seemed all around – in the heavy lattice of wood and iron that wafted and hovered above them under the floodlights, and in the constant, brilliant, silver daytime cast by them amidst the trees.

Then, once the new stretch of track had been rested down, it had to be levered into alignment with the existing rails, and the bed of ballast that had seemed so level now showed all its undulations and thinnesses. The lengths of rail had to be connected up; wedges had to be knocked out with a sledgehammer and then knocked back in. It was midnight, Greg found, halfway through the shift already, before they had properly laid the first section of track for the night. Greg ferried more barrowloads of ballast to Jeremy and the Mid Hants man from the tent, who continued 'packing the track', which meant there were still unforeseen hollows under the sleepers to be filled in. 'You can go when you like, Greg-lad,' called Les at one point as Greg blundered past him, and Greg wondered distantly how and why that meant all the rest had to stay and do it. But around one o'clock he began to notice how his empty wheelbarrow would actually be a perfect fit for a curled-up, sleeping body. 'No, no,' his mind sternly told his eyes, 'It is *quite* big enough: it could have been made for it.' Remembering too that Mel would be up at nine because they were supposed to be digging over the hostel's vegetable garden, Greg essayed a hale wave of encouragement and valediction at everyone, and groped away into the night.

The walk back, alongside the dull iron rails leading him on through the moonlight, took little time. We could all have walked to where the crane was, thought Greg: so far the rails go no distance at all. Then he thought, But we took the train. A train now runs from the platform to the crane, so we caught it! He stopped when the lights of Carrock came into view at the end of the trees, and he could dimly see the single line of track ramify into the fan of sidings in the station. Then he turned round and walked back in the other direction from the town until they disappeared again, and he was standing, wide awake again now, and calm, between these breathing, silhouetted files of oaks and hawthorns in the darkness with only the line running away from him both behind and ahead.

Why are people doing this, he wondered. There is just trees and earth and grass here, and a short walk away – if you listened hard, against the trees now, you could hear odd shouts and the ravelling clatter of the crane's chains – people are laying this iron roadway, and it is half past one in the morning. We have been laying it almost exactly as they did a hundred years ago when they built the line: by hand, with picks and spades and barrows. Except for the crane – and even that runs on steam – we have been able to work only as fast as we can shovel or hammer. We have halogen floodlights, round-the-clock shifts, a portable telephone, and all in order to do something as big as this using only our hands. Listen! They are out in the middle of nowhere. They work all night all weekend, they get ravaged and stewed around the campfire in between, they even travel all the way up from Hampshire and live in tents and old railway carriages. They choose it! They *like* being navvies! This work was harder than anything at the youth hostel, anything at the big store, and Greg had only done it for a few hours: they all did it as if they had to, and the only reason for them making it like that for themselves was because they didn't have to, because no one was making them. The work was not just for the railway, but for itself.

The industry of it! A few months ago this had been a clearing studded with tree stumps, before that an impenetrable tangle of foliage. Now they had built the first length of a railway line through it again. Greg's memory threw up the schoolboy guard down on the Dart Valley Railway: two hundred steam engines . . . hadn't he said that every one of the locomotives sold to that scrapyard in Wales at the end of steam had now been bought back for preservation? They had one themselves just back along the line. Wasn't it two *hundred*? Was that a coincidence – how could it even be only a hobby? That is an *industry*, Greg thought with proud, sardonic clarity, in mute and fierce appeal to the heaving trees. Now tell me, would British Rail have built as many new diesels during those twenty years?

The wind had got up, and the moon had faded in clouds. It was quarter to two. Greg shrank into his windcheater and followed the line quietly back to the station, where a torch in another of the tents was already throwing the erratic shadows of someone struggling into their clothes.

The next weekend was Easter, and the hostel opened, and was full throughout the Bank Holiday. In the first weeks that it was open Greg only had time to drop in at the station and take a quick walk around to see was what happening. Each week the rails reached further along the trackbed, although Greg found it difficult, when he wandered up the line until he came to the crane, and it was always the rails running between the trees, to judge how far. The Mid Hants team had retired after the third round-the-clock effort, having shown the Carrock volunteers how to do it and given the tracklaying a good start. Soon after Easter Edwards announced that the railway was to receive two substantial grants – £50,000 altogether – from the county council and the English Tourist Board, towards the reopening of the first section. A small maroon tank engine arrived at the station, and the signwriting man from the dairy led a group in polishing and oiling it, while its owner, a builder in Wetherbeck, steamed it every Sunday and gave visitors footplate rides along the length of the platform for 50p. Greg detected Edwards's authorship behind a new poster appearing in shop windows and tea shops in town that seemed to be based on the 'Lakeland Express' picture Greg had been given for the exhibition, and said STEAMING AWAY THIS SUMMER!

After the flurry of the Bank Holiday weekend Greg was able to look around at what the hostel was like under Mel's management. Mel opened the hostel at lunchtime – why shoo them away all day, he said; it's why we're here. He planted garlic and liquorice and cinnamon amongst the Warden's roses; on still days the garden was a welter of high, needling smells. He played Ry Cooder tapes at reception and questioned the hostellers about themselves from the moment they arrived, assigning all kinds of correspondences and common interests between them. 'Glasgow?' (He read their address as they signed in.) 'Got another guy in tonight from there – room five.' 'Ah, well then, you'd like Scandinavia – talk to Alice there, she's just come over from Bergen.' Whether anyone ever took up any of Mel's matchmaking initiatives seemed of no concern to him – or perhaps he assumed that everyone would.

In the evenings, now that they weren't too full, Mel pulled the tables in the dining room together into one, and he and Greg joined the hostellers for the meal, Mel holding court to hear everyone's life story and answering with baleful monologues of his own, in between leaping up to answer the phone for future bookings. Such evenings were frequently long and hilarious, and sold lots of wine, and Greg could see people thinking with doubtful relief, This isn't how youth hostels are supposed to be . . . makes a nice change once in a while . . . even the food's . . . interesting . . . Sometimes, however, Mel said things like, 'Of course soon you're going to have pensioners flogging their homes to pay for a plastic hip joint – government's already recommending it,' and got up to flick the relevant report in the *Guardian* for all to see, and then the gathering around the table froze, and you knew it didn't matter what anyone present thought about it, or even whether they considered it to be true. They were there for a meal, and remarks of that order were uneasy and out of place, and politics and such like were not to be discussed, because someone might disagree. But Mel just said, 'I thought it was a funny story,' or told them about how whenever you got on a bus in Israel you always found the guy next to you asking you as soon as you sat down what you thought they should do about the Palestinians, and when you told him that started a blazing argument before you'd even been going five minutes.

One morning a hosteller collecting his card asked Greg suspiciously if Mel was 'one of these health types'. For a few weeks Greg also wondered at the amount of brown sauce they seemed to be getting through, until he noticed how many people were drowning their wholefood meals with it in quantities that transcended habit to bespeak panic-hardened defence. But every so often a postcard would arrive from Stratford-upon-Avon or Cornwall reading, 'Hi Mel Ireland was as good as you said Thanks again S & G', which evoked in Mel neither gratitude nor surprise. 'Sandy and Gus,' he'd say to Greg, pasting the card up in reception, 'blonde girl and the Austrian guy – remember? – just after Easter.' But Greg couldn't remember. The only occasions when Mel's businesslike gregariousness disappeared were when he demonstrated his hypersensitive gift for tracking cigarette smoke. Greg could hear such scenes in the common room from reception.

Clunk. Thud. The windows being banged open.

Mel's voice: 'Thanks for lining all our lungs with tar. Can smell it in the kitchen.'

Another voice: 'We're allowed to smoke in here, aren't we?'

'We're all allowed not to smoke in here too. How many've you had already?'

'I think you're being extremely rude!'

'As long as no one else has to breathe it in I don't mind. I'm not being the boss, I'm just someone who uses this room.' A pause. 'We've got some Polo Mints in reception.' A pause. 'You could lean out the window.'

Greg waited through the tense silence that followed. Then the other voice exploded, 'I don't know why they bother to make rules!' and the man strode past out of the common room, banged the front door, and through the window Greg could see him out on the drive inhaling puff after crazed, calmative, furious puff, as Mel returned licking his finger and impassively marking up his score in the air.

And as for Edie, the sparrowlike old lady who helped in the kitchen: 'Remind you of Warhol's Edie?' Mel confided to Greg. It became evident that despite working under the Warden for ten years she appeared to have no opinion of him at all – he was just The Warden; whereas Mel, on the other hand, let her tell him all about what was happening in the Archers, but also told her, when he saw her zealous regimentation of the washing up, to lay off the baton charges, and thereby confused her completely with the example of a warden who didn't even call himself one and was both friendlier and more boorish than the one who had been a Warden, and who must have been very nice, except that he seemed to have impinged on her not at all. Since she couldn't cook any of the new-style menus either, she gradually took charge of breakfast, which was fine by Mel, who said, 'Fill that fried bread full of fat, Edie,' and went to read the paper over his muesli.

Soon, then, Greg came to see how Mel's hostel was Mel himself: always moving, always lively, entirely public – a home, a multitude. He missed Ruth – the awareness of her preoccupied, inscrutable presence somewhere around the hostel, as there had been last summer – a separate space. The relentless activity of Mel and the hostel often became exhausting to Greg: sometimes it seemed an endless round of impermeable, self-generating frenzy. Contrasting it with the previous year, Greg came to remember the stillnesses of the Warden's hostel, even if at the time they may have been fraught: the stillness of the Warden studying the snooker, staring at you through his cigarette smoke, confronted by Kipling's Cat That Walked By Himself: the still moment of morning immediately after the last hosteller had gone.

Mel seemed to have no private life. His life was running the hostel: he was how he lived, what he did. He had views on everything, but apparently few feelings. His politics were global, universally applicable – ecology, anti-vivisection – or relativist, entropic. You think you have a problem over here with discrimination? You want to go and take a look at India. He was for conservation, against pollution – but hadn't the slightest interest in the Lake District itself, fells or lakes or wildlife. His was a tireless, pragmatic altruism of logistics and convocations: to create a centre for sailing holidays, institute a programme of orienteering competitions, offer nature study facilities, build this, fix that. *I'm sure we can lay something on for you.* What was his inner life? Did he even have or need one? What you saw was what you got: a truly public life.

In some ways – the driven, assiduous impresario, the implacably confident pedagogue – Mel reminded Greg strongly of Edwards; but to make the comparison was immediately to notice the essential difference. Edwards's public project, Greg had had to admit early on, was nearer egomania than self-effacement – its inspiration and design originating less in the town, it seemed, than in Edwards's own private millenarianism. The railway was actually not his public activity but a manifestation of his private life. In this respect, therefore, Greg began to notice the affinities between Edwards and the Warden. Mel, Greg was discovering, was the same after two months as he had been in the first five minutes of their first meeting: he travelled light; he was light; he floated. Whereas the Warden, even after you had worked with him a whole summer, was a mystery, a face turned away: he wouldn't let you know him, couldn't let you know him, and yet he was *somewhere*. And Edwards: what is he on about, you thought all the time, what is he up to? It wasn't that Mel was Australian, or even foreign, that made the difference, but it was, Greg realised nevertheless, that Edwards and the Warden were English, and so was he. Both of them had *secrets* – not Cadillac aspirations to transform and displace themselves, but their own inner territories, their own islands for themselves, their own private branch lines – and Greg recognised that he shared their secrets, felt at home in the idea of them, even if he didn't know what they were, or whether he had any of his own. We're all laying down our own tracks, it occurred to him; straight and hidden and out in nowhere and only for us to travel, each of us, all of us English.

This year, then, Greg was drawn back to the railway to escape not the torpor and solitude at the hostel during the day (as when the Warden and Ruth had been away in their fells), but the omnipresent company and busying. He joined the trackbed gang. With Adrian of 'Nutbrown', who alternated with his wife in running the shop, and the shyly lugubrious signwriting man, who now seemed to spend all his time on the railway, Greg went down the line twice each week, sometimes under the cold blue skies of approaching summer, surrounded by the clamour of birdsong, on other days hacking and puddling through sweeping rain and the warm close mist of late spring storms.

The three of them worked quietly, methodically, cutting down and rooting out the weeds and seedlings that had sprung up since the main clearing effort of the previous summer. At first Greg was surprised by the tall muscular thistles, the bundles of briar, the saplings already as thick as drumsticks, all the flourishing vegetation creeping back over the trackbed again in a matter of months. At the same time they hunted out the culverts and drainage ditches spaced regularly beside the line, cleaned them of all their matted grass and mud, relined with bricks and cement those that had crumbled or fallen in. Greg became accustomed to sense with his feet the spongy, springy turf, pick out with his eyes the over-bright green of the grass, where water was not draining away off the line – sometimes actual pools had collected, waving with fronds and specked with gnats – and to trace the hidden and clogged soakaway. And this in turn led him to become aware of every gradation in the line and the land alongside it, and every variation of undergrowth and tree covering that land. The line might be level, the trees might enclose it in regular, straight walls, but here and there the trees sat on a small, steep bank, and whenever it rained the water would always run down the bank on to the line; and here and there those oak trees might rise out of a mess of hawthorn and elderberry bushes, whose spores would always be blowing across to seed in this narrow corridor of ground open to the sun.

From the start Greg found the work an engrossing, mysterious activity. Just behind them, the new parallel iron rails spiked to the massive oily sleepers, bedded in the pale grey carpet of stones: neat and new – something that had to be laid only once, and to last: something that redefined conclusively the ground it now rested on, or rather seemed to take that ground into itself: the permanent way. Ahead, a green road, a grass pathway, there for good as well, it looked, when you regarded it from afar. But the more you worked with each yard of it at a time, as Greg was now doing, the more it seemed yourself and everything were made different, quotidian and vulnerable. It was *growing*; being grown through; it was being watered, sunned, seeded, elemented; it would always be, whatever you did. The work they were now doing was no single, conclusive solution – it was merely the first enactment of a task that would always have to be performed for as long as the railway ran again. The saplings would always plant themselves, the briars creep across, the twigs and ferns wash into the culverts – would all need to be continually cleared away. And not only from an empty green road: very soon, Greg saw, such work would need to be done on the new stretch of track as well, before the railway even opened once more, and then always too: for grass would begin to spike up through the ballast, rain would settle on and rust the rails, saturate the trackbed until it became marshy, tree boughs would sag out over the line, moss cover the sleepers. Everything was always returning to land.

This was why people restored a thing like a railway, whether or not they came from a city where the ground and almost all the sky had been concreted over and bricked out, where you couldn't see where you were standing. This was as permanent as you could get, if you were still to contend with the land, to arrive at an equilibrium between what the land wanted and what you wanted. To do something that might last, although in theory and the evidence of natural attrition it never will. And as with the modern, amateur navvies Greg had joined briefly, laying their track throughout the night to get in as much work as they could, the task of clearing and weeding and draining became important to Greg for itself: you gave the land your straight, rational project, and the land responded with all the growing it would have done anyway, so you worked at that. It was both the permission and the price of the project. As the spring deepened into summer, the trees alongside the trackbed filling out with leaves, the entire hue of the surrounding fells turning richer and lighter at the same time, the house martins now skimming and dodging under the eaves of the station, the three in the gang worked slowly along the line, just ahead of the crane and the bitten-off end of the track. Their regular, repetitive effort, that new patch of the green road in front of them on that day, their quiet co-operation for which speech was unnecessary – all this became Greg's own secret, his own private line, as it was probably the others' too in their turn. The railway was a communal effort, but for each person that worked on it it was also a retreat into solitude.

Insofar as Greg, however, inside this experience, the oblivious centre of his own secret, was able to formulate it at all to himself as he worked away on the line, his thinking approximated to it from another direction, through other questions and musings.

What's so impressive, he wondered, about a disparate group of amateurs rescuing two hundred steam engines for fun — why does that seem such proper industry? — when we all think British Rail, our proper railway, is a joke? Why does the Dart Valley Railway look so smart, and the Lewisham line so shabby? Why is Lewisham Hospital closing its beds while at the big store the staff are raising money for a scanner? Why are we all brilliant at being amateurs and uninterested and embarrassed at being professionals?

As far as Greg could see, the answer was something to do with this private-life-in-the-public-life — the best, quintessential English life was both of them. Elevate only the first, and you had Thatcherism: withdraw behind your double-glazing and count the tins in your larder; the world outside was for you to harness to the benefit of yourself. Offer only the latter, and people jibbed at the presumption on their unquestioning involvement and allegiance. We like a moat round ourselves, he thought, and we happen to live surrounded by one. There was no moral or political reason why the public on its own shouldn't work, every reason why it should: but it simply ignored people's private territories, which they just *liked* to protect. It had nothing at all to do, as it were, with their gardens, or their pets, or their stamp collections. Public works, therefore, never quite belonged to them, so never quite mattered enough to protect enough. I'm the same, thought Greg, I don't lobby my MP about the local NHS cuts — I put my small change into the scanner collecting-tin. I drive my car all the way up the motorway from London in order to restore a mile of steam railway. We're amateurs in this country: our community is in our amateurism: we're only enthusiastic about things if we can be enthusiasts. For the best, we need the public *and* the private, and at best we connect them. But we only seem able to do it by acting out of our own whimsical, cussed, private selves, and hoping that the public resonance will be loud and useful enough: it is the best and the worst in us.

So when Greg, going out to answer the hostel reception bell one evening, heard Mel suddenly make the genial declaration to everyone around the dinner table (they had been talking about how you could never find a public phone box in working order) that 'England's just a group of enthusiasts running an old railway,' he silently agreed, and felt useless and shamed, while thinking that as usual Mel's mind was travelling light. But no one at the table took Mel up on it anyway.

Chapter Fifteen

There remained the gap – the gap in the line where the bridge before Force Road was down – and it turned out that for the time being the railway couldn't bridge it. This was apart from the question of the family who now lived in Force Road Station: they didn't mind trains passing their window, but they did object to people getting out there, even on the far platform, and while they were thinking of moving in fact, they weren't ready just yet. But the bigger problem, Greg learned from his colleagues on the track gang, was the bridge. The Railway Inspectorate had stipulated that professional contractors must be used to rebuild it, and even though tens of thousands of pounds had been budgeted for it in the share issue, the original estimates of the cost of tracklaying and restoring Carrock Station had proved too low. Now the railway was short: even with the two recent grants there wasn't enough money to pay for the new bridge, and there wasn't enough time to raise more money and then build the bridge by the summer, when the line was due to open.

So the Manpower Services Commission were going to help. The project they were funding had been reconceived as one to build a platform just this side of the road, and the railway would lay a run-round loop there for the engine, and the line could open in the late summer for pleasure trips after all. Ten unemployed school-leavers from Carlisle would work on the scheme for a month, their wages and their accommodation at the youth hostel paid for by the MSC.

The week they were arriving, Greg talked to Edwards about it. Edwards was ashamed and indignant – at having to accept, and connive in, the government's pathetic excuse for job creation, and because the total cost of the project, he maintained, was virtually equal to what they needed for the bridge. 'A few thousand, that's all!' he exclaimed. Greg took that to be the sum involved in either case, but afterwards it occurred to him that perhaps Edwards was merely alluding to the difference between the two. 'Work experience,' Edwards continued: 'The Tory term for giving people shitwork for a few weeks to take them off the register. We should have no part in it. I said we should boycott it, Greg, but I was overruled.'

This was the first time Greg had heard of Edwards having less than entirely his own way on the railway, and deduced that there must be boards and committees now which could on occasion vote him down.

'A bunch of kids building a Toytown platform,' Edwards finished. 'That's what we should call it! Get them to put up a big station sign while they're here: TOYTOWN.' But Edwards's righteous outrage was less conspicuous than his new, implacable serenity. The man said he was angry – and he must have known about the scheme for months – but he looked even more confident and self-justified. The exception, it appeared, proved the rule: if this was a setback, it was one which only made the eventual, necessary outcome more certain. Or maybe Edwards's sanguine glee had something to do with whoever was assisting him at his bookshop on Saturdays. Greg was too busy at the hostel at weekends to be able to drop in for a casually-planned browse.

The group arrived at the end of April, hunched-up and gloomy in a Transit minibus on a Sunday of bright sun. Les was there from the railway to greet them with Greg. How young they are, was Greg's first thought – none could have been above seventeen. In turn each of them dropped lazily to the ground from the back of the van – several carrying large ghetto-blasters – and surveyed all around with a lassitude that seemed to indicate shyness in some, in others defiant insolence. The driver, from a Carlisle minicab firm, was leaving the van for the railway's use during the boys' stay, and went back in the car that had followed. The ten youths attended to Les's bluff welcome with little interest, and to Greg, as he took them on a tour of the hostel, with less. When they looked in on the common room he laid it on about the strict rules on smoking –

convenience of other hostellers, fire precaution, only allowed in here – but by the time he was showing them their dormitory one of them had already lit up. No alcohol in the hostel apart from the wine sold with the evening meal – sorry lads, another rule, Greg apologised heartily. A youth whose sleeveless T-shirt showed off an Iron Maiden tattoo asked if the pub was near. The tallest in the party – the others called him Kenny – went over to the washbasin and set his tub of hair gel up in front of the mirror. Greg left them to unpack, and as he went out – together they all spoke so loudly! – one called after him, 'You allowed to take showers with the birds here?' and everyone cawed with laughter.

At dinner that evening the boys sat in silence and picked at their meals. Mel asked what was bugging them; they all shrugged. Mel chatted away; they obviously weren't listening. Occasionally they grinned sheepishly at each other. As soon as it was over they dived out of the front door and headed into town. Greg went and called them for breakfast the next morning; only two made it down even so – but then they all scrabbled to get ready for nine and assembled in the hall looking scared and nervous when Les came to drive them over to the line.

For the first week they came home at dusk tired and quiet. Greg asked them what they'd been doing and they said they were having to dig out a long bank of earth by the trees to make a wide enough plot for the foundations of the platform, and then haul all the bricks and sand and cement up by hand from the lorry down in the road. Greg tried to fill them in on the history of the line and the aims of the restoration project; they heard him out as if it was part of the job requirement. They continued to leave their meals every evening and head for the town – Greg heard one of them mutter to another on coming into the dining room that it would probably be more 'Paki food'. At the end of the week they all hitch-hiked back to Carlisle for the weekend because they were missing their girlfriends.

But the first, apprehensive week became the second, and the third, and fourth. The boys left every morning for the line, where, Les said, they did everything they were told, and in virtual silence. They returned in the evenings to sit around in their dormitory or go out in search of pubs and Space Invaders.

They declined offers to take them up into the fells, or down to see the lake, and accepted a table to themselves at dinner where they could talk together, and Greg now found himself waiting furiously for the next of their frequent, booming jokes about wogs and poofs. They went home every weekend. Greg and Mel had the daily turnover of hostellers to see to: it was easier to ignore the group, and it seemed to be what they wanted. Mel had soon come to hold Greg responsible, if not for their coming, which had been his decision, then, as the hostel's railway representative, for their stay. So it was Greg who regularly had to go up to their dormitory to stop them smoking (at least they confined it, along with themselves, to there) or playing their ghetto-blasters late, to find waste-paper baskets stacked with empty cans of Newcastle Brown. His admonitions were obeyed immediately and without rancour, and a couple of days later he'd be doing it again. You either contracted in, or out, was Mel's attitude: these people did not want anything from him that he had to give. When Greg suggested that they get Edie to cook them a meal they would eat, Mel said, 'Do you want to get the *Sun* delivered every day?'

The month's work was finished three days ahead of schedule, and on the penultimate morning Greg went up to the bridge with the group to have a look. The new platform, nestled under the overhanging oak trees, was long enough for perhaps three carriages; it was edged with white paving slabs, surfaced with black macadam covered in grey gravel. In front of it the trackbed had been widened for the run-round loop, and just before the bridge parapet a pair of buffers had already been set into the ground to mark the end of the line.

'This is very smart,' Greg said to Kenny, who was watching him survey it, it seemed, almost out of interest that someone could be interested in such a thing at all. 'Have you enjoyed doing it?' Greg was determined to have a conversation with one of them before they left.

'Hard work,' said Kenny. 'Guvnor seems pleased enough' – glancing over at Les.

Greg thought for something else to say. 'What next, then – what will you do after this?'

'I don't know,' said Kenny. 'Dole. This doesn't fit you up for anything. Job Centre people back home keep telling you to train for something. All they keep on about. But what for? Aren't any jobs where I live.'

Greg looked at the platform. 'Well, you've all been a great help to everyone here.'

Kenny put his hands in his pockets. 'Labouring job. 'S like working on the roads. Knackers you.'

'What sort of job would you like?' asked Greg. 'Have you ever thought of moving a bit away from Carlisle?'

'Oh, I don't mind. Anything that pays you a bit of money. As long as you've got enough money in your pocket.'

'But have you ever looked anywhere else?'

'All my mates are in Carlisle. That's why this place has been so boring.'

Greg realised that Kenny wasn't really complaining – he, not Greg, was the one speaking from the position of authority: it was Greg, in a sense, who was discontented with Kenny's prospects.

'I'm looking forward to being back home,' said Kenny.

No one on the railway or at the hostel thought of organising something for the boys' last night, so they went into town as usual, and were up early next morning waiting for the minibus driver to arrive from Carlisle. It was as if their home town were many hours' drive away, not twenty minutes. *Back home.* They made it sound antipodean. Mel didn't bother to see them off, and they didn't seek him out: it didn't seem deliberate.

The week following their departure Greg spent feeling guilty at how little he must have done to make their stay more enjoyable; how little he remembered of them already – and that was only of them as a group, their habits, as their *kind*; how little, altogether, the whole project apparently signified, except that the railway had got its stop-gap halt. If they had stayed longer . . . ? But a month had been enough for both sides. Then Greg bumped into Edwards again at the station as he was setting out for an afternoon with the track gang. Edwards, their conversation soon established, hadn't actually got around to meeting any of the boys, or visiting the new bridge terminus yet.

'You're still blacking the whole scheme?' said Greg.

'Good lord no,' said Edwards innocently. 'One knew what to expect, that was all. Hardly a great deal to find out by taking a look. Don't tell me the whole thing was in any way important, Greg, really. *It was not important.* Well – no.' An idea had occurred to him; he pushed his glasses back up his nose so he could look straight through them at Greg. 'If one wanted to get depressed I suppose one could say it is kind of important, managing to reinvent the navvy a hundred years on, in the *nineteen* eighties. Bus them in for a month's forced labour and virtually no wages – at least you feed them properly this time – wonder why they spend what you do pay them on getting pissed most of the time . . . of course, a hundred years ago you had to go all the way to Ireland to find them and take advantage of the potato famine – now you just go up the road. That is an achievement! That is historically important!'

'You don't know what you're talking about,' exclaimed Greg. 'You didn't even meet them. You talk about them as if they're animals!' But he was thinking about the racist jokes, the hours and hours spent sprawled on their bunks.

'The new underclass, Greg, that's all: slowly being cut adrift from society. People are content to leave them be, leave them alone, put them out of their minds. These blokes knew they were doing Mickey Mouse work.'

'How do you *know*?' Greg wanted to say, I knew them, *I* met them, they're not like you assume – but to be able to contradict Edwards would be to have to acknowledge their apathy, their insularity, their conservatism. How could Greg say to Edwards that the reason *he* thought one should be angry was because they were *content* with how they were? How could he say to Edwards, You didn't bother to go and meet them because you knew you wouldn't like them either?

'They had no interest in this railway,' Greg said eventually. 'Why should they? It's our hobby. That doesn't make their work any less useful.'

'The work they were doing is the government's hobby,' said Edwards. 'Call it charity if that makes it sound nicer. Pennies in a tin. To pass the time instead of creating some real jobs – there's where the money should have gone.'

In his anger Greg was about to say that he was going off to spend an afternoon digging ditches and pulling up weeds and that was fun enough, but realised it would be saying that the trouble with the boys was that they hadn't enjoyed their manual labour.

'Where did they come from, Greg? Carlisle? It's jobs *there* that are needed –'

'I thought the whole point was jobs for Carrock?'

'– their own communities that should be revitalised. It's that precious sense of *community* we should be preserving. That's what's valuable.'

Greg couldn't argue. They wouldn't talk to anyone, he wanted to say in self-justification; they never came out of their dormitory. They didn't want to know. He could only counter Edwards's look of pained concern with silence. The alternative was to say, '*You* haven't the first idea about anything, you smug bastard,' which would only have admitted that Greg hadn't.

Now it was only a couple of weeks until Ruth came back – June already – and in the meantime Mel had discovered Wainwright. The Warden had taken his old, foxed volumes with him, but a hosteller had suggested to Mel that the hostel library ought to have the whole set – a Lake District hostel without them? – so Mel had fixed it up: now he was profoundly absorbed in them himself.

'*A Pictorial Guide to the Lakeland Fells: being an illustrated account of a study and exploration of the mountains in the English Lake District*,' he read out to Greg one evening, strangely contorted into his armchair, a smirk and wonderment competing on his face. 'Seven volumes! All in his spare time! All in his own handwriting! Every single route up every damn mountain past every single sheepfold! And you see – look – all the text is hand-written – but it's justified, Greg!'

'I know. He did all the walking at weekends, wrote it up in the evenings. He worked as the Treasurer for Kendal Borough Council – he's retired now. He took the first bus out every Saturday morning and the last one back on Sundays.'

Mel was riffling through *The Western Fells*: '"Some personal notes in conclusion" – this is the last book ... blur blur ...

blur . . .' He sat up straight: '*"Thus a thirteen year plan was finished one week ahead of schedule"*!' Mel was reeling in bewilderment, the book fallen to his lap, hands clutched to his head. 'Oh wow . . . oh man . . . This is an *Englishman*, Greg . . . this is a *great* Englishman . . .' He swayed to a halt and stared ahead in silent homage.

Of course he is, thought Greg. Everyone should know that Wainwright is a genius. But he was still surprised at Mel, and more so during the days that followed, when Greg would come upon him in reception with one of the books, turning the pages carefully.

'I thought you would have found Wainwright really daft,' Greg said to him after several such encounters. 'I expected you'd say something about, how the Lake District was hardly the Himalayas – and you're not interested in hill walking any-way.'

Mel was thinking. 'Most of the time it cracks me up, Greg,' he said with uncommon hesitancy, 'everyone over here spending all their free time doing their gardens, training their roses. Clipping their poodles for Crufts, training them to be a good boy . . . This ridiculous drive and ambition – this amazing self-education. Going all out to make the small time, you know? But then this guy . . .'

Mel didn't seem to want to talk about Wainwright any more, only read all the books about all the fells, which he himself had no desire to explore. He was at home with them, read them as if they were a fiction, a long and diffuse novel of many characters, painstakingly creating and filling in its own complete world – and soon he began advising hostellers about walks and routes. 'You want to watch it coming down off Crinkle Crags – Wain-wright's got this priceless bit about The Bad Step . . .'

There were two sides to Mel, then. There was the dinner-table commentator, delivering his regular Letter from England, pro-nouncing, 'Only a matter of time before they call the Queen a communist for dishing out the Maundy Money – you've got a socialist Prince Charles already according to the Tories.' And there was the serene student of Wainwright – just as detached from the Lakeland fells as he was from Thatcherite Britain – who still fulminated over the standard of photo-reproduction in his *Guardian* after the move to new printing presses, and pored over a series of guidebooks inscribed, drawn, cartographed and engraved entirely by hand; whose conversation was all caustic cynicism, but whose equanimity was plainly evident: a cosmopolitan who thought Britain was a parochial, old-fashioned joke, but lived there, and liked it.

It was yet one person. Mel, it seemed, was tired of travelling: had been everywhere, and no longer wanted to know it. Now he was happy with smallness, and had found somewhere where he could be: a small English town in a small region of mountains and lakes; a youth hostel to run; a continually renewed audience for whom he could map and mark out and illustrate and expatiate upon all he saw around him – whether they saw the same place as he did, he didn't mind. The smallness of the country he had ended up in maddened him, and suited him. When it was maddening you could just switch off, like everyone else did. When it suited you, everyone let you be. He wasn't cramped: there was plenty of space around. He had retreated from covering the world, in order to do his own small thing, and watch everyone else do theirs, and to cultivate, like them, a faith in making something big out of something small, while not losing touch with its smallness, and Wainwright's example was more than that.

All in his spare time. A man who had spent thirteen years of it, every moment, to do his proper and chosen work of researching and writing his seven books; who wrote about the mountains as if they were people, not because they spoke to you or surprised you, but because they didn't; a silent community discovered on his first bus-trip holiday from industrial Blackburn, whose presence meant simply, *This is as it is*: an other, larger land – just land – whose surprise was its stasis, whose openness gave you privacy, your own time, from that moment, every moment, always to be found.

So Wainwright compiled his private story, his immense archives of the fells and valleys he walked, and Mel read them as though they were the Narnia books, and Greg went to the railway with the track gang.

Soon he and Adrian and the signwriting man came in sight of the new platform as they progressed up the line; another couple of weeks and the limit of the rails was further enough on for them to see it from there. During their customary amble along the trackbed each day to identify the work to be done they began to chat about when the railway opened. As the destination ahead became more and more distinct, and their knowledge of this stretch of line to it increasingly complete, so their ruminations became more specific. You could see by now what there was to work with. How many trains per day, then, they wondered, and how many passengers would they attract? Which set them to working out how long the journey up to the bridge would take, and how long to run the locomotive round the train, and then back . . . and how long would people want up at the halt to have a look about . . . and ought there to be a refreshment kiosk there? (They should paint information boards to put up on the new platform, said the signwriting man, with pictures for the passengers waiting there of all the birds and trees and plantlife to be seen from the train.)

Then the three of them would separate, each to work on his own particular task, and to continue his own personal speculations and plans for the line. Hunkered down to claw slimy poultices of blackened leaves out of a culvert one day, Greg came to realise that all they were doing was trying to predict how people wanted to spend their leisure time. What would people want to do? Would they come at all? How to entice them? How to occupy them? That was the crucial question for the railway this summer: that was all.

It was a depressing discovery for Greg, because it was not a new one. These were the same questions Mel and he circled around all the time. Worse, they were the same as Greg had heard all through the winter in the sports department at the big store. Do you think people will buy this? How should we display it? Is this how people want to spend their free time? (Greg threw clods into the bushes.) He had been considering the railway an institution, somehow monolithic, its own task of creation: like Wainwright, *serious*. And now suddenly, even as the gang were tramping the line to prepare it for the rails, it seemed not a secret, or even different activity, but common; not forward-looking, or even backward-looking, but merely and most suitably contemporary; not work, but leisure. Do people prefer boating or orienteering or riding on old railways? Do they like Mars Bars or Wispa Bars or Milky Ways? Would this pass the time for them or that?

Greg clambered to his feet and brushed the mulch off his hands. If it seemed a depressing revaluation of the railway, it was also an interesting redefinition of himself. Greg had commemorated this last year to himself as variegated, switch-back, admirably maverick: running a youth hostel; selling sports gear in a London store; rebuilding a disused railway. Alternative: not a career but contingency. Now it stood revealed as both coherent and symptomatic: he had been working at the same thing all the time. His entire year had been preoccupied with leisure. He had been its servant, salesman, employee, customer and practitioner. Buy your swimming costume in the big store, come and stay at the youth hostel, and if the water in the lake's too cold you can go for a ride on the railway. Restore the railway in your free time so that others can ride on it in theirs, and buy ice creams and badges whose manufacture can take up yet more people's time with work that gives them spending money for their free time. Here was one good reason for the new Railway Age he had recognised down on the Dart Valley: himself. There was your new industry: a lead-mining line become a tourist joy-ride and a nature trail. The Leisure Age. He was trained in it.

Greg's mind spooled on to prefigure a new and alarming future. A new series of Railway Acts. The government-sponsored construction of dozens more preserved railway lines. Pension fund money; property syndicates: the maximally-profitable length of track computed in terms of potential tourist through-flow . . . sites matched to catchment areas and major arterial roads like out-of-town shopping centres . . . a new Swindon works for the centralised overhaul of steam loco-motives and the training of engine drivers . . . massive MSC schemes for rebuilding viaducts and tunnels and mainline cuttings to mop up the enforced free time of the longterm unemployed with bursts of enforced labour . . . a Con servative minister addressing the House: 'In the light of current increasing levels of disposable income and the growing trend towards part-time work and job-sharing, it is clear that

Britain, while no longer under-shopped, remains substantially under-railwayed . . .'

Greg's gang reached the new platform, and marked the occasion by walking up and down it a lot, and from it the signwriting man thought he saw a deer on the slopes of the next valley – but by the time Greg and Adrian came over to follow his pointing finger it must have tiptoed away amongst the rowan trees. Adrian, stripped to the waist and pink in the hot afternoon sun, waved his shirt as a flag and a banner and a fly swatter.

Close behind them were the rails, due to run in beside the platform and complete the tracklaying in two more weeks, and a party was already planned for that day. It was also the day of Ruth's return – the postcard of Paul Nash's *Landscape from a Dream*, propped up on Greg's windowsill, had announced:

Train gets in Sat 10 at 4.30 or some ridiculous hour.
Can you pick me up

l. R

x.

But a phone call to Wetherbeck Station allayed Greg's shock: there were no arrivals at that time in the morning; Ruth was just complaining about travelling all day – and it was Saturday the 9th anyway.

During the week leading up to her return Greg dwelt on the card, feeling he ought to see the painting as somehow instructive, portentous, unconsciously apt. The strange barred screen in front of the sea cliffs . . . intersecting with that vast picture frame, or was it a mirror, enclosing the distant tumuli and hills and the rosy sunset sky and the bird soaring on the air . . . and these odd, outsize ball-things levitated above the ground, that could have been topiarised hedges or tumbleweeds or Fyling-dales Early Warning Station . . . Greg offered himself inti-mations of wildness and imprisonment and nameless, sourceless admonition, all of which seemed both relevant to the picture and entirely inappropriate to him and Ruth. Or there was the matter of the two birds: the great hawk that stood at the intersection of the barred screen and the picture frame – at

the centre of the painting, staring straight ahead, out of everything, at you; and far off, outside the screen but inside the
frame, the small wheeling sea bird, for that was what it seemed.
Was it flying away from the hawk, or was it sweeping in to land
alongside? And could it ever do so – could it ever breach these
framings and barrings? Was Greg the hawk, or Ruth? Eventually
Greg told himself he should think that Ruth had probably
given the purchase of the card about ten seconds and as much
premeditation as she gave to anything, and that if she could
have heard such speculation she would have been baffled with
boredom, which was why he liked her. But the postcard stood
before him through the days, the pitiless arrow-stare challenge
of the great hawk constant and unresolved.

On the afternoon of the 9th Greg drove to Wetherbeck via
Force Road, stopping there to climb up the embankment and
inspect the line. The new halt was deserted – they must have
been working through Friday night, and finished in the morning.
The crane was gone. The rails ran alongside the platform and
up to the buffers. The platform smelt of new tar, heated and
moistened in the heavy sun; here and there the air wagged a
single leaf. The railway had a complete line: a terminus to a
terminus: tracks running from the town to a small station in
the country. From one of the buffers was hung a piece of
cardboard of the shape previously packed inside a new shirt, on
which was written:

THE NEXT TRAIN TO DEPART FROM THIS PLATFORM
WILL BE IN TWO MONTHS TIME.

And then on to fetch Ruth, who leapt out of the carriage and
into Greg's arms, and apart from whooping 'Oh my bag!' and
managing to claw her suitcase out just as the train was about
to pull away again, said nothing for ages but only beamed and
sang 'Mannish Boy' at Greg, with guitar-riff improvisations, in
a high, light voice.

During the drive back to Carrock Greg chatted warily to her
about the work on the railway, since except for duvets and
wholefoods he couldn't think of any other news he had. But
this time Ruth didn't seem to mind, or at least idly listened, and
when, completing his progress report, he said, 'They're having

a party tonight up at the station to celebrate the end of the tracklaying,' to his surprise she said, 'Oh, let's! *I* want to party!'

At ten that evening, therefore, they met at the hostel porch. Greg had gone into town for a bottle of whisky to take with them, while Ruth was getting ready; now on his return she stepped forward out of the gloom and rested her hand on his shoulder. Greg had never seen Ruth dressed up before. She had rolled up the sleeves of the oversized cricket sweater into woollen waterwings; the red-and-blue-edged V-neck showed it was being worn next to the skin. Just there it clung, and from there it billowed and lost her inside, until finally it hugged her thighs, where it met her metallic pink tights. A pair of lime green wraparound sunglasses with mirror lenses were pushed back above her forehead. As far as he could make out in the moonlight she was wearing yellow eyeshadow and her lips were indigo and her cheekbones were spangled with glitter.

Greg couldn't begin to think about what he saw. Ruth was here when she hadn't been for months; here was the person who hadn't been here. Why hadn't he seen her since Christmas – why hadn't he been to see her, or even written – for *six months*? She stood revealed, and disguised, and hidden, and there, in the closest, sheerest mouldings of her: this was this was this was she was this was she was this: it was all he knew. Her hand stayed on his shoulder all the way to the station; sometimes it seemed as if she was steering him or steadying him, at others that he was the still point of touch for this precarious amalgam of pink and bagginess and sleekness and cricket beside him.

Coloured lights circled the booking hall; the stationmaster's office was wet with drink and gritty with squashed peanuts; the waiting room was a disco; the whole building was thronged with people.

'You can meet Ashley,' said Greg in a you-remember-I-told-you-about-him tone, after he'd introduced Ruth to Adrian and Les and Kevin and the signwriting man. 'I suppose we'd better say hello.' He wanted everyone to meet Ruth, and he wanted just himself to be with her. They pushed through the crowd until they found Edwards, who was talking to Peter Fellows about Tony Benn's challenge for the Labour leadership, and

Fellows was absently crackling his empty plastic cup. Greg made the introductions, Edwards turned a frank smile on Ruth, and Ruth arched an eyebrow in return.

That done, the two of them found the barrels of beer, hid the whisky under Edwards's desk, and jostled around some more. After a while Ruth said, 'You needn't keep me company all the time, Greg, if you want to say hi to everyone. No, go on – I'm quite happy getting tanked.'

So Greg had to take himself off and talk to Jeremy and Les about the final night of tracklaying, and the culverts, and the sycamore saplings, when he only wanted to be with Ruth. Several times he caught sight of her across the room. Once she was listening to the signwriting man, who was pointing sternly at the red-and-blue V-neck of her jumper, which appeared to be the inspiration for his subsequent mournful speech – perhaps they were Lancashire colours and a reminder of David Hughes and twenty-four off an over in the Old Trafford murk. Later Greg was amused to see Ruth in animated conversation with Edwards. What were they saying to each other? Could she really be, *telling* him?

Eventually Ruth drifted back to him with the whisky bottle, already well started.

'Beer all gone?'

''S piss,' said Ruth.

'What were you saying to Ashley?'

Ruth smiled and shook her head in wan helplessness. She pressed the bottle neck down heavily on the rim of his plastic cup and sloshed a cataract of whisky into his beer.

They stood together, helping each other every so often with a top-up, and peacefully watched everyone around them. Then, dreamily drunk, they tugged each other into the heaving disco and danced, and danced with each other, and at, and round, and near, and by each other, until suddenly the room was stirring and swelling with the drab, weary groaning of 'Nights in White Satin', and Ruth stood still and said 'Oh fuck!' They laughed and ran their hands down each other's slippery-wet arms, and went outside on to the platform.

They wandered along past the single gas lamp that glowed and spat under the canopy – all the others were out – and then they stopped. More whisky – and eventually the churning dirge had died behind them. The carriages and wagons were scattered hulks of blackness, silent solids in the dark, and Ruth was staring ahead. Greg followed her stare, but only as far as her face. Her yellow eyeshadow made her eyes wide, seem gelid and anxious in their bright surrounds. Her sparkling cheekbones seemed infinitely delicate; brittle and scintillant like a crazed wineglass. She glanced suddenly at Greg, her hand at the pale glistening V of skin bordered by the red-and-blue, a look of appeal and reassurance, and lightly clutched his arm. And now Greg was holding her tender at her temples, clasping her neck under her hair, feeling the faint crusting of glitter on his finger-tips, and he kissed her gently, and again, and again. Ruth smiled him a strange, sad, passive smile that seemed to say, 'I accept you.'

They sat down laboriously side by side on the edge of the platform, passing each other the whisky bottle and speaking quiet words between long silences, any words, it was only the voice you needed to hear. After a time all Greg could remember was that Ruth, or had it been he? had said something about the Moody Blues, or perhaps it was what she was saying now – he couldn't see her any more, because although her pink legs still dangled over the edge next to his the rest of her appeared to have lain back flat on the platform. And he began to confide in her all his thoughts and worries that he had ever had, or would ever have, which with her he would have no more, but the confession came out only as a general affirmation that he would from now on at some point confide everything, because that seemed much easier, and because for the time being he couldn't recall any of the specific worries or thoughts that a moment before he had needed to share.

And later Ruth was sitting up and saying something, and all he could catch was 'Greg', which was all he wanted her to say, and now she was walking away, but by the time he raised himself upright, for he seemed to be lying down too, the platform was empty, which meant that whatever she had gone to do she would be back soon. Since he now felt awake again he had some more to drink while he waited, and occasionally he noticed how cold it seemed to have got, but the whisky would soon warm you up, and eventually he couldn't wait for Ruth any longer, so he got to his feet and flung the bottle away with all his might, which crashed through the darkened window of Dorothy's in a glorious, exultant shower of glass, just where he had aimed it, but then he realised – he could see! – that Alec – he was starting already! – was going to have to sweep it all up, which wasn't the idea, and now here was Les in his new shirt, you could still see the creases where it had been folded round the cardboard, shining the floodlight through the jagged hole so that the floor of the café flashed and glittered like an ice-crazed pond, but there at least was Ruth, sitting in the corner at the back, beyond the reach of the light, although she shouldn't be there at all, because she was due in at Old Trafford, the ninth wicket was down, never mind how dark it was, or Lancashire would lose, which at least was why she wasn't here now with him, but it didn't matter, it didn't matter, it *didn't* matter, because at *least* she was still holding the whisky bottle . . . And now someone's hands were grasping under his armpits and hauling him backwards and up, which meant his head must have been down between his knees, Kevin's hands, because Kevin's voice was saying '. . . out like a light', and the music seemed to have stopped, but that might have happened a long time ago, it had the last time he had heard it.

Chapter Sixteen

Love was not a last brick suddenly in place, no crystallised absoluteness: love was realising the potential consequence of loss. When minutes of someone's presence calibrated the calamity of their six months' absence; when there was no reason for feeling something except that you felt it. You could list endless reasons and evidence for why you didn't fit together, how you didn't know each other – but you couldn't add up like that and hope to judge. Love was imagining the other being taken away and seeing whether the place left by them bled. You could only imagine the taking away.

It was easy for Greg to imagine the taking away, since in the days after the party, which had now accumulated into weeks, Ruth had hardly spoken to him. This was nothing unusual: she was exactly as she had been the previous summer. There was no reason for her to change along with the hostel's regime: indeed, the replacement of the Warden had only changed things for the same. Ruth didn't like Mel either. She didn't like the food he made them cook and then eat, and she didn't like it that when she was airy and disorganised and messy in the kitchen he wasn't silently, furiously tolerant like the Warden, but shouted and stood over her, and she didn't like it that if she got angry in turn, since she was trying her best, he found her torrential comminations hugely funny. So Ruth on all hostel duties was sullen and petulant, and Greg cast uncomfortably as mediator and consoler. Once again Greg found himself running Ruth out to the fell every morning – she had presumed upon it this time, as before the party he had expected and wanted her to – and the mutually silent drive was accompanied by her sunny humming; but this summer Greg wasn't to come with her on her traversing of the slopes, because she had too much to do and he'd be in the way: she said it as a favour. And, as before, Ruth used Greg's room in the evenings: it appeared that her aim was to work hard on writing up her field notes right from the start – but by the time she returned from the fell her tranquil, imperviously gay mood of the morning had often become a distracted taciturnity, and Greg suspected that like last time she was sitting up there for long hours and doing no work.

It didn't appear that he was the problem – indeed, that there was a problem at all. On his apologising the day after the party, as he thought he ought to, for getting so drunk, Ruth said in surprise, 'Don't be so silly!' and added sombrely, 'You saw how I was.' Altogether, as far as he could see, she was just the same towards him as she had always been, and he to her. So that was the problem: he *was* the problem – to himself. He seemed to have remembered an evening that hadn't apparently happened, although he was fairly certain that some of it had, and he seemed to be the only witness. Where had she gone – and why? When he had asked her she had only said flatly, in embarrassment or apology or was it any of his business anyway, 'I'm sorry I left you.' That was the closest they came, and Greg could do nothing with it, as he seemed to have been unable to do anything with their entire friendship, to seize or use any moment of it to carry forward to the next, to do anything but let each one go and wait for another. And all the while, over his thoughts of love, and his thoughts of thoughts of love (since that, he wondered, was perhaps all he had, or all it was safe to have), over it all there was the momentary minute glitter-feeling on his fingertips – he had felt that, the only important thing was that he could say, *I felt that* – and also the aloof, elusive Ruthness of Ruth herself, whom you were always waiting for while she was always simply being Ruth, whose whole existence still said to him, *You think too much, when you can never know*, but left him nothing else to do.

So Greg became solitary, and took to walking by himself in the fells. He would drop Ruth at Scale, and then drive away over the fell roads to the farther shore of the lake and the range of hills clustered along it. Now that the railway had completed its tracklaying the new task was telegraph poles, to be erected the length of the line, so that when the trains started running the signalman at Carrock could be in touch with the bridge halt at the other end. Mel's only comment was a strangulated impression of Glen Campbell singing 'The Wichita Lineman', but Greg preferred to reply by going off on his own during the day, and came to enjoy the first morning strides away from the car, to turn his back like the Warden and hunch his shoulders into the slow plod upwards. Sometimes he found himself setting off up a gentle gully scoured out by a curling mountain stream; sometimes there would be a gradual, blind ascent across undulating sheep pasture and through straggling wild orchards; sometimes a stony fellside came right down steeply to the road. And the summits he pulled up on to: there were sharp, splintered outcrops, where the highest point was a finger of rock you could only slap with your hand; wide boulder-strewn plateaux like sports fields, where a view was only available from the perimeter; or domed mounds from which vast sides of scree draped away, and seemed to be forcing you up to where you were as you stared down.

Each day Greg took a new route, gained another peak, and worked his way round from the fells at the base of the lake – abutting the ridge where he and Ruth had walked the previous summer – via those bordering the western shore, and the ranges behind them, to the mountains due west of Carrock, that swept round to the Thunacar range to the north. He became accustomed to testing the view from each summit – straight away he would look across for the Irish Sea, and sometimes when neighbouring peaks were in the way it showed only as discontinuous, one-dimensional segments of grey. On hazy days the Solway Firth was a creamy blur; in bright sun the smoke puffed rich and white from Heysham power station against the gilded sea. Gradually, from looking out over the Lake District to these distant boundaries, Greg came to scan within them and see the whole region as one. From each summit he learnt to pick out the Coniston fells to the south, the Helvellyn range to the east; beyond them, over on the far side of Ullswater, High Street and the far-eastern fells. Every day all the fells were there, but every day in new places. The configurations were constantly different. One day Coniston Old Man would be almost invisible, because other, smaller but nearer fells were in the way; the next, there was a clear sight, but it was the other side of its neighbour Wetherlam, because Greg himself had moved round. Some days Greg started out into fells bright and green in sun after rain, and found himself on a peak around which the cold fog still seethed, and the adjacent mountains were only dim receding masses, no more than darker bodyings of the clouds, and thirty feet below the way down had disappeared. Every day, even as he got to know it better, Greg had to rediscover the landscape. The mountains realigned around each other; they appeared out of drying mists and vanished into distant slanting rain; they grew green with grass and red with heather and grey with scree, and striated and knobbed, as the sun moved round and touched them; they lapsed into iron solidity as the clouds moved, into a continuous wobbly scissor-cut of silhouette as the sky filled in. You could never look and see the same thing.

On the summit of Silver How one day, the northernmost fell of the lakeshore range, which Greg had reached up the long spine that ascended from the river valley in which Carrock lay, he found an axehead. A piece of turf had been scuffed back from a rock, where a previous hiker had perhaps slumped down and thrown his feet out too heavily, and the sliver of grey rock, threaded with white like cream poured in coffee, was protruding for Greg to ease it out of the gritty soil. He rubbed his thumb over the pewter-hammered blade, and put it in his pocket. Finding it felt almost expected, almost anti-climactic. It was like seeing a woodpecker in your garden, or an airship over London; the familiarity of the thing itself – you knew *about* it so well – superseded the rareness of its actual occurrence, and the simple fact of its presence disallowed any questions as to its sudden provenance. Stone axeheads: they were in museums and Ladybird books and Alan Garner novels; primary school taught you to discover one some day.

But in the evening Greg wondered if some local history society might be interested – there might be a small museum in town that would want it as an exhibit. The next morning he went to seek out the librarian who had helped him with the railway research.

Revolving the axehead between thumb and forefinger, the

librarian led Greg back down the marble stairs to the basement with the yellow bulbs. Installed behind his desk, and Greg again in the interviewee's chair the other side, the librarian clasped his hands together and began his address, as if Greg were the television viewer he couldn't see, but averting his eyes slightly up and to the right just in case.

He spoke of axe factories, four thousand years ago, when the Lake District was forest; of Neolithic men who had unearthed the hard grey rock in shallow quarries, on sites acres-large, or even thousands of feet up on fell tops. They had shaped the shards into axeheads, mass produced axeheads in thousands, it would seem, for the job of clearing the trees from the mountain-sides, to give wood for building, for boats, for burning. The region was covered in axe factory sites: it was the main source of supply for the whole of Britain, and the axe-heads had even been exported to Europe. The trees had been cleared, the fell peaks opened to the weather – no longer secret summits amongst woodland and scrub. This axehead that lay on the blotter between the two of them would have cut down the trees that had covered Silver How.

'There would have been no view from the top,' said Greg.

'There would not,' said the librarian, staring beyond Greg's shoulder; the question could have been beamed into his ear by satellite. 'A sea of forest all around you, if you could see. Just the highest summits poking above the treeline. You'd be looking for the lakes, not the fells.'

Then the librarian spoke of how there had been settlements on the site of Carrock since the Bronze Age: a stone circle still stood in a field to the west of the town; there were ancient burial cairns by the lakeside; petrified soil humus preserved at the bottom of the lake contained the residue of elm trees cut down in the third century BC, washed down from the mountainside in the soil erosion following deforestation.

'Last time I was here we were talking about how the railway created Carrock,' said Greg.

'So it did.'

'But it has also been growing since prehistoric times.'

'Indeed.'

The librarian got up and spread his hands out to behold the

walls of old volumes behind him. After a long moment he rammed them into his pockets and jingled his coins, and then withdrew one again to hoick open the bottom drawer of his desk. It wasn't clear if his glum expression derived from there being no more detailed reference works to hand that he could assign them both to for the day, or rather an impossible, desperate surfeit. In any case, Greg's time was up. The librarian was pushing the axehead back across the table and motioning for him to keep it, and from the drawer was taking out his lunchbox.

That afternoon Greg climbed another route to the top of Silver How – this time from its western slopes, his back to the coastline. As he tramped up the slender, little-used path that zigzagged across the scrubby heather, he was looking towards the Lake District, rather than out of it at the flat pastures of West Cumbria, but he couldn't see it. From the top would be revealed the lake, the town, all the central mountain ranges. Yet this time Greg was not making such anticipations, but took with him, in the axehead still in his pocket, another new view of the Lake District. The axehead had proved as common as he had expected – no rare find, indeed – but now its commonness was phenomenal. It was like discovering that the airship you had seen whirring above the Thames had been running scheduled cross Channel services for the last forty years.

That everything had started with Wordsworth. This was what you assumed. You had the Industrial Revolution – factories, foundries, mining and quarrying for raw materials, back-to-back terraces for the workers; you had tourism – day trips, walking holidays with walnut staffs, guest houses; you had the railway conceived to service and develop both; and you had Wordsworth, who liked the mountains, hated the factories, liked the walking, hated the day trippers, and hated the railway because it would defile the mountains and bring in the day trippers. Everything had started with him. Before him the Lake District had been untouched, unspoiled: as it had always been. He had happened to live just at the time when everything had started to happen in the Lake District.

And now here was an industrial revolution that had taken place in the Bronze Age; during which the Lake District had sent its product across the country and overseas; which had defoliated an entire region when even the Lancashire cotton trade had only managed to transform one valley. All this bare rock, these tussocky, windy slopes of wiry grass and boulders, these vast sliding falls of scree: what else would grow with no soil to grow in, because there were no trees to hold the soil on? This was Amazonian destruction: forests hacked down to bare hillsides, down to the bare rock, with stone axeheads.

I don't know, thought Greg as he pulled up to the grass horizon above him, which seemed likely to be the summit, people made the Lake District like this – I suppose. The imaginative comprehension was too great for him properly to make: at best you could tell yourself, At one time the Lake District looked *like* British Columbia, or something. Now it looked like it looked. The new knowledge yet made the small town and the railway seem not merely scratchings, but new and humble: all the buildings huddled together; a single narrow line. Anything you could still see felt new.

You can't think of the Lake District-now as a denudation of Lake District-then, can you? said Greg to himself, whether from our vantage point or Wordsworth's? It was always being started, so far back that prehistoric destruction had time to become our untouched wilderness. How could there ever have been a time of which you could say, It was all right *then*? All you can do is be astonished by the number and breadth of different thens contained in our now. All you could do was what you wanted to now: that was all people would do, anyway. They would tow in caravans behind their Rovers, preserve old railways, fly supersonic fighters through the valleys, handwrite guide books containing every fell – because they thought they needed to. Now, for this moment, Greg began to see what Ruth had meant when they had walked the ridge that day. All people would do was what they wanted to.

He strode over the brow of the fell and the first thing he saw from the top was the railway. Ascending from the west he found himself looking out straight over Carrock at the green road leading directly ahead. Now there was the checked ribbon of track between the trees, running out of the edge of the town. But beyond, beyond the gap where the bridge was down and the grey road cut across, was the green line still curving evenly to the left round the embankment and out of sight, and then the huge brown mound of Scale Fell, from here its base, and the bricked-up mouth of the tunnel, obscured by the lower slopes of Thunacar. And beyond the fell?

Still Greg had not walked the rest of the line. Somewhere the other side of Scale Fell was the viaduct, and over there, far ahead somewhere in the haze, was Wetherbeck Station and the main line. Still he had no sense of how they all joined, of what the complete journey would be – and since Easter it had seemed as if the mile they had cleared and relaid to the bridge was the whole line.

'Tomorrow I'm walking to Wetherbeck,' Greg said to Ruth that evening, 'so I can't run you out to Scale. But we can walk together as far as there.'

Ruth said that was good, because she wanted to talk to him about something.

At the deserted station the next morning there were two carriages at the platform that Greg hadn't seen before: one had already been repainted from its British Rail blue into maroon and cream. Ruth opened a door and peered in. 'Just like the one I came up in, only dirtier.'

They dropped down off the end of the platform and followed the rails between the trees, Ruth striding ahead from sleeper to sleeper, Greg keeping pace to the side of the track. Not until they were in sight of the bridge platform did Ruth say, 'How many weeks have I been back, Greg?'

'A few weeks, Ruth. Five and a half weeks.'

'I think I want to leave. Tell me I should leave.'

'Why do you want to leave?'

Ruth strode on. 'I don't know.' Another silence. 'Don't you think Mel's a *fuckhead*? He keeps calling me Janice, Greg – why's he keep calling me Janice? A whole fucking summer under the same roof as him . . .'

'Janis Joplin.'

'It makes me screamingly mad, Greg.'

'That's what's wrong?'

'Oh, no,' said Ruth. 'I'll throw some shit in his face one day.

I just want you to tell me I should leave. Chuck all this stuff
up.'

'You're bored with the thesis again ... The food? Just
bored?'

'Mm, all of that. But no.'

'Why should I tell you you ought to leave?'

'Because I just asked you to!' said Ruth gaily, straddling the
rails: suddenly she seemed to have cheered up. 'I really like you,
Greg. Forget all that crap I just said.'

'I didn't do anything.'

'I'm all right now. I'm glad to be with you walking now.'
Ruth had become severe. 'That's all.'

'I – don't see how you can ask me – to tell you to leave.'

'I'm O K now. You want me to be O K?' Ruth shook her head
and her eyes were soft with tears. Their walk together reverted
to silence.

Ruth turned away when they reached the cutting and disappeared into the trees at the foot of Scale Fell, waving at Greg
without looking back. Greg waited and breathed in hard; then
he climbed up above the cutting and walked around the side of
the fell, trying to keep to the line of where he judged the tunnel
to be running deep beneath him, and walk until he saw the
other end. This will falter on and on, he knew all of a sudden:
every encounter a fresh start, and exactly the same as all the
others: it will never be any different. How could someone like
you best when you didn't say anything?

The trackbed was stretching ahead again below him. He
skidded down the steep fellside until he was standing to catch
his breath in front of the tunnel's other portal, a mile on from
the entrance at the Scale village end. He walked on, the line
now along the side of the fell, which rose away from him on his
right, and declined into the river valley to his left. A long steady
curve to the south, away from Carrock and the river, and the
green track ran into a scattering of houses and past a weedgrown
platform, where the tall grass had reached above and nearly
hidden the remains of its half-demolished station building. Greg
checked his map. This would be Tollerthwaite – there was the
narrow fell road just ahead passing underneath the dotted line
that marked the course of the railway trackbed – six miles out

of Carrock. He got up onto the platform to look over at the small hamlet. Perhaps a dozen dwellings: not many passengers from here – you had to imagine livestock being brought in from the surrounding farms to go to market, milk churns, parcels . . . Or perhaps there had never been any traffic; perhaps the station had been built only in the hope of some. It occurred to Greg too, swishing through the knee-high grass, brushing away the flies that skimmed up at him, that if Tollerthwaite had had its own station, why not Scale village as well? At neither time he had walked past had he seen any trace of one; there hadn't been any mention of one in the last years' timetables people had given him for the exhibition. Had it existed once long ago like the navvies' tunnel mess there, and been obliterated just as thoroughly? So three stations this far, maybe, apart from Carrock and the new bridge halt; the places where people got on and off the railway: one now someone's house, with a Volvo estate parked between the platforms, one a high, waving ledge of grass, and one completely vanished.

He reached the viaduct in another mile, and stopped to rest and gaze out again over the river and the sweeping dale that enclosed it. A single track earth road wound up onto the fell from the south – it was the only access Greg could see to the viaduct, and the only way the railway builders could have approached the site. Everything up that track. Not a building to be seen all around: the hills hid any. The arched span still stood for itself, the thistles and poppies spreading along it now in purple and red flower. A hawk bumped and sagged and bored on the air above. This was the stage of the line to attain, Greg could see – what came after would be consolidation. Bring people as far as here.

A mile past the viaduct he came upon people working on the line. A wooden platform, a boarded-up station cottage, and a yellow JCB digging out the ground in front of them. Here was Knarfoot Station – Knarfoot village the map showed to be two miles away over the fells, in the next valley. Three men – Greg recognised with surprise the signwriting man in an orange waterproof – stood around as the digger bit into the earth; two more were mending the platform fence with new palings. As he came up the signwriting man said, 'Hello Greg,' and then his

head returned to following the rheumatic delving and swivelling
and dumping of the JCB. Greg watched with him.

'We're doing well,' said the signwriting man after a while.
Several more clawfuls and he explained, 'People who lived here
before filled in the trackbed for their lawn. Was level with the
platform. We've nearly dug it out. And John and Mick in there'
– he pointed to the open door of the cottage, and now Greg
heard a scraping and knocking within – 'they're doing well on
the plastering, and' (over to the platform) 'those chaps'll be
creosoting the fence later on.'

'Whose idea is all this?' asked Greg. This was extraordinary!
Eight miles from Carrock! 'What for?'

'Oh, Mr Edwards is organising it. Decided it had to be done
now before it got even worse.' He led Greg to the doorway of
the cottage and showed him the scorched and blistered front
door. 'Got burnt out a few years ago. Black horrible mess when
we started. He said renovate it now before it goes altogether.'

'Who does it belong to?'

'I don't know that,' said the signwriting man. 'I've just been
turning up here with the rest of the gang when he told us to.
He sorted it all out.'

Inside the station cottage the two men – apart from the
signwriting man Greg didn't recognise these new volunteers –
had been laying new floorboards on the ground floor, and above
them the ceiling timbers were fresh yellow wood. They had
plastered two walls downstairs already, and one man was beginning on the third while the other was filling in the ceiling. 'Burnt
beams lying everywhere when we opened it up,' pronounced
the signwriting man. 'A ruin.'

'But what's it going to be used for?' exclaimed Greg, 'and
when?'

'He just wants it ready,' the signwriting man said. 'Told me
he wants to keep things moving.' He looked out past the far
end of the platform. 'Used to be a signalbox down there – he
wants that put back.' Then he went back over to the JCB
spectators, calling to Greg, 'You walked all the way out here
from the town?'

'Walking the whole line.'

'Not many people do that,' said the signwriting man. 'He

comes out here sometimes of a lunchtime,' he added, 'but not today, it looks.' Greg left him there in superintendence, now after each new bite of earth pointing mutely to the spot where the JCB should dig next. Greg went on a few hundred yards until the station and its work party were small in the distance, and then sat down under a tree to eat his lunch. From there he watched the yellow digger nod, and rear, and pour its soil to the side in a heap, and the two men with their invisibly tiny brushes work slowly along the platform fence, which was turning dark at the same speed.

After Knarfoot the countryside around the railway began to flatten out: he was nearing the pale, hazy plain where the line had first emerged when he had looked across from the top of Thunacar. The craggy, fissured mountains became low, dumpy hills, and then subsided into undulating fields. Nearby, the river ran level with the old line. Along the trackbed Greg now found hay dumped in circular black plastic rolls, discarded tangles of rusty barbed wire, and heaps of hardcore, smashed tile fireplaces and giant perished tyres. One stretch of the line was a brown quagmire where farm tractors had left deep castellated furrows. At several places Greg had to pick his way over fences that barred his way. He passed through one more station – Lower Keldale was the nearest village in the map – which was a stone platform in a small wood. He almost didn't recognise it, because the trackbed had shrunk to a snaking path between the trees that actually went up on to and along the mossy platform itself. There was nothing else left.

Then, three miles from Wetherbeck, the line disappeared completely. It went below a bridge carrying a minor road, was blocked by a gate underneath, and nothing came out the other side: the other side was a flat hay field shimmering in the sun. Greg took his bearing on a single tree ahead, in the direction of where the line should lead, and stumbled round the bumpy edge of the field. He picked up the trackbed again beyond a second large field, and another fence: altogether about a quarter of a mile of the line looked to have been obliterated. What was the railway going to do about this?

Greg checked his watch and found that he had less than an

hour to reach Wetherbeck before the last bus left for Carrock. Suddenly stiff and weary, he noticed little about the final stages of the line, but there seemed little to notice: flattish farmland, scattered copses of trees, a yard full of lorries and trailers. He kicked on, and eventually the trackbed crossed a low bridge spanning the Wether Beck – he had to push through the shoulder-high rhododendron bushes that had colonised it – and Greg came out in Wetherbeck Station opposite the main line. The Carrock branch trains, he now saw, would have run in along the other side of the platform where he had met Ruth.

He had time to sink down on to a bench outside the station for ten minutes, and see that Wetherbeck's main street was a terrace of houses, a garage of corrugated sheds with engines being revved inside and a tail-less dog pacing at the end of its rope, and a General Stores with tins of peas in the window, and then the bus picked him up outside the Station Hotel. Having taken seven hours to walk from Carrock to Wetherbeck, he travelled back in forty minutes.

But it was the time and length of the day's journey that stayed with Greg. To walk the line had taken him all day. Fifteen miles: so far they hadn't completed restoring one of them. Restoring the whole line meant coming all the way that he had come – cutting down more woods, clearing fourteen more miles of culverts and cuttings, laying track along every yard, and in places the line had gone altogether and would somehow have to be built again, if at all, as though it had never existed. It had been a long cross-country walk – a deserted long distance footpath through the mountains, dales and fields. This was all there was. Greg relaxed on the bus and reran in his mind the views from the embankment, the viaduct, across to the eastern plain, rebuilt for himself the small stations out in the country, remembered how the scenery and the course of the line had changed continually the whole way – how he had started in the mountains and ended in the plain, gone high over the river on the viaduct and later travelled alongside it, walked round the side of the fells when the line tunnelled deep underneath and then further on found the line itself hugging the fellside. He was euphoric and fatigued at completing the walk he had set himself, and at the same time found himself being distantly and sadly rational about the railway, for in putting the whole journey together for himself he was also recalling the stillness, the solitude of the day. He had come upon the men at Knarfoot, and no one else, the whole way to Wetherbeck. Perhaps Greg was too tired: now the quietness seemed to say not that this lost green road was waiting for a railway again – why should it be? – but that the railway had gone, had been before, and the people who had been with it, and what was left was too much for people to do, except if they wanted to walk it as he had done, for it was a fine walk.

Greg went up to the station at lunchtime the following day, on the offchance of finding Edwards. Les was there, unloading some large drums of wire from his truck – for the telegraph poles? – and rolling them into the booking hall, but no Edwards.

'I was hoping Ashley might be around,' Greg said, 'so I could brag to him at having walked the line now. I did it yesterday – all the way. I suppose he's out at the other station, is he?'

'What other station? You know what his nibs thinks about the bridge platform.'

'The . . . work party out at Knarfoot,' said Greg, the penny dropping at once, and Les leant on the tailgate of his truck and stared back, and Greg went on and told of the hired JCB and the ruined cottage and its new ceiling and floors and the plastering and the fence outside and the plan to rebuild the signalbox, and soon Les was very still and tapping his fingertips lightly on the top of the tailgate.

'The idea was to, stop it, deteriorating any further,' ventured Greg, 'apparently. I could see what they meant . . .' But he thought, What for?

'Some people – live in their own – little world.' Les heaved off another drum and staggered with furious momentum into the booking hall. Greg, lugging one down from the truck himself, heard Les's bomp to the floor. 'We are trying to get this line ready for opening,' Les called as he emerged and Greg tottered past, 'and we've only got a couple of weeks left, and money is very short, and there is too much still to do. He's helping little enough with that. And we're supposed to be running things by committee.'

Les threw the last drum through the booking hall doorway and banged the doors shut on it, then got into his truck and drove off, and Greg knew where he was going.

The hostel phone rang a lot for Greg that evening. First Les, then Victor Senior the accountant, then Adrian Shillingworth, then each of them again at least once more, until eventually Mel answered the next call, glaring at Greg, and said, 'Crewe Central', but this time it only confused a hosteller wanting to book. Les rang to say thankyou to Greg, but Greg said he'd only been for a walk, and Les said he'd been out there and, we'll see . . . Victor Senior wanted to hear all the facts again, and then said that matters had been coming to a head for a while, and that the whole thing beat him, and Adrian wanted to hear them as well and said to Greg that Edwards treated the line 'like his own toy railway'.

'Don't you worry,' Les assured Greg. 'None of those blokes out there knew we didn't know. All'd had their ears bent by him. You haven't dropped him in anything.' But Greg, feeling half guilty, primarily because he felt half pleased too, knew he had.

Chapter Seventeen

As Les was starting into his address from the stage to the packed Church Hall, Edwards – he was next to speak – was unloading a large number of books from his briefcase and piling them into a rampart on the table in front of him.

'Without Ashley's efforts,' Les was saying, reading gruffly and tonelessly from his prepared speech on a pack of index cards, 'there would be no railway. He was, as the phrase goes, the prime mover. He got things going. It was his idea. We should remember that, and I would like to express our gratitude for it.' Shattering applause exploded with nervous suddenness.

This was the first Extraordinary General Meeting of the railway company's shareholders (Greg was sitting at the back), convened, following the discovery of the secret Knarfoot operation, to vote on a motion of no confidence in Edwards. A week before the railway was due to reopen, it was proposing to dispose of its Chairman and founder.

So far, however, the meeting had listened quietly and reasonably to a succession of respectful, even doggedly fulsome tributes to Edwards's leadership, and had applauded recklessly. It had heard how a recent local paper's survey had found that a majority of Carrock's population not only knew about the railway (nearly five hundred had taken out shares in it), but wanted to see it reopened all the way to Wetherbeck. How already three steam locomotives had been attracted to the line. How the share issue had been completely successful, and fundraising for the volunteer restoration effort consistently effective. And how, in the space of a year, a mile of track had been relaid, and the station rebuilt, and the initial section of the line made ready for the first passengers in sixteen years. Edwards had endured all this with an expression of injured boredom.

But Les was reading on. 'But I must now come on to the matter in hand, namely the unauthorised and underhand misappropriation of company funds to institute the renovation of Knarfoot station. Ladies and gentlemen, I have to say that this is only the latest in a catalogue of recent and – strange, I have to say – preoccupations on the part of Mr Edwards. During the last couple of months, for example, he has been urging my fellow directors and myself to draw up detailed plans for introducing freight traffic on the railway. The reason given was that it would take heavy loads off the roads, and be a source of new employment for the town. Ladies and gentlemen, we still have fourteen miles of track to relay before the connection with British Rail can be reinstated. Mr Edwards has also been lobbying our local MP on the railway's behalf, and on a regular basis, for a national tax on cars and lorries to pay for maintenance of the road network – to redress the anomaly, as he puts it, of the railways having to pay for the upkeep of their own track. He has been meeting with the Lake District Tourist Board to press for the introduction of quotas limiting the number of cars allowed within the national park boundaries. And now, above all, we have money being spent – secretly – on restoring a station, which is not even the property of the railway company, which is on the far side of the Carrs Viaduct, and which is some seven miles from the current end of the line. And when we can't even afford to reconstruct the bridge over Force Road.

'Ladies and gentlemen, it is little wonder that nowadays Mr Edwards is rarely seen up at the station when restoration work is in progress. He is too busy with these other utterly irrelevant schemes. We all know about his political opinions, but, ladies and gentlemen, the railway is supposed to be opening to the public *next week*! And the unofficial activities of our Chairman are distracting attention from this, and diverting essential funds from it. At the present time we need democratic decisions in the management of this company – decisions that everyone knows about and agrees with. Not autocratic and secret ones. We need realism, ladies and gentlemen, financial and practical realism, if this severely under-capitalised company is to survive at all. Next week we will be committing ourselves to running a passenger service every day except Tuesdays for the rest of the summer.

TRAIN, TRAIN

To running a proper railway, with stations and track and engines and carriages, even if it is only a mile long. It is a big risk. That is all we can do for the present, but it is quite enough. For the foreseeable future the railway can only be a short, summer-only, steam-operated line for tourist rides. We cannot afford to do any more. And ladies and gentlemen – we haven't *done* any more. So far this is all we have managed to do! To be thinking of anything more at the current moment is irresponsible and ludicrously premature. To try to do it, to try and extend any nearer Wetherbeck already, would jeopardise the entire project.' Shattering applause again as Les sat down.

Edwards got slowly to his feet. He patted the pile of books together, rested his knuckles on them and leant forward for a long moment, scrutinising every part of the audience. 'In Britain,' he began, 'we're more interested in our past than in our present. We exalt Victorian values over modern values. We like stately homes better than a housing policy. The National Trust more than the National Health Service. We like steam engines better than railways. We're so busy thinking that things must be the same as they always were, *because* they always were, that we don't see what is actually happening now – we don't see how all the time we're allowing the present to damage the future.

'This is the country we live in. A *private* country. A privatised country. A country which respects the privacy of people's great wealth. Which respects the privacy of their right as private citizens to private health care. A country which, right now, is preparing to sell off its nuclear power industry – *nuclear power* – into private ownership. And then its water supplies. Private water: and we all thought it was ours. Having already, this country, sold off its gas, its telephone system, its bus services, the Trustee Savings Bank, and now – we've already seen the announcement that the Settle and Carlisle must be sold off, or closed – is now talking about privatising British Rail . . .'

A murmur was travelling around the hall. Greg felt a tap on his shoulder. It was Fellows, now noisily exchanging seats with the person in the row behind. 'Extorted fifty quid from me for his share issue swindle,' said Fellows into Greg's ear in a loud stage whisper. 'High time to get after him.'

'. . . A market-led country, then: a consumerist country – hospitals aren't to have patients, but consumers: if it can't be sold, it can't be needed. A country of theme parks, hypermarkets, marinas, Metro Centres – a country which now spends every minute of its time being *sold* to . . .'

'Ashley –' said Victor Senior, who was chairing the meeting.

'Twenty years ago,' continued Edwards quickly, 'we closed down a third of our railway system: not profitable enough, according to the government then in power. A few years ago we shut down most of the steel industry, and put tens of thousands of men out of work: not profitable enough – and so the great Consett steel works is now a ploughed field returning to grass. These days it's the turn of the coal mines: not, according to a recent chairman brought in from America on a million-pound transfer fee, not profitable enough: close them down too. Now, who are these industries for? The stock market? People with Porsches and portfolios? Or the country? –'

'This is not the place for preaching politics,' someone called out.

'– And in so doing, by letting things go to the wall, Devil take the hindmost, Darwin and natural selection and the law of the jungle, by ignoring the evidence of our own eyes, all that happens is that things slide, and the more we let them the more they slide, until eventually recovery is catastrophically more difficult, if it is even still possible at all, than if we had kept our eyes open, and looked around us.

'But of course, says our prime minister, there is no such thing as society. No such thing as society, only – individuals. And people must fend for themselves . . .' (coughs and sighs punctuated his words; chairs scraped on the floor) '. . . if they end up with a lot, that proves they must have earned it. If they end up with a little, it proves they don't deserve any more. So we live in a country which can cut the top rate of income tax to forty per cent, and give the chairman of the Burton Group an *extra* quarter of a million a year, rather than spend a penny more on our hospitals. So we *reduce* housing benefit for the old and disabled: we actually reduce it – if they need any more let them seek charity from the church. No such thing as society. This is the fair, equitable, democratic country we live in. Is this the future? Does all this seem like progress? Improvement? Advancement? Or *does* it indeed remind us, this litany of decay, complacency, neglect, division, exploitation and simple callousness – does it remind us rather of previous eras, of the workhouse, of the Jarrow marches, of Florence Nightingale in the Crimea – of the distant, dirty, disgraced, past?'

'Are we going to sit here being lectured all night?' cut in someone.

'What does all this have to do with the railway?' someone else called.

Edwards stopped, momentarily speechless. 'What does it have to do with the railway?' he repeated incredulously. He paused. 'OK. Let's look at it another way. Think of it in terms of pollution – in terms of public health, even. We have entire forests in Scandinavia, all over Europe, in fact, dying as a result of acid rain: reduced to blackened, scorched stumps. Lakes in Wales entirely lifeless, dead, for the same reason. Who is responsible? Who refuses, in the face of the concerted opposition of the rest of Europe, to modify the emissions from its power stations? Great Britain. The North Sea: overflowing with raw sewage. Or we could take the lead levels in the blood of children living near the intersection of the M25 and M4. The *tens* of *thousands* of deaths on our roads every year – all this is sheer madness –'

'Go on, tell us the Test Match score as well!' yelled Fellows.

'I'm ready to vote now!' a man near the front was calling out.

What were they going to do, thought Greg. He has to have his say – but how much more? Now the hall was ringing with shouts of protest, and several people were on their feet.

'Let me – let me read you –' Edwards was shouting above the hubbub, perspiration standing out on his pink forehead, 'let me read you something – let me read you something said in 1973 by none other than Edward Heath.' He extracted a paperback from the pile in front of him and held it up. '*English Culture and the Decline of the Industrial Spirit*, by Martin J. Wiener.' People were craning forward to peer at the book's cover. 'The point is this,' Edwards continued as he leafed through for the page. 'Quite simply, what is a railway *for*?' He looked up again. 'Edward Heath, 1973, then:

"The alternative to expansion is not, as some occasionally seem to suppose, an England of quiet market towns linked only by trains puffing slowly and peacefully through green meadows".'

There was a beat of silence. Then, 'Exactly!' exclaimed Les from the platform, his arms outraised. 'What do you think it means, then, Ashley?'

'It means,' said Edwards, 'what is the point of a railway that doesn't go anywhere? OK – you see, I'm trying to show you, since people seem to think I'm masterminding some kind of clandestine Marxist conspiracy, that what is at issue here is the entire future of the railway, the whole point of running it at all. Is it going to be of the slightest use, at all, to anyone? So OK, here's someone else – it's not just me saying all this stuff; I haven't made it all up . . .' He fished among the pile for another book, and then brandished it aloft. 'The former chairmain of ICI – yes – yes' – Edwards held his hand up to hush the anticipated outcry – 'Sir John Harvey-Jones, now regarded as the most able and dynamic industrial strategist for years, I gather. His new book, *Making It Happen: Reflections on Leadership*:

"If we think we can rejuvenate industrially by attracting foreign tourists to visit ancient castles manned by people standing around in suits of armour, we must be out of our tiny minds".'

'Come and work for me, then!' shouted Fellows.

'Ashley, we agree!' said Victor Senior. 'Why do you think we wouldn't? Of course he's right! Look . . .' – his voice became quiet with embarrassment – '. . . you're cutting your own throat. This is your only chance to defend yourself against a potentially irreversible vote of no confidence in your Chairmanship of this company. For heaven's sake use it – please!'

'Of course Sir John's right,' added Les to the audience, as if the man with flowing locks gazing keenly out from the book jacket could hear the debate. 'We're not trying to turn the clock back and run the railway as if the main road and thirty-nine ton lorries didn't exist. It's been closed twenty years. *You're* trying to pretend this is still before the war and we can reopen as if nothing's changed. We're just trying, for the time being, to run a small railway for holidaymakers to ride on. You do what you can.'

'*No!*' pleaded Edwards. 'You have to do the whole thing. It's *nothing* in bits. I'm trying to safeguard the future of the whole thing. It's decayed away so far already, if we don't preserve what's still left now, soon there won't be anything. How much longer before the viaduct becomes unsafe? How much longer before that – *that* – actually falls down? If the railway isn't complete, it's nothing. I've compromised enough – I accepted all the luxury Pullman plans, the industrial heritage holidays stuff, all this . . . necessary, *wealth creation* for the line. But you just water it down, and water it down, until eventually you forget about the original point of doing it all, and become satisfied with useless, twee, picturesque smallness, and think that's all there is, and all there need be.'

'We want to do the whole thing,' said Les. 'But for the time being there's no money. *You* tell us where to get it! We have to be cautious. For the present we have to compromise.'

'The middle way!' jeered Edwards. 'The British genius for moderation. Never go too far . . .' He was reaching for another book. 'Is a mile-long joyride going to help Carrock's traffic problem? Is it going to be a crucial new link for Carrock when the Channel tunnel starts sending trains straight through from Europe? Is it going to take a single heavy lorry off our roads?'

'These things take *time*, Ashley,' said Senior. For the moment the hall was hushed and engrossed. Heads turned left, then right, then back left. 'Years and years – more than we can conceive. It's an immense project. We can hope that one day trains will bring people to Carrock again. We can only hope. That's the best hope of all – but it's an immense project.'

'So let's *start*, for Christ's sake!' Edwards held up the new paperback: 'Kenneth Morgan's *Labour in Power 1945-1951* –' and the hall erupted again.

'You really think Tony Benn's going to be the next Labour leader?' cried Fellows. 'You *really* think that?'

'Aneurin Bevan –' Greg could hear Edwards shouting into the uproar, 'Aneurin Bevan –'

'This isn't the *News on Sunday*,' called someone, 'and it's not going to end up like it.'

'You used shareholders' money, in secret, on a preposterous and wasteful venture,' insisted Adrian from the stage. 'That's all. That's all we're concerned with.'

'*You're* stuck in the past, Mr Edwards. That's your socialism – 1945.'

'Not a movement, but a monument!' A wave of laughter broke out. 'Mick McGahey said that, sir, *Mick McGahey*!'

'This has nothing to do with anything!'

'– for *half* a Health Service?' Edwards's voice was hoarse and quavering into a screech. 'Did he try for a *bit* of a Health Service –?'

Behind Greg, Fellows was on his feet and roaring, 'You're mad! You're mad!'

Victor Senior waved his arms for order. 'We move to a vote. You've had your chance, Ashley.' The shouting stopped, and people sat down again. One arm remained up and waving frantically for attention. 'The last comment, then,' said Senior, pointing the hand out.

The man stood up, and the hall was quiet. 'I am a shareholder in the railway – a comparatively modest amount – and, um, I am also a history teacher at the secondary school here, and –' The man swallowed. His eyes darted nervously. The audience waited on his words. '– And, um, I would just like to say that – um – contrary to his original plans and his own deeply-held convictions, and er, the reason why it is still there now, er – owing to the recalcitrance of the doctors and the BMA – and I have myself read the particular book to which Mr Edwards refers, incorrigible recalcitrance – Aneurin Bevan was in fact forced to incorporate private medicine into the National Health Service.' The man sat down hurriedly to a baffled silence, muttering, 'Most people *don't* know that . . .'

Then Fellows began chanting, 'Vote! Vote!' Edwards was shaking his head in amused disbelief. The chant was taken up by others, and slow handclapping as well, and Edwards, sprawled in his seat now and gazing at the picture of Attlee on the cover of *Labour in Power*, called back repeatedly, 'Tell me I'm wrong! Tell me *anything* I've said that isn't true!'

TRAIN, TRAIN

Victor Senior eventually restored order by seizing two of Edwards's books and slamming them together with a report like a gunshot, and the show of hands in favour of the no confidence motion was unanimous. Edwards stared ahead, then shrugged his shoulders and began packing his books back into his briefcase.

'Well, Ashley . . . ?' said Victor Senior after an expectant silence.

'Well what?'

'What next?'

'You tell me,' scoffed Edwards.

'Are you planning to . . . can we expect your resignation?'

'Oh yes.' Edwards stood up with his hands in his pockets and looked at the ceiling. 'I hereby resign as Chairman of the Carrock trainset.'

Chapter Eighteen

So Les had become the new Chairman, Fellows had grabbed Greg's hand and shaken it hard, and as everyone surged for the doors amid a crashing of chairs, the two of them had been borne out into the street.

The next morning Mel woke up with a soaring temperature, and by lunchtime was in bed sweltering and raving with a bad dose of flu, and doctor's instructions to stay there for at least two days. '*I walk the line,*' he ranted in a flat, throaty rumble as Greg went in with aspirins and honey drinks; at Ruth he snarled something about the Aga Khan making all his money from selling kitchen ranges. On the third day, past the fever but still not well enough to get up, he croaked, 'New Wainwrights!'

'Not new,' said Greg, 'except if you want coffee-table books,' and Mel looked ill again, but Greg sent Ruth into town that morning to see what she could find. She came back with a thin pamphlet on the old drove roads of Eastern Lakeland, which she said according to Edwards was the latest Wainwright-Wainwright, you could see how shaky the handwriting had become, and Flannery O'Connor's *The Violent Bear It Away*, which she said looked interesting. But Mel, emerging blearily from his twisted hump of blankets at the end of the day, said with the frail wonder that succeeds delirium that it was the weirdest, most depressing, most *demented*, book he'd ever read.

'I should ring Ashley,' Greg said to Ruth. 'Did he seem all right?'

Ruth shrugged a disinterested yes and stared back, which Greg took as meaning she hadn't noticed or didn't care. Not everyone cares about this railway, he reminded himself humbly.

There was no time to call in on or even phone Edwards, though let alone go up to the station. Mel was ill for nearly a week, and Greg was left in charge. Every day was busy all day: as well as organising meals, buying the food, taking bookings and doing the accounts, he had to look after Mel. Soon he began to suspect that he would miss the first day of trains at Carrock altogether.

But two days before Saturday's opening ceremony Mel appeared in the kitchen to take over dinner again quietly and deliberately, muttering agitated recollections of his fever and its nightmare revelation of the Hair-grease Party: 'Shining, smoothed-down, slicked-down hair, all over the Cabinet, Greg, everywhere you look, count them all off . . . Energy Secretary, Education Secretary, Transport Secretary, Employment Secretary, Tory Party Chairman, even . . . Smothered in Brylcreem – gleaming, dripping with it . . . Shut my eyes and listened to their voices and could *still* hear their hair . . .'

Later that evening it was Edwards who phoned Greg.

His voice was flat and heavy. 'I can't stay here, Greg, I can't stay here.' The words sounded sighed out rather than spoken: no breath in them. 'How can I stay here while they open it like that? I can't be there then.' There was a slow, audible drawing-in of breath. 'You're the only one who's not mixed up in all of this, Greg, all this stupid business over a J C B . . . All that work . . . no one else in town who knows about the whole plan of how it should have been but didn't ruin everything in one evening . . .'

Greg opened his mouth, but Edwards was already saying, 'If we could just go for one last walk along the line, since you haven't been along it yet, at least I could show someone. Would you do that? Could we do that tomorrow?'

Greg didn't want to reply with silence, but words still failed him. Finally he said, 'In fact, only a few days ago I went –'

'I know I'm imposing,' Edwards broke in. 'I know I put people's backs up, just blunder on. Then I'll leave. I ought to leave.'

So Greg said yes.

On the Friday, then, the two of them drove out to Force Road in the middle of the day, and Edwards parked by the old bridge. He sat in the car while Greg scrambled up the bank to take a quick look down the line. Telegraph poles draped their wires away back towards Carrock. A large signal gantry stood over the track just beyond the platform, a frame of heavy levers alongside. On the platform itself were two new maroon painted wrought-iron benches, several tubs of flowers, and a large signboard in maroon letters that read FORCE HALT. There was no one about.

'It's all ready for tomorrow,' Greg said quietly on returning to the car, and Edwards swung his door open and said, 'Let's go.'

They set off towards Scale, skirting Force Road Station, where Edwards peered glumly through the bushes at the Volvo estate parked on the old platform, and the sunbeds on the smooth lawn where the tracks had been, and said, 'Sunday supplements.' All the way along the embankment he talked wistfully of how tracklaying here would be so simple, the whole earthwork was so well built there hadn't been a subsidence this century – and imagine the view from the carriage as the train curved out towards Scale Fell! And right now British Rail were getting rid of some two-car diesel trains that would be ideal for the branch – probably even worked on it when it was open – and next year or the year after would be too late, they'd have long gone for scrap by then. And just think (further on) how much petrol that trainload of people was saving now that they didn't have to use their cars! And what a start to a holiday, if this was your approach to Carrock! Then as soon as the Volvo-owners got out . . . and just rebuild that bridge back at Force Road . . . Edwards's burgeoning good mood faltered, and as the sun gilded his glasses and effaced his eyes his mouth became surly. 'A good idea like this – a pure, social idea – and you let people in on the act and they start sticking their oar in, their politics, their personalities . . .'

'The local people all bought shares!' protested Greg – it was the first thing he'd said since leaving the car. 'You wanted democracy. The hall was packed.'

Edwards was shaking his head. 'They prefer a toy railway to a real railway,' he pronounced. 'To go with the coffee shops and the car parks and the coach parties.' He said it as an apophthegm, as if a gnomic admonition against idealism: a simple distillation, newly-perceived, of how people were. *They prefer a toy railway to a real railway.* But to Greg it only seemed like Edwards's private talisman, his personal mantra, and Greg's mind wandered to thinking again, with dread and amazement, How can he not know I was the one who shopped him?

Edwards was quickening his step as they approached the tunnel mouth, seemingly wanting to put some distance between himself and Greg.

'The last time I came along here I . . .' Greg tried again, but as Edwards hauled open the iron door and turned to face Greg doubtfully Greg could see he wasn't listening, and that there was nothing for it but to go with him.

Edwards pulled a torch out of his pocket and switched it on as he lifted one leg inside the door. 'I put my own money into the Knarfoot renovation,' he said, so quietly that Greg, yards down the cutting, could hardly hear, 'as much of my own as I used of the company's' – and ducked inside.

So Greg went after, and, a year on from the first time, when he had briefly followed his own torch beam as it wavered in his hand, and then later sheltered from the rain with Ruth, again found himself stumbling through the pouring blackness that closed in and shrank away and plipped and dropped and rang out, and skidded and splashed under your feet, and this time listened to Edwards's hollow voice talking about England and its past.

'Take the Falklands,' it boomed. 'The typical, hopeless in-ability to look to the future, to see anything coming – so eventually it happens. But then you can think you're fighting the Second World War over again, and everything's brilliant efficiency.

'Look at the steel industry. Look at the inner cities. Let it all decay until it requires a superhuman effort to build it up again, and what you finally take credit for rejuvenating is always so much *less* – so much irrevocably lost – so much irremediable human loss . . .

'Appeal to the past . . . we idolise *past technology*.' The words rippled and faded in the blackness. Edwards's torch beam bounced on ahead.

'Slow down, can you?' Greg panted out in agitation. The

torch beam swung round into his face. 'Just slow down a bit.'

'Here,' said Edwards, and with a few gritty footfalls the torch came into Greg's hand. So Greg led the way, treading unsteadily into the dark – you needed one torch shining ahead to show you the arch of the tunnel roof and the way ahead, and another for where to place your feet – and now Greg could sense Edwards at his heels, a stride pattern shuffling and breaking to adjust without success to Greg's slower pace, and Edwards's voice now dogging him at his shoulder, newly confidential, urging and insisting, '*Past* technological supremacy – not a sentimental yearning but a genuine attachment – truly thinking that, in some serendipitous, stentorian way, the steam engine still represents the pinnacle of British enterprise . . . "When did we start to go wrong?" we say, finding that we have nothing to look to but back – and don't realise that *things have always been this way . . .*'

Swirling, reboant, the words crowded in around Greg, flapped and pecked at him, settled and clustered on him from nowhere in the darkness: were everywhere. *Who am I?* he came to think in dull panic, *who am I?* All I am is someone people talk at: what does that make me?

And all the time that Edwards's voice rolled around the walls, a guided tour of nothing but his own words, selling you a different line, *his* line, treating of the past, it only made Greg think of the present: how some things changed, and others didn't, and what you ended up with was how things were. The past of a year ago was Carrock Station boarded up and its platform showered with glass, and a mile of thicket and winding dog-walk leading to a bridge parapet; the present was a station full of rolling-stock and a mile of track leading to a new halt –

'. . . The nation that invented the railway,' resounded Edwards's proud, amused voice, 'now become a nation of trainspotters . . .'

– But the year-ago's past of this tunnel was also its present: nothing had changed, except that another year's worth of water had streamed down its slimy brickwork. 'What is significant, Ashley,' Greg said suddenly, his words crying out sharply and bringing them both to a halt, 'is the pace of things. The potential momentum of things.'

'I'm sorry?'

'The evidence of how slowly things happen. How slowly things have actually been able to happen,' Greg said with deliberation, trying to let the words come to him. 'The *cost* of things. This tunnel took three years to build. People got cholera working out here. Ten of them died. Just for this. One tunnel. Something can't be important and easy. Or difficult and quick. If something's been staring people in the face for years – and it still is – and everyone knows it is – that's because no one's managed to do it yet.'

The trickle of water lined the silence.

'The lesson is in how things are,' said Greg. 'In what people have actually been able to do. In what they've actually let happen. Even the bad. It's really easy just to let rich people go on making even more money.'

The trickle of water.

They shuffled on, until eventually Edwards asked for the torch and said they were near the end, and soon the door was clanging open. As they stepped out into thin sunshine spreading through slow-curling clouds Edwards said, 'You're right, in fact. The lesson is that some things *are* always going to be there because it was right to do them in the first place, and this will always be here – a secret, if you like, almost forgotten – but closed up and ready for whoever comes to reopen it.' He eased the door to again solemnly. 'You can't gainsay the true past.'

It wasn't what Greg had meant, to be offered a glimpse of King Arthur and his knights slumbrous beneath Glastonbury Tor, and anyway to his raw and fractious mind of the moment Edwards's words only cast him again as the reactionary, came only as another prepared speech, delivered for the speaker's benefit, and pious and sentimental too. To Greg the dank, ravelling tunnel said that once was enough: if it stood for anything outside itself then it was for something that should never have happened – a man who should never have been in charge of public projects back then and ten more who needn't have died: something that was at least past – and no one need ever go in there again, and the last year hadn't changed that. *You don't listen, do you?* he thought, as Edwards strolled alongside, smiling into the sun, all the desperation of the night before gone. You only called me out here to lecture me, and you wouldn't even let me tell you what I'd done to you. You never listen to anything; you just constantly assure yourself that everyone is listening to you, and that one day they'll all come round, if they haven't already.

'How much further, Ashley?' Greg was getting tired. Four miles already without stopping . . .

'Just to the viaduct.' Edwards strode on.

At least they were in the open air again – new air, amongst trees and hills, and a grassy track under their feet. 'Leaving aside the past, Ashley,' puffed Greg, 'you have to deal with what there is, with what you can actually do, with what people will really listen to. You can't do what you can't do.'

'So you do a little bit and then stop and say, *phew*! Aren't we clever!' Edwards shrugged his shoulders. 'Wilsonism, Greg. Callaghanism. Get elected to do something, and then sell out.'

'You can't go faster than people will let you. Right now people aren't very interested in socialism, in notions of community. This country simply isn't interested – it just voted so. I don't know what you do.'

'So to turn that tide – to counter Thatcher's revolution with any momentum – you need radical measures.'

'And either people won't listen in the first place, or you'll turn them off altogether.'

'So what about this?' said Edwards, and they climbed up onto the platform of waving grass at Tollerthwaite Station.

'What about it?'

'Do you think there should be a timeshare estate right here? This station building to be restored as "Porter's Bistro"? Yes – nice little timeshares, nice little Alpine-style chalets, ever so nice in this nice spot for a nice break from stockbroking and oh *look!* must have been a nice little country station here once – *right where we are now?*'

'You're kidding.'

'Lake District Planning Board threw the application out three times. Never seemed likely.' Edwards scratched his beard. 'This week the Environment Secretary reversed the decision. Done the same thing ten times already this year. It was in the local paper – the only chance now is a public inquiry.' He gave the grass a slashing kick. 'You can't *wait*, Greg. It'll be too late! These things are happening – this country *is* what it is – being changed for ever.'

There was silence between them.

'You're saying I'm out of date, Greg. Railways are out of date, community's out of date, socialism's out of date. This is the modern world-market world: those things have gone, closed down, been abandoned. Not a movement but a –'

'No!' exclaimed Greg. But what else? How could he say, You're right, but you're the last person who should be saying this? That Edwards was pathologically self-absorbed, deludedly, romantically idealistic, potentially demagogic, got his ideas from books . . . but right? The person people should listen to, though they never would? Or that in any case rebuilding an old railway would serve nothing, was just playing games, merely totemic – that the only radical measure was an anti-Tory majority in Parliament?

But Edwards saved him. 'At the moment there's no one,' he was saying. 'It needs some *prophetic* figure: no one like that on the left just now, and no one in sight . . . but no one less will do . . .' and he was walking on.

Greg couldn't see any point in going on, and his legs were stiff and sore. 'Ashley –' he called.

'It's not much further. Viaduct's just up ahead.'

So Greg trudged on, yards behind, but soon he stopped again. 'No,' he shouted ahead to Edwards. 'Can't. Too far. Too tired.'

Edwards sauntered back with desultory steps, glancing back over his shoulder to where the line curved on, level and green, and out of sight around the side of the fell. 'Bottling out,' he said amiably.

Greg shook his head, and stood with hands on hips.

'It's just up ahead,' said Edwards after a pause. 'Mile, mile and a bit. We must see the viaduct. Just round this bend.'

'I'm sorry, Ashley.'

'But it's the finest thing on the railway. Finest thing you'll ever see.'

Greg shook his head again. The two of them stared ahead together, to where the green road disappeared, and where, an uncertain distance on and hidden from them, would be the viaduct.

'Beautiful icon,' said Edwards. 'Like a causeway in air: taking everyone across: raising them high. People built it once. It was used once. We can still use it again. I'll always believe it'll be reopened one day.'

In his mind's eye Greg saw the same – the march of soaring arches joining together to carry the one line, always to be there – but what Greg saw was an empty viaduct in the middle of nowhere, grass where the track should be, and nothing leading up to it, and nothing leading on.

He turned round and started back towards Tollerthwaite, his legs lighter now that he knew they were going back, and a long while went by before Edwards began to scuff along reluctantly a distance behind. Once Edwards muttered out of the silence, 'The English – just think in these narrow straight lines . . .', and then again later, 'Just take fright. Want safety. Never deviate.' And by the time they were nearing the tunnel he had become maudlin and peevish and out of breath. 'Railways in the Lake District,' he panted, '– two were never meant to mix . . . Short life for'm all – all closed. Coniston branch, lovely station above village . . . shut in '58 . . . now industrial units 'n' *bungalows* . . . Lakeside branch – severed by a – road improvement . . . Cockermouth and Workington . . . Silloth to th'north . . . All gone . . . Even Windermere branch, only one left, Kendal's derelict . . . 'mere station shed'sa *super*market . . .' and within sight of the tunnel mouth Greg led the way up off the green road, and round over the fellside.

Back in Carrock Greg left Edwards to the loneliness of his own talk, the glass in his shop door trembling after he'd let himself in. Greg plodded back up the hill, his head heavy and stale with railways, sullenly bored by the prospect of tomorrow's opening ceremony, another trains day.

And here was Ruth, as he came up the hostel drive, sitting in the porch with her head in her hands, saying without looking up that they had to go for a walk that evening.

It was the last thing Greg felt like doing, but a rescue all the same, even if Ruth, as it appeared, was in one of her morose moods and probably wouldn't say a word. 'We could go down to the lake,' he suggested. It was a pity his feet had to come with him.

'I can't bear your room a moment longer,' said Ruth, fearful and grave. 'Or me.' But to Greg just then she seemed funny and quaint and young — or perhaps the feeling was somewhere between them, and nearer him.

A few hours later they were making their way down through the town, and for once Ruth let Greg lead; her face wore a look of secret determination he hadn't seen before.

On a narrow spit of sand between a reed-bed and the open water of the lake Ruth sat down and hugged her knees, and Greg knelt by her side. To their left the reeds were sudden instants of shivering; out ahead the water was choppy and muddy in the twilight, slapped at the sand in front of them. Gradually, as the two of them scanned the reeds and the waves, they became aware of the number of different birds scattered about the water; quietly they began to point them out to each other: a dark grebe bobbing and diving in the middle of the lake; a pale spot-sprinkling of duck over the far side; long-legged waders sifting amongst the rushes; swallows skimming the waves in silhouette. Here, that had shone immense copper at them looking far down from the ridge: here, where Ruth had swum in a haze of sun: now changing, as the sky and the water were closing together into darkness, from a lake of light into a lake of sound.

Moment by moment: the lake was vast and empty, and there was all the time in the world to wait for it to reveal its intricate, random life. Ruth was still, hadn't moved but to cock a finger at a duck subsiding out of flight on to the water, incline her head in the direction of a swallow's low fizz. It made Greg feel perfectly relaxed. She breathed in deeply, and out silently.

I am happy with you, Greg thought. This moment, in moments like this, I am happy. You are all I need. She made him the best of him, it felt, did away with the earnestness and the caution and the passiveness and the thought: let him be like this, let him be . . . And then he was clutched again with shame at how ridiculously reticent he'd been, how much time had been wasted, how none of this had ever got shown or said.

'I wish I could be like this for ever,' said Ruth suddenly. She brushed a midge away, and looked at Greg, then got up. 'You'll probably laugh or something when I tell you this,' she said, lifting a lock of his hair lightly with her finger as she went away from him. 'I couldn't tell anyone else. I've been in despair to tell someone – you're the only one I know I can talk to.' She crouched down by the water's edge with her back to him. A breeze went through the trees behind them; Greg felt it on his face. 'I've got myself into a jam with – someone you know. I don't even like him. And I wish I hadn't met him. I mean, I know how you feel about him. But . . . it's been I suppose several months now – it's still now, anyway. I don't know what to do.' She said it to the water in a drear monotone; now a heavy thrill came into her voice: 'I don't know how I managed to fall in love like this.'

Why these canting soap-opera sentences? Ruth was dabbling a twig in the water. 'We're not talking about Mel, are we?' was all Greg could find to say, and when he saw Ruth's back stiffen added, 'No, of course.'

And as some things become perfectly clear in an instant because their apparent impossibility seals them, reserves them until that instant to be fully imaginable, so Greg's brain first ran past the why, that didn't matter, and processed furious, efficient answers, it took only a few seconds to recast months. She was at the hostel during the evenings, so he must have driven out to her during the day . . . on the way to inspecting the Knarfoot work – after Greg had first introduced them at the station party – when Ruth had disappeared – and Greg running her out to Scale every morning . . . driven out there in his lunchtimes, and there, *there*, Ruth and Edwards, out on the open fell . . . in the *tunnel*? *You don't know*, Greg told himself desperately, *only you've thought that*. He just felt tired, tired to speechlessness, wanted to curl up into sleep, and there was no one to go to except the person who was telling him this.

'Now you know me,' said Ruth.

'That isn't you.'

There was a faint splash as Ruth's twig was flung into the water. '*All* me is me!' She was suddenly angry.

'But, when I saw you over Christmas you said he sounded
a –'

'I can't remember what I did two days ago! I talk *shit*, Greg!
You know that! You try and *hold* me to things. You can't stand
still like that. You build these *monuments* to things, Greg . . .'

'You don't know what you're doing.'

'How do you know? *I* don't know – so how should you?
What's that got to do with doing anything?'

'Why are you telling me this? Why conceal it till now?'

'Oh fuck off, Greg.'

Ruth moved away along the shore, and Greg sat on. Now a
question returned: why, after they had been together so much
and come to know each other so well, had they not come close
to each other? But when he looked back to their individual
encounters in turn, he couldn't see how they could have got any
further. Of which moment could he have said, *If only I . . .*, or,
That was because she . . .? Get the minds in gear together, and
the bodies would follow. It had to be like that: you couldn't do
it the other way round. So how had she and Edwards?

Ruth came back. 'Why are you being like this, Greg? I didn't
expect you to be like this. I thought you didn't mind what I
did.'

Greg got up, put his hands in his pockets.

'I wanted you to think it was nothing. I've been hating myself.'

Eventually, looking out over the lake, Greg said, 'Because
you're the person I care about most. And I thought if something
happened with you . . .' – he could sense Ruth listening with
horror, tried to shut her out and plough on with these exhausted
drab words that weren't what he meant and shouldn't ever be
said – 'I thought I could have been a better person, with you,
for good . . .' But his whole experience of Ruth was telling him
that things never happened for good, only momentarily, one at
a time . . .

'What the fuck are you talking about?' said Ruth in a low
voice, and then, 'Oh Greg . . .' – there was shock and knowledge
in it now. She held him tightly, her hair in his eyes, hugged him
hard: it seemed like a comfort. And then suddenly she was
shaking against him, shaking in his arms, and already she was
heaving out hard, coughing sobs that were loud in the night

around them, and now it was Ruth that clung on to Greg and Greg that held her to him as tightly as he could, it felt as if she would cry herself apart.

The wind was lifting white rims on the waves, and the water was slumping onto the sand in heavy slabs. When Ruth became calm again they stood side by side in the moonlight looking out over the reeds. The midges had become a persistent gauzy hum, skeining the air around the two of them. At last she spoke, with a dull, self-protective airiness, standing apart from him. 'You couldn't ever rely on me, could you, Greg? You know that. We had a lot of whisky at the station. Greg, you know *nothing* about me!' – she said it with sympathetic wonder – 'about the facts of me. You never asked me anything about myself. I thought you liked not knowing about me, me being different. You never wrote to me – you never *told* me how you felt ...' She let Greg listen to what she'd said.

'But if I had, it wouldn't have made any difference – would it.'

Ruth said no.

Then she said, 'I never thought ... I always assumed your mind was in the way. When you kissed me ... it was as if you were trying to kiss me with your mind.' She shivered. 'I still don't know what to do. I truly hate this place.'

A duck flapped away into the air. A wader was treading with tiny picking splashes through the reeds. There was a fluttering above them in the trees; something settled on the water in a light slow flurry of wings. Anything could come; anything could go: you waited, you looked, but it would come, or it wouldn't, when it wanted. (What was she talking about?) There were the parallel iron-silver lines you laid down for yourself, level and even and fixed for you to run on, your journey to a certain and preordained end – and there were creatures flying at you, all kinds, landing near you or far off, coming suddenly or on a slow descent or not at all, bobbing on their own wave, collecting in their own groups – oh, where could you go? Who would be there? Picking away in precious, slow, dreadful determination, that insane, slow, separate settling, wheeling in the semi-darkness either in approach or retreat, you couldn't see, there was no knowing ...

TRAIN, TRAIN

'Don't be crazy about me, Greg.' Ruth struck out at the cloud of midges thick and acrid around them, and said they'd better head back or she'd be bitten to death. 'You'll get fucked by someone else,' she added gently, 'if that's what you want.'

Chapter Nineteen

So Greg went for a ride on the railway the next day, which took ten minutes from the station up to the bridge halt, and a quarter of an hour's wait there, and ten minutes back: longer to wait at the halt for the locomotive to run round the train than the actual journey along the track. A year to build it; ten minutes to travel. All year in Greg's mind a longer and longer train had been preparing to leave the station, building up steam: a greater and greater articulation of history and hopes and effort and needs, of people and places – everything that had happened around the central thread of the railway, each event a new link, until on the day it would all pull away together. But on the day a little two-coach train, pulled by the puttering diesel because the hotel was still objecting to steam engines, was creeping up to the gap before the bridge and back every hour throughout the day. Along a little way, and slowly, and then back, and then over again, but no farther, and that was all.

And not even as far as the mountains. Greg looked out of the carriage window with the young children and the mothers and fathers, the teenagers with notebooks and the men with zoom lenses, and saw a wall of trees all the way. A railway in the Lake District, the great spaces of water and mountains around, such openness, such wideness – and they had rebuilt the line only through a short corridor of oak trees.

And then if things weren't the sum of their parts, if things didn't lead to things, if days didn't accumulate, but only succeeded one another . . . ? But Greg was thinking about the railway – and getting depressed – to avoid thinking and getting depressed about Ruth, and therefore was thinking and getting depressed about Ruth. All it was saying was, the obvious was what you already knew, but didn't let yourself know: it wasn't time or history tripping you up.

And how could Edwards's notion of the railway ever have received a minute's credence? Had anyone other than Greg ever given it any, rather than just ignoring it? How had it ever had anything to do with anything? You *betrayed* it, Greg had wanted to accuse Edwards afterwards: you had the chance to make something of it, and you blew it – but of course that was rubbish. Of course it had been a non-starter – something you could always imagine, something you could look at in that light – but you were the one who was shining the light. This was not how things were now, only how you wanted them to be. At any present time: it was the only way you could judge – but your judgement of the present may not accord with someone else's, and they may be the necessary fact on which yours depends. Material for a blues, perhaps – sing a blues to yourself, for itself, if you like – but that was all.

Greg sat in the sun on one of the benches on Carrock Station, watching the platform milling with people, all these people, waiting for the short train to pull in again so they could be taken up to the halt at Force. A young couple – hardly older than Greg – walked past him pushing a pushchair, taking their son up to the end of the platform for the first sight of the locomotive, the small boy perhaps two years old, half-captivated, half-scared, trying to pull one of his shoes off.

'. . . Should never have closed,' the husband was saying to his wife as they went by.

It was the third time Greg had heard the words that afternoon. What did they mean? The couple wouldn't have been old enough to remember steam trains, to remember Beeching, as he didn't – so how did they know? How did everyone know? There's your consensus, Greg said to himself, thinking of Edwards waving a load of books at the gathering in the church hall, perceiving truth but no significance: there's your community. People do know what you're talking about. And yet – there had been Mel at the breakfast table first thing, reading out from the newspaper about a government thinktank proposal for the individual privatisation of hospitals, about the Transport

Minister announcing a jamboree sale to the highest bidders of personalised car numberplates like COL 1 N and D 1 ANA.

It should never have closed: a myth of sanity and safety: a caution: democracy constrained by a fixed track: the myth its own community, as the railway, Greg realised in surprise, had been its own. The year had been all of them building the railway together, knowing how to do that. You just wanted that to take you further, to translate. The young couple were crouching down beside the pushchair and pointing out for the little boy where the train would appear from among the trees.

Warmed and dreamy, Greg watched the locomotive draw its two carriages alongside the platform, and the people get out and the people get in, and, inspired now by a new sad optimism, thinking again of Ruth, of things, things like hedgehogs and cricket sweaters, thinking not of the journey but the destination, a somewhere to go, joined the train himself for another ride up to Force, for hadn't Ruth, on their very first walk along this trackbed, all that time ago, the briars snagging back into his face as he followed behind her – hadn't Ruth said that *force* was the ancient Norse word for *waterfall*?

At the bridge halt Greg slipped away into the trees at the back of the platform, to suspicious and reproving looks that said he was either an escapee on the run or disappearing for an uncouth pee in the bushes, and came out into the rolling dale behind. He wandered up to the top of the field, looked wide around him for ravines or gulches that could lead up to a waterfall. Here was the bed of a stream, but it was pebbly, shallow, dry; elsewhere a spring seeped smoothly out of the grass; beyond, in the direction of Scale Fell, he came upon the ancient rowan copses and the slopes of heather. He pushed on over the meadows, ochre-winged butterflies dancing up the air, rounded the steep slopes of hills, dropped down into the next broad grassy gorge, splashed into concealed marshy troughs, alternately pleasured at the sanguine tranquillity he sometimes felt he was feeling, and hollowed by the other emptiness that wouldn't speak to him out of these open, sun-soft fells, that would have said that people are projectiles on different trajectories, coming from different places on different paths at different speeds: that some things don't happen, and that things don't happen more often than they do.

And with each summit he pulled up to from which to scan below, every valley wall he skidded down, the waterfall, still unfound, grew in his mind's eye ever more palpable, grew higher, faster, insistent, *somewhere* – until eventually the regular, distant horn of the small train was lost to him, and somewhere would be this sudden, crashing torrent, misting the air, this constant, releasing, thunderous tumble of water, instantly redefining the landscape, shimmering, falling like hair, stumbled on with a quietness, as you rounded the next green hillside, there, until the cloud shadows were chasing the afternoon sun fast across the slopes, and there it would be, feathery and iridescent, and Greg hadn't found it.

ABOUT THE AUTHOR

Graham Coster was born in Croydon in 1960 and read English at Cambridge, where he still lives. Until 1987 he was Assistant Editor of *Granta*; since then his stories have been published in *Granta*, the *London Review of Books* and the *New Yorker*. TRAIN, TRAIN is his first novel.